La Lady Fund

Also by José Muñoz

To See It Through

La Lady Fund

José Muñoz

Shawmut Peninsula Press

Boston
Massachusetts

Books that will amaze you!

Dedication

La Lady Fund is dedicated to my beautiful wife, Alma Delia Muñoz, for her love, support, and the keen ability to run a household with so much on her plate.

Chapter 1

Diana Solis finished her meeting at two thirty in the afternoon. It would take her a little over an hour to make it back to the office. Happy it was Friday, with a little luck, perhaps she could entice the girls at the office to go to Happy Hour. Lord knows, it had been a long week. She was impressed with the work ethic of her two employees, and if they could meet up for drinks, she was going to tell them.

Diana walked into her office from the back entrance and placed the yellow manila envelope on the right-hand corner of her desk. The real estate papers could wait until Monday. Diana looked out from her office window and smiled as she saw the sun glinting off the Franklin Mountains. Since moving to El Paso immediately after high school, she felt at peace in the desert. Diana was mentally tired; her week had started with a Monday meeting in Mexico City, followed by a Wednesday one in Brownsville, Texas, and then a meeting in Bakersfield, California. This was in addition to her own business, Solis Realty. Even though she was tired, she was going to enjoy the downtime of the upcoming weekend. Going to happy hour would help kick it off.

Diana opened her office door and saw the receptionist cleaning up her workstation. "Hi Raquel, are you ready for the weekend?" asked Diana with a smile.

Grinning, Raquel Ramblas replied, "Diana, I'm always ready for the weekend."

"Good, because I want to take you and Yuli to happy hour with me. My treat," said Diana.

"What, happy hour?" inquired Yulisa Bermudez, Diana's office manager.

"Yes, happy hour. I want to take my hard-working girls out for a drink or two, if you can make it," announced Diana.

Yulisa smiled in the direction of Raquel and nodded her head.

# # #

Diana took the two ladies to an upscale restaurant/bar where they were seated at the corner of the bar. She was in no mood to hear loudmouth drunks whooping and hollering and wanted something quieter. Both Yulisa and Raquel had never been in such a beautiful place. The walls were made from dark maple, with grand designs carved at every corner. The tables were just as dark as the walls, which Yulisa made sure to check by moving the white linen tablecloth. The place exuded money, thought Raquel as she looked around at all the people in their business attire.

A Latino waiter, a man who looked to be in his late twenties with thinning black hair and a starched white jacket came to their table to take their order. They all ordered a Cadillac margarita. A small clamor rose near them as people relaxed and imbibed their drinks. Diana smiled at her hard-working employees, and said, "I just wanted to thank both of you for holding down the office while I was away. I really appreciate your hard work."

Both ladies smiled; Raquel was twenty-six-years-old and a recent graduate from the University of Texas at El Paso. Yulisa was thirty-one and had been working with Diana for six years. She had started as a receptionist and worked her way up because of her strong work ethic.

"Thank you, Diana," said Raquel, just as the waiter came with their drinks.

"Yes, thank you for your kind words," replied Yulisa, before she licked some salt from her glass.

"A toast to las trabajadoras y amigas," stated Diana. She raised her glass with the others. Their glasses clinked together then they took a sip. There was nothing better than the first drink after a long work week. Diana continued, "I really appreciate you two. I know I don't have to stress when I'm away because you two take care of business."

The two ladies smiled because they understood what Diana meant. Yulisa was mentoring Raquel on the ins and outs of office work, and Raquel was appreciative of Diana for working around her college schedule until she had graduated. They both felt loyalty to her, and knew Diana was a good person who treated her employees with fairness and respect. Yulisa had worked at other offices where bosses, both male and female, treated their employees with contempt and who should be happy that they were even employed. So they busted their asses for Diana because she was a kind and genuine person.

At the same time, both said, "Thank you."

They all enjoyed their girl time, relaxed, and appreciated the camaraderie as the alcohol took effect. They had two drinks apiece; it felt good to relax, and it was even better to be in the company of people without pretention. Before leaving, Diana asked if they needed a ride home and offered to call an Uber, but both declined.

\# \# \#

Diana got home at seven. She walked into the foyer, placed her car keys in the black ceramic dish next to the lamp, and headed for her liquor cabinet. She mixed one more margarita with the hope that it would help her sleep. She sat on her black leather sofa and looked at her bookshelf. Her eyes focused on Tales from Lamont, written by her friend, Bobby Martinez, and a smile came to her face. Had it not been for his help, she might not be here today. She recalled the turning point in her life when she had to kill or be killed. Her thoughts then turned to a Russian named Alexander Tupov, who helped her to gain her life back, but thinking about him made her sad because she never saw him again after surviving her ordeal in the desert. She reached for the remote and turned on the television, just to hear some background noise. She tried to think of her realty business, anything but her immigrant smuggling operation. She knew that she had put her time in and she was looking to find and personally train someone to take her place. Diana was almost fifty-nine now, and she wanted to step away from the business. But she had to find the right person to keep it going, and if she couldn't find that replacement, she'd never get to leave. That's why she needed another drink, because it seemed that she always had something to worry about and was growing tired of it. Her last thought before going to sleep was her victory in the Sonoran Desert, where she claimed her life back. She smiled, then finally drifted off to sleep.

\# \# \#

Diana awoke at seven thirty in the morning. She felt refreshed, having the two extra hours to sleep in on the weekends. She showered, brushed her teeth, then dressed before going to the living room. She used her iPhone to connect to the Bose stereo, choosing some smooth jazz to build a calm ambiance. Diana made a pot of coffee, then put a slice of bread in the toaster as she reached into the cabinet for a coffee mug and saucer. When the toast was ready, she took out a jar of peanut butter and placed it on the counter. The toast was ready before the coffee, so Diana placed the slice of bread on the saucer. She liked her toast cool before spreading the peanut butter. Then she walked to the refrigerator, and took out one Red Delicious apple, her favorite variety. Before heading to the patio, she took a paring knife and her coffee. Then she opened the sliding glass door with her left foot and stepped out. She set the food and coffee mug on the table and pulled out a chair. This was her quiet time where she felt the cool El Paso morning air and enjoyed the morning breeze rustling through the trees.

After she finished her breakfast, she pushed her chair away and kicked her feet up onto the table. Alone with her thoughts, she wondered if she was happy. She had a home, a thriving realty business, and had been selfless for the last twenty-seven years. But all it got her was grey hair that she had to dye once a month. Lately she noticed even the little joys of life like these weekend mornings only helped her for a few hours; then thoughts of how she might extricate herself from her immigrant smuggling organization would creep back into her head.

There were many joys that Diana felt as she helped people start their American Dream. Her organization kept records of the progress of the people they brought into the United States. All their people had been vetted as being hard work-ers with an unbreakable sense of providing for their families. The people they brought in believed if a person worked hard enough, eventually good things would happen. That brought a smile to Diana's face, because she knew what she was doing would be okay in God's eyes. She was providing a helping hand to these people, but they had to do their part to succeed.

She divided her life into two parts: the time before she liberatd herself from Rodrigo Flores, who preyed after her because she witnessed his cold-blooded murder of an innocent man; and after, when she ended his life ten miles south of the United States border after facing the biggest fear of her life. Afterwards, she threw herself into college and earned a finance degree from UTEP all while still being the head of an immigrant smuggling organization. She was still doing the same thing twenty-seven years later, only now from a safer distance. No longer did she bring immigrants in herself. Now there were people on her payroll who bore those risks. Plus, she had a thriving real estate business that she hoped to use as cover if she were ever investigated by the authorities.

In 2017, she had entertained thoughts of getting out of the immigrant smuggling business altogether, but then an odd thing happened. People began donating small amounts of money which allowed the organization to bring in more immigrants and helped defray the operating costs. Transporting immigrants into the United States was a lot easier in 1995 than it was today because the United States Government now had incredible technology at their disposal. Another oddity about those donations where that a lot came in the form of checks with Anglo sir names. For a while, the organization didn't cash those checks for fear of being set up. It wasn't until the third month of this after people left notes inside the envelopes asking why their checks hadn't been cashed that she felt brave enough to deposit them. In at least twenty donation envelopes, notes were left that stated they stopped tithing to their church and instead were sending their money to her organization for the children who had been separated from their parents and placed in cages. That was when Diana knew these donations were coming from people who felt guilt about what the cruel and racist presidential administration was doing to other humans.

Diana recalled the sudden plethora of money. While

what she was doing was illegal in the eyes of the law, her operation was supported by a lot of people. Thus she felt a little ashamed for thinking about retiring, but she was tired of putting herself second. The real toll was that she'd date men, some who were good men, but because of the line of work she was in, she could never be honest with them about what she did. What good would it be to be in a relationship if you had to hide the truth from your significant other? This is what was eating her up inside. Diana had plenty of money, more than she could ever spend, but there was something missing in her life, and that is what brought her anxiety, sleepless nights, and the feeling that she was missing out on her personal happiness. It felt like dark clouds always loomed around her.

Chapter 2

A green 2003 Ford F-150 pulled into the driveway, its hood beginning to rust. The man took his time getting out of the truck, slowly shuffled onto the porch, and went inside the home.

"Hi dear, how was work?" asked Reba McDonald as she kissed her husband.

"Well, let's just say, thank God I can start my weekend now," gruffly replied sixty-one-year-old Archie McDonald, as he put his keys on the table.

This caused Reba to bite her lip, because she knew her husband was tired. However, she needed him to run one last errand. "Archie, baby,"

He knew that his day was not finished anytime his wife called him 'Archie baby,' and he knew he had something left to do. He sighed deeply, then replied, "Well, what is it?"

"I know you're tired, but can you go to that Mexican bar and drop this off?" she asked.

Archie took the envelope and opened it as it was not

sealed. "Goddamn it, another check to these people. How much are you giving them and how often?" he inquired.

"Look Archie, you can stop and pick up a six-pack on the way home," countered Reba. "Archie, both you and I know what a racist ass you have been for most of your life. Look at this errand as a way to make up for all the wrongs you have done in your life. You'll score points with Jesus, and Lord knows that you need them."

Archie looked at his wife, his eyes beadier than usual, sighed then asked, "Well, who do I meet with?"

A smile came to Reba's face, and she kissed her husband on the cheek. "His name is Ramon Cruz. He'll be the best dressed man there. His hair is all white, combed to the back, and his skin is tanned. He'll be wearing red and white checkered pants, a black sweater, and…"

Archie interrupted, "Who in the hell wears a goddamn sweater in El Paso during this time of year?"

"Honey, he's an elderly man, and you know how old people are," explained his wife. She patted her husband towards the door.

Archie grunted as he walked out of the door and back into his pickup truck. A smile came across Reba's face when she thought of how much her husband had changed in the last two years. Before he was an insufferable bastard, filled with rage and hate. But since he learned immigrants had been separated from their children at the border and that children were being kept in cages, his hate melted faster than the Grinch's on Christmas morning. Reba had even caught him wiping tears away when he first learned of this tragedy.

Archie found a parking spot then walked into Cheto's Cantina. The bar was old but inviting. The floor had a checkerboard pattern, and the bar had two pool tables with games going on. He walked up to the bar, sat down, then looked over and was happy to see they carried Modelo on draught. The bartender walked over to him and took his order. As Archie waited, he looked at the liquor bottles displayed: plenty of tequilas, gin, plus the obligatory Jack Daniel's Whiskey bottle that any bar worth their weight had to have. Or was it even a real bar? Archie looked at his reflection and smiled at himself. He was happy to run an errand for his wife as he viewed it as serving penance for all the pain and anger he had caused her. The funny thing was they weren't even Catholic, but he knew that if his wife wanted to donate money to a cause, then it was worth it.

"Here you go sir, that will be five dollars please," said the bartender as he placed a coaster down before setting the perfectly poured beer on top of it.

Archie gave him a five-dollar bill then put two single dollars on the bar top for the tip. The beer had just enough foam to cover the top of the pilsner glass. He took a drink and enjoyed the cold liquid as it went down his gullet. He liked a beer or two on the weekends, but nothing like before when he raged with hate and spewed racial indignities at anyone who was not white. He turned around and looked at the people around the room. It was a blue-collar bar, and most of the men drinking and playing pool where still in their work clothes. A year ago, he'd have counted how many minorities were there, but now he noted how all the people looked like him: blue collar people just relaxing on a Saturday afternoon. He could tell which people had to work on Saturdays by the clothes they wore. The new Archie looked at these people and understood that they shared more similarities than differences.

After drinking some of his beer, Archie turned his bar seat around and scanned the bar for this Ramon Cruz, 'just look for a man who has a tan with white hair combed to the back,' he remembered his wife saying. Suddenly, someone scratched on the first pool table, knocking the eight ball into the wrong pocket. "Chingada madre," the player yelled as he reached into his wallet and slammed a twenty-dollar bill onto the table. Laughter came from the others who were enjoying their beers and watching the game. Then Archie spotted the man he was looking for. He was sitting at a table looking down at his phone. Archie's wife was right, this man did have a tan. The man's face was the same color as a hamburger bun, and his white hair contrasted nicely with his skin to give him a regal look. Archie took his beer and walked over to him.

"Ramon Cruz?" he asked.

"Yes, how can I help you," replied the man who did not look up.

"I have an envelope for you," said Archie. He removed the envelope from his pocket and put it on the table.

Before picking up the envelope, Ramon scanned the bar to see if he was under surveillance. Then he slid the envelope into his breast pocket and said, "Thank you."

"My wife didn't know who to address it to, so she just wrote out the check to La Lady Fund," explained Archie.

A smile came across Ramon's face, upon hearing the name then repeated, "La Lady Fund? I like that. Tell your wife that the organization thanks her. And thank you for dropping this off."

"Yes, it's terrible to separate children from their parents, then to put the children in cages. That's just disgraceful," replied Archie.

Ramon nodded his head and pursed his lips as he thought about the tragedy that was unfolding across the United States. He had piercing green eyes which gave him an even more distinguished look.

"Well Ramon, you have a good afternoon," said Archie with a smile, before walking back to his seat at the bar. He resumed enjoying his beer.

It took Archie thirty minutes to finish his beer. It relaxed him as he looked at the pool games going on. While he couldn't understand all the Spanish that was spoken there, he understood the whoops of glee after an amazing bank shot or the frustrated grunts when a player scratched. After Archie finished his beer, he peered over to where Ramon had sat, but he was nowhere to be found. Archie thanked the bartender then headed home.

Reba was waiting for her husband when he got home, and she thanked him for running her errand. "Honey, I'm going to make you the biggest New York steak for dinner with a fat baked potato and a small salad on the side," she said. She hugged him. She was happy he had changed and thanked God for his turn-around. Yes, Archie was still sarcastic and a little moody but nowhere near like he'd been a few years before. She had faith in God and had always prayed for her husband to become a more decent human being. She was grateful that her prayers had been answered.

Archie smiled at her because he loved having a steak on a Saturday night, then said, "Thank you, Love." He excused himself to shower and clean up.

# # #

It was just after three in the afternoon, and Diana was cutting some tomatoes, onions, and cilantro for the pico de gallo she was making for a six o'clock barbeque. Her friend Elizabeth was coming over with some carne asada, and they were going to have a relaxing evening with some food and wine. Elizabeth had been Diana's closest friend since Diana moved to El Paso. She was also her confidant; whenever the pressure became too great for Diana, Elizabeth would listen as her friend unload her pressing problems to her. Part of Diana's organization since its inception, both ladies enjoyed helping other people. But both were looking forward to retirement. Elizabeth was a high school history teacher who was retiring at the end of the current school year, and she had made it a point to tell Diana that she would be leaving the organization as well. It was ironic because back in the day, she was the most gung-ho of all the members, she would be the one to take the most risks. But like an aging tigress, she was getting long in the tooth. And they were all tired.

After mixing the pico de gallo, Diana walked to the dishwasher, retrieved a container and lid, then scooped the pico into it, closed the lid, and put it in the refrigerator. Diana then walked to her patio, swept the leaves that had accumulated over the past week, and finally, made sure her propane grill was full, clean, and ready to go. She liked to keep busy because it was a respite from the issues she faced.

With everything prepared for the evening, she walked back into the living room and sat on her sofa. She looked forward to the chisme that Elizabeth always shared with her, like what teacher was in hot water for being incompetent or what teachers were hooking up. She then propped up her head on a pillow and laid down and took a short nap.

Chapter 3

Diana got up and put three more corn tortillas on the grill then walked back into the house for another bottle of wine. The evening had been relaxing with good food and wine that put Diana and Elizabeth into a reflective mood, but both knew by the end of the night, they would have to talk about Diana's exit strategy. It started right after Diana opened the next bottle.

"Boy, that Pico had some kick to it, what kind of chili did you use?" asked Elizabeth, as she scooted her wine glass towards Diana for a refill.

"I put in some serranos and habaneros. I like it a little hot," replied Diana.

Then both ladies looked at each other, racking their brain for the best way to broach the subject of Diana's retirement. Diana went first. "I want to find a replacement so that this time next year, I don't have to worry about anything but my realty business."

Elizabeth listened and nodded as she chewed her food, then said, "I think it's a good idea, if you don't have a plan now, you'll be stuck here forever." She took a drink of her wine and continued, "Do you have anyone in mind?"

"Not now, and I don't want this to be a steppingstone until retirement. Ideally, I want to pick someone I can trust, who is willing to learn all the ins and outs of this business, and someone with a lot of patience," Diana replied.

"Too bad you can't sign up with Indeed.com, and get your replacement there," joked Elizabeth.

Diana smiled, but it really wasn't funny to her. She racked her brain, mentally compiling a list of the skills that her replacement would need. "Yeah, too bad we can't," she replied, with a heavy sigh.

"What's the first thing you want to do when you get out?" asked her friend.

Diana, after a long pause, smiled, then said, "I want to go to Europe, I want to see the London, Paris, Munich, and of course Berlin."

"Ah hell girl, I want to join you on that trip," as both began to laugh.

But as quickly as the laughter came, it was gone again, leaving them at square one of trying to figure how Diana would get out of the smuggling business. Diana knew she'd have to make that decisive move and the sooner the better. The rest of the evening was spent watching a movie and drinking more wine, but neither one could really enjoy the movie as each one ran different scenarios through their heads that would allow Diana to be free of the overwhelming stress, that she had endured for the last twenty-seven years.

###

The bus announced its arrival from a quarter mile away as its loud exhaust blew the dirt away from the old road. The cadre of Mexican men and women were ready to get the next group of people off to their American Dream, but for risk to be minimized, everyone was put through a weeklong crash course in English which Diana's Organization called the Language Institute. The purpose was to get people to understand American culture from different regions, so when they got ready to cross the border, they would not be tense or nervous when being questioned by the Border Patrol or TSA agents at airports. The chance of being arrested were slim because the people were prepared, and more importantly, confident. In the early days, Diana would lead groups in through mountains and deserts, but since 9/11, as heightened security measures were enacted, the organization had to jump into the twenty first century as well, and the Language Institute was part of that process. This group was managing twenty people from various parts of Mexico, some with complete families and some going at it alone. Each person had been recommended to the organization by various sub-contractors who saw these people work hard in their community and felt that if it was their wish to go North, then they should be given the opportunity. These sub-contractors were picky because there was a thousand-dollar bonus for them if the organization chose their nominees. This was an actual award that could not be bought since vouching for a lazy sack of shit would be detrimental to the economics of the sub-contractor. The Cadre lined up the group in four rows of five, then the man in change said, "Ésta es la última vez que van a hablar español. ¿Entienden?"

Everyone nodded in the group because they knew the importance of this week. They all knew this was a test which was a critical part of the process. As they passed each step, they grew closer to their dreams. Little did they know that this was their final test. The cadre showed them to their quarters for the next week then gave them a tour around the compound.

"Mamá, tengo miedo," said nine-year-old Veronica Valaderas as she hugged her mother as soon as the door was closed.

"Tranquila, Vero, todo va estar bien, pero, en inglés, in English," replied her thirty-two-year-old mother as she playfully wagged her index finger in a scolding manner.

Veronica replied, "Yes, mom," with a smile.

The first four days were everyday interactions in English that people would have in a grocery store, at jobs, or when visiting the doctor. It was repetitious. From asking questions, like, 'Can you tell me how to get to 10924 San Emidio Street?' To verbally communicating, such as answering the question to, 'Can you explain what types of symptoms you are having?' They did this so the cohort learned to pay attention to detail. Then the training would start again. Diana's Organization believed that the least these people could do when coming into their new country was to try and assimilate, to become part of the community, so as not to live in isolation in a strange country that they knew little about. There had been some philosophical differences even within the organization. Some thought they should not push people to assimilate because of the possible loss of culture while others felt it was necessary for progress. The final decision on assimilation came from Diana Solis herself. She reminded her colleagues that the reason there were Spanish magazines at the checkout stand wasn't because corporations wanted to keep Latinos informed, but that the media had finally discovered that Latinos had money. Diana thought the exploitation by the media was part of the problem, so she pushed for training on the benefits of assimilating. It was up to the people whether they wanted to assimilate, but they were given tips on ways to start the process if they so desired. The organization presented pamphlets and produced videos of people who had been in their exact shoes touting the advantages of assimilation. But the organization knew that it was an individual decision, so like a safety officer at compliance training meeting, they pushed the play button and let the people make up their own minds.

At noon on Friday the English training had ended, and now the cohort would be fitted for clothes to appear like Tejanos, Chicanos, or hip-hop loving children. It was at this time that they were presented with legal documents, which included a state driver's license or identification cards. This group was scheduled to cross the International Bridge between Juárez and El Paso because of all the ways to cross, this had the least amount of risk than other points of entry. Here, the US Border Patrol would be too busy to scrutinize every person returning from Juárez.

On the last night, everyone came together for a feast of carne asada, rice and beans. It was only then that they realized they had passed the final hurdle, and that by this time tomorrow, they would be in the United States. There was great joy, but there was still one hill to climb for the group. It was of utmost importance that they use what they learned all week to be able to walk into their new country.

Upon hearing the news that they had passed their final test, Jacinto Jimenez hugged his wife and eleven-year-old daughter. "¿Escuchaste? Manaña vamos a estar en los Estados Unidos," he said to his wife.

"¡Sí, no lo puedo creer?" replied his wife, Mercedes, as she brought her daughter's face closer to her with her hands; the warmth from her mother's hands was internalized by eleven-year-old Jenny as a sign of pure love—the warm feeling she felt told her that their lives were going to improve.

"I cannot believe that we will be in, ah, los United States tomorrow," announced Jacinto, in his best English, as he hugged both his wife and daughter. Jacinto was going to work with his uncle Reynaldo Jimenez, in Puget Sound, Washington, His tío worked for a company that provided boat tours of the Seattle area. His tía Rocio, was the chef on board. They had a thriving business due to people requesting his tours and, as an added bonus, the exquisite Mexican cuisine. Jacinto was also aware that his tío, tía, and prima had made a much harder trip into the United States, some twenty years before.

Perhaps the best privilege of being nominated to come to

the United States through the organization's process was that each person had a guaranteed job at a living wage waiting for them, plus there was support for the people in adapting to the new culture. Being brought into the United States by the organization was no small feat, and these people had been thoroughly vetted as hard-working people, but they were warned that they needed to keep the same work ethic that got them noticed to be successful.

This is what excited Jacinto. He thought if his uncle could have his own boat, then why couldn't he? He learned a long time ago to be a good listener, paid attention to detail, and he had extreme confidence in himself. Plus, he had already been working as a crew member on a fishing boat, but even more of a bonus was that his wife and daughter were with him, and he felt happy to come to the United States.

There was one last meeting before the night was over. The group was told to be ready by seven thirty in the morning for a two-hour bus ride into Juárez. Once there, another cadre would be waiting for them. They were instructed to do everything that was asked of them. With that, everyone went into their rooms lost in their own thoughts. Many were excited and couldn't sleep, thrilled to be able to start a new life while others worried that they would be the ones to be singled out by the Border Patrol, so they quietly practiced their English until they could finally fall asleep. Others silently wept in their beds at the thought of leaving the only country that they had ever known and having to leave family members behind with no guarantee that they would be able to see them again. But what was done was done, and there would be no turning back now. The future was always something to look forward to, and that meant that their lives would change for the better with more opportunities. All they had to do was continue to work hard, take care of their family, and stay focused on their goals.

###

The hallway lights came on at six in the morning. Some of the group had been stirring in their bunks since five, and with the lights now on, some got up to start their most important day of their lives while others tried to get more sleep until the last minute. The group lined up for a buffet style breakfast at six forty-five⊠the meal consisted of eggs, bacon, potatoes, biscuits, and gravy. For many, it was their first American breakfast.

Chapter 4

It was a back to work Monday, and Diana awoke at five thirty in the morning. She laid there stretching out her arms, shoulders, and back. After five minutes of procrastinating, she hopped up from bed and walked to the shower with today's schedule already running through her head. She had a nine forty-five meeting at City Hall followed by an eleven thirty meeting near her office and a four o'clock meeting in Las Cruces.

After dressing and blow drying her hair, she walked into the kitchen for a fresh cup of coffee. She looked in the cupboard and had several cups to choose from. Feeling a little sad today, she chose the purple mug and filled it up with coffee. She was still tired, but the weekend of lounging had helped her.

When she finished her coffee, Diana called her office and left a message. "Yuli, this is Diana. I forgot to tell you that I have a mid-morning meeting and won't be in the office until later, so can you put that business envelope that's on my desk in the mail today? Thank you, bye." Diana then packed up her laptop, put it into the leather satchel, and placed it by the door. Now that she was ready to start her day, she gave herself the once over in the living room mirror. At fifty-nine, she had developed a spread around her waist, but she'd always been beautiful. So now she looked like an older lady who had kept her looks.

Before heading out the door, she poured the rest of the coffee into her silver UTEP Miners travel cup. She locked the door behind her.

###

"Ms. Solis, it's a pleasure to see you again," said the Mayor of El Paso, as he took her hand into his.

"Thank you, Mr. Mayor, I'm so glad we could make this work," replied Diana with a smile. The mayor had proposed an idea to her about saving an old building with historical significance to the city, and Diana was able to broker a deal between the owner of the dilapidated building and the city. Her policy was to always try to be on good terms with as many people as possible.

###

Diana's eleven thirty meeting was with a home builder who wanted to show her his plans for a new community. She always liked to be ahead of the game when it came to real estate, plus she enjoyed the networking that came with the job. They met at Adrian's Tacos.

"Diana. ¿Cómo estás?" asked Frank Moreno, the forty-five-year-old Tejano who took off his black cowboy hat before giving her a hug.

She smiled, then replied, "Estoy bien, Frankie."

They were seated, and after the waitress came with their

drinks and the salsa and chips, Frank moved everything to the edge of the table, then unrolled his blueprints to share his joy. He described what it would look like when it was complete like a father bragging about their child. Diana listened to his presentation and smiled at the conviction that Frank Moreno had in his eyes because he believed in his creation. He had barely finished his presentation when the food arrived. Both ordered the lunch special of three carne asada soft tacos with rice and beans.

"This looks good," said Diana, pointing to his blueprints, before taking a mouthful of Mexican rice.

"Yes, I'm glad you see it. You're like me Diana. We both have vision," replied Frank. He was a tall dark-skinned Tejano with short salt and pepper hair.

"The passion you have for your creation says a lot about you. I can see the hard work Frankie, this is going to work."

Frank Moreno smiled so big, his eyes almost shut, but this was a proud moment for him, and he didn't care what he looked like. Getting Diana Solis's blessing meant a lot to him, but more importantly, he could remove all doubt from his mind now; his endeavor was validated by an El Paso realty owner. "Thank you, Diana," he said with a smile. They exchanged business cards and got back to lunch.

Afterwards, Diana went back to her office because she had time before her next appointment. The office was a beehive of activity with agents on the phone with prospective sellers and buyers, so she stayed in her office and took a twenty-minute power nap. After waking and taking care of some paperwork, she drove north to Las Cruces at a leisurely pace. The upcoming meeting dealt with her immigrant smuggling business, and she was driving to Las Cruces to pick up donations from the area. Diana always enjoyed visiting Las Cruces as the nearby Organ Mountains offered up some spectacular views that always put her mind at ease. She couldn't pinpoint it, but seeing the rocky hills with its sharp granite and rhyolite rock formations made Diana feel at home.

She met Ramon Cruz at AJ's Bar and Grill at four o'clock sharp. She gave him a hug, and they were quickly seated. A waiter came over and took their drink order. Then Ramon opened his briefcase, removed a large, heavy business envelope, and dropped it on the table. It was so heavy it landed with a thud. "Here are last week's donations," replied Ramon, as he slid the envelope towards Diana.

"These envelopes are getting heavier each week," stated Diana, just as their beers were served to them.

Ramon laughed, then said, "Many of these checks are written to La Lady Fund," then he laughed again.

"La Lady Fund?" was Diana's reply. The name sent shockwaves through her, knowing that a female had been identified as the immigrant smuggling leader. Her heart was beating a mile a minute.

"Tranquila, Diana. Don't be upset by the name. People are appalled at what is happening with the child separation acts, these people," Ramon picked up the bulky envelope and waved it to her face, "They hate what is happening right now." Ramon raised his pint glass and toasted her. "I think La Lady Fund for a name is great. But more important, you have fifteen thousand dollars in checks in only one week's time."

Diana understood what Ramon was saying, and she was amazed at the size of the donations. This extra money helped to defray costs incurred by the organization for extra security measures and the added cost of hiring extra personnel. She nodded her head in agreement with Ramon, then said, "La Lady Fund? Humm, that's catchy." Diana had come a long way since first bringing in immigrants herself. But these were not just any immigrants, these people had stood out in their communities because of their strong work ethic and had demonstrated they were serious about improving their lives. She was proud of what she started and what her organization did.

"Diana, Diana," said Ramon, waving his hand in front of her trying to get her attention.

She smiled, then said, "Sorry, I was just thinking of the old days."

"Then I take it that you like La Lady Fund?" asked Ramon, before taking another sip of beer.

"It could be worse, they could have named me La Vieja Fea," replied Diana. They both shared a hearty laugh, then planned for their next meeting.

After the meeting she drove home with the traffic not too bad for a Monday afternoon. Her workdays had begun to blur, something different every day, yet time seemed to fly by. Keeping busy was what Diana did best because it kept the monster at bay. The monster being finding someone to take over for her. It was five thirty in the evening when Diana stepped through her front door.

###

Basilo looked at his watch and noticed that the bus was late, and of all days, too. But just as he was about to make a call, he saw the bus come around the corner. He took a deep breath to calm himself. He was responsible for twenty people: seven men, eleven women, and two children, aged eleven and nine.

There had been a small hiccup in the schedule, so this group had stayed longer at the Language Institute. As they stepped off the bus, he identified himself to them at the City Square, then escorted them into a Mexican restaurant to get the final details of how they would cross into the United States.

"Voy a hablar inglés, porque tienen que practicar. Okay, we are going to cross the bridge at six tonight. We will all be spread out, but we will be in the same line," announced Basilio, who looked to see if everyone understood, and with no questions, he continued. "Families will be driving across together, and everyone else will walk, but spread apart. Remember, don't be nervous or scared, look them in the eye, and play the part you were given. Keep practicing your English and have confidence in yourselves."

The group nodded their heads in the affirmative. Some ate all the food they could because they were nervous while others couldn't eat because they were scared and filled with dread. After the pep talk by Basilio, the group followed him into a store, and everyone was instructed to buy something to carry across the border as they tried to blend in like other Americans. At five-forty, the group split up, some would be walking into the United States with Basilio while the families in the group would be driving across the border.

In the end, the group was successful. All remembered to look the Immigration Officer in the eye and not hesitate in their answers. This was due to the confidence they gained as they practiced their English; this was why the Organization's Language Institute was so important to the process.

Once the group came across the border, they were met by their contact from the organization who would be with them for the next forty-eight hours for support. This was done to relieve any anxiety the person felt when they crossed the border. It was customary for the organization's contact to take the people out to a steak dinner to celebrate their new country. The second day was for instructions on how to get to their assigned locations followed by a run to a retail store for enough clothes to last a week.

For Jacinto Jimenez, it meant that he would drive from El Paso to San Diego, California, with his family and then fly Southwest Airlines to the Seattle-Tacoma International Airport where they would be picked up by his uncle, Reynaldo Jimenez. With their anxiety levels lowered, they were able to look at all the possibilities they had now. The best part of coming into the United States was that these people had guaranteed jobs and plenty of support, this was their reward for their work ethic.

###

Diana received an email at seven-ten in the evening. She would check it later, but an email at this exact time signaled that another group had safely crossed the border.

Chapter 5

The organization provided two days of instruction on the ins and outs of traveling for the new group, then Vicente Valaderas packed up his assigned truck and prepared his family for their new lives. He'd been loaned a 2014 Ford F-150. The organization provided their immigrants with vehicles for a year, enough time for people to get on their feet and save, after which Vicente would turn his vehicle in. The Valadares had been the third family to use this truck.

Vicente and his family were headed to Arvin, California. He was a farm mechanic by trade, and was going to be working for one of the biggest farmers in California's Central Valley. The organization's Arvin contact had already leased an apartment for the family which worked the same as the vehicle. The organization paid their rent for a year enabling the family to save as much money as possible. Many times, these people would return the vehicle and the keys to their apartment earlier, because they were eager to start their new lives, and they wanted to see how far their work ethic could take them.

Vicente took Interstate 10 and headed west. "¿Lo puedes creer mi amor?" said Vicente. He looked over at his wife, then patted her knee.

"Amor, en inglés," replied his wife Oralia, as she took his

hand into hers. "Yes, my love, I cannot believe it."

"I want to take you and Vero to Disneyland for our one-year aniversario of coming to America," announced Vicente with a smile on his face.

"Okay Apá, I am going to remember that," replied his daughter Veronica from the back seat.

Ecstatic, the Valaderas family focused on doing as well as they could in their new country. Little Veronica was excited to start school in her new country and had been practicing English for two years now. But no one was happier than Vicente. All he ever wanted was to have a happy life and be able to take care of his family. His wish had materialized, and he would not waste his good fortune.

###

Jacinto Jimenez and his family were boarding their first flight ever. The drive from El Paso to San Diego was an easy one, and now they were on their last leg of their journey before starting their new lives. They walked through the aisle of the plane where Jenny claimed the window seat, Mercedes took the middle, and Jacinto took the aisle seat. Jenny looked out the window, saw the tarmac workers loading luggage onto the plane, and said, "Look Mama, I think I saw our suitcases," as she buckled her seat belt.

Mercedes smiled at her daughter. She was happy that Jenny would have more opportunities and hoped it would equate to a better life for her daughter. Mercedes already had what she wanted, a beautiful healthy daughter and a man who loved her unconditionally and getting to live in America was the cherry on top. She didn't know how she'd like all the rain in the Pacific Northwest, but she would be content with her life. What she wanted was for Jacinto to have the best opportunity for success, and with his work ethic, she wondered how far he could go. She was excited to begin their life in their new country.

Jacinto's heart was beating a mile a minute with excitement. He had really done it. After being nominated to come North, he was with his family starting a new life. Being chosen to come to the US was never planned. He worked just as his father had taught him, but it was still quite a shock when he was asked if he wanted to come to the United States. He accepted immediately because he knew there would be more opportunities there to achieve all he wanted.

Jacinto was also happy for his wife as she had always been a hard worker, and now she would be rewarded with a better life. Everyone would have a better life. As the plane climbed into the air, he wondered what it would be like to work with his uncle Reynaldo. Jacinto had experience working on a fishing boat, and now he was going to be a member of his uncle's crew. He smiled at his good fortune and swore that he'd keep working hard because that's the way it was supposed to be. He had no clue exactly what he would be doing, but it didn't matter because he was smart and confident. Jacinto learned long ago that work was work, no matter if you were herding cattle or working on a crew. He always paid attention and quickly picked up on things, but his best asset was the attitude he had about work. Jacinto couldn't understand how people could be so lazy when the money they earned helped to support their families. In every job he ever had, he was always the first one to be promoted over others who had been hired before him. It was because of his work ethic and self-confidence. "Mi amor, ¿te gusta el avión?" he asked his wife.

"Sí, pero en English. I am so happy Jacinto," said his wife, as she reached for his hand and gave it a squeeze.

"I wonder how you will like ah... Wachingtón?" he said, leaning over to the right to give his wife a kiss."

"As long as I have Jenny and you, estoy tranquila."

Jacinto looked deep into Mercedes' eyes, their eyes

locked, and a smile came to their faces because they knew they had become one

Reynaldo Jimenez was waiting at the Seattle-Tacoma International Airport to pick up his nephew, his wife and daughter. He was excited to see his brother's son. It had been over ten years since he had last seen him. Reynaldo had closed the cruise service for the weekend to spend time with his nephew and family. He wanted to devote all the weekend to his new guests, give the family a tour of where they would live and explain to Jacinto what he would be doing.

Reynaldo's first job after coming to America was working on a fishing boat in Puget Sound. He quickly rose to the head of the crew due to his hard-working nature. He and Rocio saved as much money as possible, and after five years of pinching pennies, Reynaldo was able to purchase his own fishing boat. He felt blessed, and soon word got out that he had the best charter fishing boat, as everyone who went out with him, usually caught their limit.

Perhaps it was in the Jimenez genes to have strong work ethic because Reynaldo was rewarded again. Soon he had his own charter fishing boat business that was always filled to capacity, but then one day he met a man who changed his life forever.

Jimmy Parks was a software multi-millionaire who lived in the Seattle area, and he was in search of a captain for his harbor cruise business. He was six foot two with thinning blond hair and weighed a hundred and sixty pounds. He hated the sea, and buying the yacht was strictly business, but he had heard a lot about a fishing boat captain who was always booked and wanted to know why, so he took a motion sickness pill and boarded Reynaldo's boat. Parks observed him from afar at first, then he went out again the next day, just to see if there was a difference. But there wasn't any, just another packed charter. Parks liked the way Reynaldo carried himself and introduced himself to Reynaldo. He was impressed as Reynaldo always seemed to be cleaning or wiping down a table. The man was always busy. To Jimmy Parks, that showed a man who took pride in his possessions, and that meant a lot to Jimmy. Needing a captain soon, Parks asked Reynaldo if he was interested in the position.

Parks got down to business. After hearing the starting pay, and the fact that he would be the Captain of Parks' Harbor Cruise business, Reynaldo Jimenez jumped at the chance. He was even more elated upon hearing that it was a four-year contract. He couldn't believe his good fortune on how God continued to bless him with opportunities. The best part of his new job was that he got to choose his own crew, like a football coach who gets to hire their own staff. Many of his crew went with him as he started his new venture.

Over time, Parks wanted to expand the business and asked Reynaldo if he knew a Mexican cook. He smiled and said his wife had been a seafood cook back in Mexico. After a few dishes as a test, Parks hired her.

That had been seven years ago, and since that time Reynaldo and Rocio happily went to work, each doing what they loved and being paid well for it. The couple smiled at how their life had turned out. Reynaldo loved to go out on the Puget Sound at night when the air was cool and fresh, and he always enjoyed the view of Seattle. He savored being at the helm, while guests enjoyed their night on the harbor, and he felt the freest when he was out on the water.

Rocio Jimenez also enjoyed her new life immensely. Never in her dreams could she picture the life she was now leading. Growing up poor, she was rescued from poverty by her now husband Reynaldo. He convinced her to come to the coastal city of Manzanillo, Colima. He was already working on a fishing boat and could provide for her. Rocio accepted his offer to escape rural living without indoor plumbing.

She much preferred the coast to the stifling mountains. Reynaldo was always a good provider and a hard worker. They already had a good life compared to how she lived before. Then the night Reynaldo came home with the news that their family had been chosen to come to America, was one of tears of jubilation for the opportunities they would have.

Rocio was excited that their Mari would be educated in America. Since they came to Seattle, little Mari, forever to be known to her mother as her Chiquita, became a successful attorney practicing in Los Angeles. Mari always excelled in school, but once they came to America, she became a sponge for knowledge.

Rocio felt fortunate to be working in the field she loved, since there were many people who woke up pissed off at having to go to work at a place that they hated. Not Rocio. She always loved cooking and even had a seafood restaurant in Manzanillo, before their family came to the United States. Now she was the chef on the dinner cruise while her husband was navigating the yacht. They were a true team, and at least once a day Rocio thought about how her life would have turned out had she never met Reynaldo.

Rocio was truly in love with her husband. Everything he had promised her when they were married had been delivered. What she loved most about him was his compassion for others. Rocio wondered if his compassion had anything to do with them being chosen to come to the US, though it didn't matter because she had a healthy and successful daughter and a man who treasured her. She couldn't ask for a better life, and she wanted to show Reynaldo's nephew and family how great life could be.

"¡Ahí están!," shouted Reynaldo as they waited for Jacinto and his family to come off the jet walk. "¡Jacinto aquí!" shouted Reynaldo as he waved his arms to get their attention. They finally found each other. He gave his nephew a heartfelt welcome, then the extended families were introduced to each other. After gathering their luggage, they loaded it into Reynaldo's Ford F-250 and headed home.

Rocio took Mercedes hands into hers and said, "Te va encantar el estado de Washington."

Chapter 6

Diana received the call while in her office. "Abalardo, tell me what the hell happened?" she asked. She had a pen and paper to take down the pertinent information.

"Well, Ricardo requested transportation on the wrong day," replied Abalardo Avilas.

Diana heard the news and sighed deeply out of frustration. "You mean our people were exposed in the street, and the goddamn fucking bus never showed?" Diana tried to contain her anger by taking a deep breath.

"After about twenty minutes, we moved them back to the safehouse, and that's when we learned of the wrong date for transportation," reported Abalardo.

"Goddamn it. I'll be down there this evening. Thank you for letting me know, Abalardo." With that, she put her phone down and surfed the United Airlines website for the next flight down South.

With that phone call, Diana's day had turned to shit. She had Raquel call clients to reschedule appointments. This was another reason for her wanting to leave the organization, she was getting tired of dealing with the stress. Diana left her office and walked to the breakroom for a bottle of water.

"Hi Diana," said Yulisa, as they passed each other in the breakroom.

Diana stopped and returned the greeting, then explained that she would be out of the office for a few days. "I have a fire to put out."

"Anything I can help you with?" inquired Yulisa.

Diana smiled at the offer, then replied, "No, just keep this place going." Then Diana left the office to pack a bag for Monterrey, Mexico.

# # #

Diana was sitting in her seat on a United Airlines flight to Monterrey, Mexico, when she read the entire Incident Report by email.

Ricardo Resendez, the leader of the Organization's Transportation Department, had stepped out of the office. Then the phone rang, and a junior member answered the call, took down the message on a Post It note, and placed it on the desk. About thirty minutes later, the junior member could not locate the Post It note and panicked. This is where the cog broke down in Diana's organizational system. He couldn't remember the date or time, so he guessed as best he could. Unfortunately, he had written it wrong. This was later confirmed when everything in the room was moved and the note in question was found on the floor near the bookshelf. Evidently, the Post It note had become detached from the desk when another junior member turned on an industrial-sized fan to get some relief from the stifling heat. Everything was written in the investigative report.

Diana was able to read the full report before having to switch her phone on airplane mode for her flight. The end result had not been catastrophic, but it was still sloppy work. Diana thought it was time to make her presence known to the Mexican contingent of her organization.

# # #

"Diana Solis, ¿cómo estás?" asked Ricardo Resendez, the forty-eight-year-old who was six foot tall and wore jeans with a buttoned-up shirt. His hair was jet black, and he had a thick mustache.

"Estoy bien. ¿Cómo está todo?" replied Diana, as she looked around his office.

"I'm sorry for the mix up, Diana, perdóname," said Ricardo, putting his hands together to beg forgiveness.

Diana waved him off and said, "Ricardo, todo está bien, eso no es necesario." She gave him a big hug. "I'm just here to take a tour of everything we do down here. I never want to be too far away from all the work that everyone does."

Diana was finally able to calm Ricardo, and she even got to speak to the junior member who started this whole chain of events. She told the probationary employee that his job was safe, but reminded him that had he just been honest, this whole incident could have been avoided. Diana then toured the transportation depot. Buses of various sizes were being washed. She walked into the bay doors of the garage and observed mechanics assembling an engine while other workers were in the pit servicing vehicles. Diana noticed the place was abuzz with activity and wondered if this display of work was to impress her. It didn't matter for Ricardo Resendez. He understood the consequences. Like a Navy captain who wrecks their boat and then resigns their commission, Ricardo understood that his dream of succeeding Diana was now dead. He'd still be employed with the Organization, but the top sport had disappeared like that Post It note in his office.

There was a silver lining to Diana's problem in Mexico.

She now had an opportunity to refamiliarize herself with the Mexico operations which she could share with her incoming replacement. If she could ever find one. But she was also troubled and pissed off because this reminded her of the personal danger she lived through. A cold feeling went through her and frightened her as she thought of the repercussions of her actions. Had it not been for a quick-thinking worker, the problem could have exploded in her face. Diana was growing tired of the risk, and that only made her angrier because she felt she was in a holding pattern with no replacement in sight.

# # #

After a day touring the Mexican operations, Diana went back to her hotel for the evening. She ordered room service and had the enchilada plate that came with rice and beans for dinner. The Transportation Center was running at maximum efficiency, minus the snafu that brought her to Mexico, but she was over managing the entire operation. She wanted to find a replacement. She took out the organizational chart to see who she would consider. She mixed her Mexican rice with her refried beans, then took a bite and savored the flavor, detecting a hint of lemon in the rice. She unfolded the chart to study the pictures of the senior management of the organization. The faces that looked back at her were all near fifty. Ideally, she wanted to hire someone young to take over for her so that there would be continuity. Plus, the last thing Diana wanted was for this to be someone's steppingstone towards retirement, like some school administrators in their last years before collecting their pension.

After dinner she opened a bottle of Merlot and considered who was worthy and smart enough to take over for her. Then it hit her. How in the hell was she going to hire a person from outside the organization? Logic dictated that the next leader should come from someone inside, and Diana wanted it to be her choice. But who could she trust with this operation? Her head was telling her that if she was serious about leaving, the transition would be easier if she promoted from within, but her heart was hoping she could find someone on her own. If she didn't care, it would be easier to name her successor, and it would no longer be her problem, but this was her baby. She had invested too much time. She just needed to find the right person so she could slowly slip away and finally start her own life.

# # #

Jacinto Jimenez was on the side of the yacht with a bucket of soap and water, cleaning the sides of the boat to remove the salt build up while he dangled on a rope seat. This is how he spent his first three hours of work. The other crew members hurled insults and laughed at the new guy, but Jacinto took it all in stride. He'd worked harder for much less pay, so he was just being Jacinto, doing his job without complaint.

After lunch his tío gave him a choice of assignments for his first cruise on Thursday evening. He could either help his tía in the kitchen, or he could walk around serving drinks to the guests. His uncle gave him some time to decide. On one side he could work with his aunt, helping with whatever she needed, or he could breathe the fresh air and walk around. He chose being a waiter because he wanted to see what a night cruise was all about.

At three in the afternoon, Jacinto got a tour of the yacht from his uncle. Jacinto noted that his tío always carried a towel with him, and was always wiping down the cedar wood, protecting the boat from the elements. He got to see his tío in action. His uncle was always on the move, always with a bounce in his step. His tío reminded Jacinto of a person who was always hopped up on coffee, but he saw a lot of himself in his uncle. They were always in motion, eager to take care of the next thing on the list that needed to be done. That's how work was thought of in the Jimenez world.

Jacinto was pleased with his new job, and he didn't care if they made him clean toilets because this job provided a stable life for his lovely wife and daughter. He'd been taught at a young age that a man was a piece of shit if he couldn't provide for their family. His wife Mercedes was enjoying her new surroundings, and if she was happy, that meant Jacinto was too.

Today was Jenny's first day of school. Jacinto hoped her day would go as well as his. He was thankful for their new life, it almost seemed like he was living in a dream that he did not want to wake from. Jacinto and Mercedes were excited to come to America because of all the opportunities their daughter would have. Plus his daughter's attitude about learning was amazing, and he prayed that Jenny Jimenez would have a good life.

The Jimenez living arrangements were beyond what they expected. They stayed in the guest house that his tío and tía owned. It would be home for the next twelve months, as they'd pocket all the money Jacinto would make, until they could start their own American Dream. They had use of vehicles to take Jenny to and from school, and for groceries or other trips, but Jacinto was stubborn, too. There would be no sightseeing until they were on their own. Until then he would work hard to provide for his family, for the two people who were his entire world.

# # #

Jacinto put on his white jacket and looked into the mirror, then he adjusted his black bow tie and smiled. He looked pretty good, if he did say so himself. He walked into the living room to show his wife his uniform of the day. She took a picture of him, and then he left for his first evening on the water. This was the best uniform he'd ever worn. As he drove towards the harbor, he recalled the very first day of his working life. He'd been assigned the exhuasting task of stacking one-hundred-pound sacks of grain onto a pallet. By lunch time his back hurt; by quitting time, he wondered if he wanted to return. But when the sun arose the next morning, Jacinto was back at work. He pulled up into the harbor, took one last look at himself, and reported for duty.

He walked onto the yacht to meet his uncle. "Mira tan guapo," his tío said to his nephew. "Una muchacha te va decir lo que vas a hacer, está fácil."

"Lo que me están pagando, limpiará mierda," replied Jacinto with a smile.

"You will enjoy tonight, walk around, do your job, but make sure you take in the sights, te hace tranquilizará aquí," replied his uncle as he pointed to his chest.

Jacinto got his assignment from a young blond named Melanie. He circulated around the boat to make sure that the guests had drinks. It was a good evening to be out on the Sound. The guests were dressed in formal wear, and everyone was having a festive time enjoying the evening. The social hours were busy, and everyone became more excited as it grew darker and the Seattle lights came into view. The guests took pictures, and Jacinto kept the drinks coming, trading the empty glasses for full ones and then making a bee line back towards the kitchen. In total he made four complete circuits around the yacht. He had a quiet moment to himself as he heard the water hitting the boat's hull. He recalled his first job again, and smiled because his back no longer hurt.

Chapter 7

When Jacinto got home from his first night of work, he was so excited he woke up Mercedes, because he couldn't keep his joy to himself. His evening had been one of the most enjoyable shifts he'd ever spent working. The guests were cordial, the work light, and the best part of the evening was getting to look at the city of Seattle from the water at night. The blueish hues corresponded nicely with the amazing structures the city had to offer. It made Jacinto feel like he was watching a magic show with different lights intersecting at just the right moment. "No lo puedo creer mi amor," stated Jacinto, as he kissed his wife on the forehead.

"Que bueno Jacinto, hablamos en la mañana," replied the sleepy Mercedes before turning over on her left side.

"Sí amor, en la mañana," repeated Jacinto, as he gently tucked the blankets under his wife's shoulders.

Jacinto was too excited to sleep, and he went to the sofa to sit down and go over his day. His whole body felt encased in warmth and comfort from his heart all the way down to his feet, a feeling that everything would work out. It was more a vibe than anything else, an aura of peace and tranquility that Jacinto did not want disturbed. He was so happy and cried tears of joy at his current place in life. He had a job that paid well, and that would help to springboard his family towards their American Dream. It made Jacinto so thankful that he got on his knees in the living room and thanked God for everything his family had. The reason he was so emotional was that he had a feeling since he was a boy that one day he would find his fortune. It would happen because of the work ethic that had been taught to him by his father and uncle. He would do all he could to keep the good fortune going.

To Jacinto, it wasn't that this job was less laborious than those he had had before, it was because he was now making more money than if he had he stayed in Manzanillo. He was grateful to God for being chosen to come to America. He promised God he would continue to work hard and to always take care of his family, he walked into the bedroom and undressed. Tonight had been a good evening.

# # #

Diana landed at El Paso International Airport at ten in the morning. All she had was a carry-on bag so she went straight to the curb for an Uber back to her home. She turned the key to her door and walked into the house, then into the kitchen and looked at the patio which was still covered in shade. She opened the door and stepped out onto the patio. Diana was always big on positive energy, so she took a small piñon incense brick, picked up her lighter, then lit the incense, and placed it into a small ceramic kiva in the middle of the patio table. The grey whiff of smoke gave off an aroma of burning wood, and Diana waved her hands to bring the smoke closer to her. She loved the smell of burning piñon wood, native to New Mexico, and hell, she needed all the help she could get. She called Elizabeth, and in less than thirty minutes, she appeared at Diana's front door with two bottles of wine. Upon seeing the bottles, Diana said, "You know, I have to go to work."

Elizabeth scrunched up her face, and with one eye open, à la Popeye said, "Relax, tell me everything that happened, and what are you going to do?"

Diana looked at her friend and frowned. There was no need to hide what she felt and Diana said, "I need your advice on who to name as my successor." The shade still covered the patio as Diana took her organizational chart and handed it to Elizabeth.

She scanned the chart, which was complete with pictures, years of service and ages. Elizabeth noted the crossed out picture of Ricardo and asked, "So, no Ricardo?"

Diana shook her head, then said, "It's too bad, but así es la vida sometimes. Plus, look," as she pointed to the chart, "What do these guys have left, five years, seven at the most? Then we'll be back to square one."

"Five or seven years from now?" Elizabeth had a perplexed look on her face. "Why would that be any of your concern? You just need to get out and not worry about this anymore," admonished Elizabeth.

"What we need is some new blood, bring in some smart youngsters. That would be perfect," replied Diana, as she took a drink of her wine.

"But where can you find them?" asked Elizabeth.

Diana shook her head and said, "See my problem?"

"Chica, you want your cake and eat it too. Since when in life do we get to have it all? Just name a replacement from within and start your new life."

Diana smiled and nodded, her friend was right, it would be much easier to name a replacement from within the Organization, be done with it, and start the life she was longing for, or at least leave this life behind. Why was it so hard for her to understand that? The organization would no longer be her problem, and she reminded herself that nothing lasts forever. "Yeah, you're right, I have to call the office and tell them I won't be in, but you're mala influencia," she said with a smile.

Diana called Yulisa informing her that she would not be in today, and before she got off the phone, Diana invited her to join the party. It caught Yulisa off guard, and she saw her image in the office mirror; forehead farrowed with one eye was shut, as she tried to figure out the invitation. "Sure, I'll be there after four," Yulisa replied, still in shock.

# # #

When Yulisa arrived at Diana's, Elizabeth and Diana were in the middle of a debate on whether immigrants should assimilate. Diana poured her a glass of wine. The breeze running through the trees from Diana's patio gave the table an appealing ambiance. "Elizabeth here," as Diana pointed to her friend, "is a Social Studies Department Chair at an El Paso high school. Yulisa smiled at Elizabeth, and they shook hands. She informed Diana's friend that she was Diana's office manager, before Diana continued about the importance of learning a new culture. "Why in the hell would you travel to a new country and live on the outskirts of society? That's not good for anyone."

"But you can't forget your culture," pointed out Elizabeth, with a wagging finger.

Diana smacked her lips and said, "Oh shit, here we go with culture crap." She looked at Yulisa, then continued, "Look, most people don't forget their culture unless they want to. My point being is why wouldn't people want to learn about their new country? They will always have their traditions, but assimilation is the key, in my humble opinion."

Yulisa listened to the debate. She could tell they both

liked to play the debating game. She took the more diplomatic route and said both had made some valid points.

"No really, where do you stand on this assimilation issue?" pressed Elizabeth, before taking another drink of wine.

Yulisa smiled, took a drink from her glass then said, "Personally, I feel that people should at least try and assimilate a little, at least try to get to know their surroundings. I don't think they should hide and live in fear," as she placed her hands flat on the table.

"See, that's exactly my point," interjected Diana, using her index finger to make a point. Grudgingly, Elizabeth conceded that those were good points. Thankfully the conversation steered to her opinion on animals and other less intense subjects. The wine kept coming and everyone had a good buzz. At six in the evening, they ordered Chinese to soak up the alcohol, and by eight, the party broke up.

# # #

It was Friday afternoon and Vicente Valaderas was in the shop servicing the farm's tractors when his boss came up from behind and tapped him on his shoulder with an envelope. "Good afternoon, Vicente, I wanted to thank you for the job you are doing. We've never serviced all our tractors at the same time, only when it were needed. But this makes so much more sense," announced the boss, as he handed Vicente his paycheck.

"Thank you, sir, I want to show you that I am not afraid to work. I no lazy. Thank you very much for hiring me," was Vicente's reply, before moving on to the next tractor.

Everything was perfect for Vicente, he enjoyed his job working on vehicles that needed servicing, and on a farm this size, he would always remain busy. On the home front, his wife and daughter loved their new lives, and they were adjusting well to their new country. Vicente was given five work uniforms, a forest green long-sleeved shirt with his name on the chest with five sets of green pants to match. Vicente laughed because never in his working life did any company give him clothes to wear for work, much less a name tag. He liked his new country even more.

Oralia Valaderas was a delighted wife. She was at home in their new apartment, a two-bedroom, two-bath unit. It was the biggest place she had ever lived in. The apartment was carpeted wall to wall, something that she had never experienced before. It was her mission to have a clean apartment as a way of saying thank you to her husband for helping to better their lives. Vicente was always a good provider, and he'd often worked two jobs to make ends meet in Mexico; and that is why Oralia loved him so much, because he put his family before his own comfort. Oralia was also grateful that Vero was having a good time in her new school. Their daughter had always been smart, but the attitude she carried about learning was making this move to the United States even more rewarding. For that she was thankful for Vicente's work ethic, because otherwise they would never have been able to come to the US.

Vicente was home by five in the evening, he kissed his wife and daughter, then headed to the bedroom to shower. He had a tradition that he learned from his father that when he got home from the end of the work week, he always shaved, so his family could see him at his best instead of the scraggily version during the work week. He came out of the bedroom, clean and smelling of aftershave. He walked up to his wife and hugged and kissed her again, then he did the same to his daughter.

"Hoy, vamos a ordenar pizza, y cada día de pago, vamos a comer la mejor comida, va a ser una nueva tradición," he said to his wife and daughter.

"Papá, in English," reminded his daughter.

"Yes, okay," he replied with a smile. He looked at his wife

and daughter, the only treasures he had, and reached out for a group hug. His heart was bursting with joy at how much their lives had improved in the short time they had been in the United States.

Chapter 8

Yulisa Castro and Sergio Bermudez had been high school sweethearts since their junior year when they had the same classes and friends. Yulisa was a cheerleader and Sergio was the star quarterback. They were well liked by the student body because they treated everyone well, from the cheerleaders and athletes to the cliques of skateboarders, geeks, and even the loner students. They were voted Homecoming Queen and King their senior year and everyone celebrated. They were also voted the Cutest Couple in the yearbook at Andress High School.

After high school Yulisa went to El Paso Community College to take classes in business administration while Sergio worked in construction. They were as close as ever, and soon they became engaged and focused on building a life together. To have a huge traditional wedding would cost lots of money, and Sergio wanted to save money for after they were married rather than spend a fortune commemorating the ceremony. Yulisa had also been raised to be practical, so she agreed to a small wedding. Eventually they bypassed the traditional route of a Catholic Church wedding and were married at the County Courthouse, much to the chagrin of both mothers. The fathers understood the enormous cost of a wedding and reception, so Yulisa and Sergio compromised with family and had a small ceremony for their parents, with a limited number of family from both sides attending. Yulisa didn't care for a big wedding because she saw the big picture. The wedding day was the first day of a life together and not like the grand finale at a Fourth of July fireworks show, which was what some newlyweds tended to forget.

They lived a blessed existence enjoying their lives together. While most couples needed a break from each other from time to time, Yulisa and Sergio never did, and their shared experiences brought them even closer because they got to see how each reacted to situations in life. Most people only want to think about the good parts of their relationship, but Yulisa and Sergio felt like a team, and their love only grew for each other. That's how it was for a year. Then came their little angel, Rosita. She was the love of their lives. Sergio's priority in life was now his lovely wife and their beautiful child. A few months later, he got a promotion and soon after, they moved into their own house.

The Bermudez family was living their dream and anyone who came to their barbeques would see a proud man as he hugged his wife and child, bursting at the blessing the man upstairs had given him. Sergio had the same happy grin at birthday parties, football parties, and during the holidays. Yulisa could always feel Sergio's love for her and their daughter, and she felt the same as her husband, blessed. From the time she was a senior in high school, all she had wanted was to marry Sergio and raise a child with him, and since she already had that, she was content in life. After Rosita started school, Yulisa got a job as a receptionist. She'd always had good diction, and she paid attention to detail. It was mostly so she would not be bored at home alone until it was time to pick Rosita up. She enjoyed the work and was getting mentored, which made her job easier as she got to see the big picture of running a business. Sergio didn't mind because he wanted his carída to be happy. They used the extra money to provide family vacations to Disneyland and Sea World San Antonio. They spoiled Rosita. For Sergio, it was about showing his daughter the love he'd been given by his parents. His childhood had been filled with joy, and he wanted his daughter to experience the same. His heart melted seeing Rosita enjoy herself. Yulisa understood Sergio's point of view, and she pampered their daughter as much as he did.

Rosita had her own personality, and she had a sense of how to make her parents laugh and exploited it for her benefit. She was a hit with both sides of the family. Rosita was smart, quick-witted, and she enjoyed sharing her joyful antics with her grandparents, uncles and aunts. Every school afternoon, Yulisa would take her afternoon break from work and pick up Rosita from school and drop her off at her mother's home until she finished her workday. This was a way to share Rosita with the family and enjoy the convenience of a babysitter. Everything in life was perfect, and Yulisa would not have changed anything in the world until that fateful day.

Yulisa had a feeling of dread as she started work that day. It was a Friday morning with the weekend coming up. Usually Fridays were light days as everyone prepared for the weekend, but that day was odd and off putting in a way she could feel but not explain. She looked out the front door of the business as a Texas Highway Patrolman pulled the door open, and her heart skipped a beat. She knew right away that they were coming in with bad news. She felt a violent tug in her heart and gut. It was a feeling of apprehension, like when a glass slips from a person's hand and shatters into a million pieces. This is what happened to Yulisa's hopes and dreams.

Unfortunately, Yulisa's intuition was spot on, and when

the patrolman asked to speak to a Yulisa Bermudez, she fell to her knees even before hearing the news that both her husband and daughter had perished in an automobile accident. Her coworkers did their best to provide comfort and support, but Yulisa could not be consoled. She wanted to go to the scene of the accident, but the officer shook his head. The only information was that a man and child had died at the scene. The patrolman was correct, it would not have been kind to drive Yulisa to the scene of her family's demise. Only charred remains were left, and the scene was gruesome even to the officers. The worst part, they thought, was learning that one of the victims was a six-year-old child.

Cellphone records indicated that this is what occurred. As always Sergio took Rosita to school on Fridays after their weekly doughnut and chocolate milk stop. On this day they had left ten minutes earlier than usual, and when Sergio received a call from his boss to pick up the keys to a new job site, he had the extra time to drive to the Northwest part of El Paso. It was on the way there that tragedy struck, three miles from his destination. Witnesses traveling in both directions saw an unsafe lane change by a person driving east, followed by an overcorrection that led to the fiery crash. Sergio's Ford F-250 was hit head-on, and then careened into a gas station where the vehicle was engulfed in flames. Witnesses had no doubt that the poor victims had been killed on impact.

Yulisa's world came crashing down on her. The happy life she had was no more. The funeral and the whole first month was a blur for Yulisa. She was present physically, but mentally she lived in grief. Both sides of the family checked up on her, brought her food, and reminded her to eat. But her heart was broken and could not be repaired as part of her died the day that Sergio and Rosita passed. Now she was alone with only memories of what was before. Yulisa went into fits of crying, which would quickly lead to anger. She was mad at God, mad at Sergio's boss for having called him on that day, and mad that it had to be a goddamn fucking Friday. It had been her belief that people were placed on earth for a certain time, and once the person's final mission was complete, God called them home. But that's for the people that died. Yulisa had never thought about it from a survivor's point of view. She was furious and having a hard time accepting the upheaval that had occurred to her.

Yulisa finally made a family appearance almost seven weeks after the tragedy. She accepted hugs and well wishes, but she didn't really want to hear them anymore because it always took her to that dreadful day, and talking about it still made her feel like shit. She had pieced together the last month of her happy life and still held on to those feelings. She went back to work eight weeks after the funeral. She didn't need the money, but she needed to keep busy and keep her mind off her catastrophic situation. Work was an escape for Yulisa, so this was her first step in trying to regain some sort of normalcy in her life.

Two months later, Yulisa was offered an Administrative Assistant position at another company. She had grown bored of her receptionist job, so she jumped at the chance. Change was good because people had to continue with their lives, no matter the pain and mental anguish a person had to withstand. During this time Yulisa was learning new tasks that she knew would help her rise in the company, and the more responsibilities she learned, the less time she had to dwell on the loss of family. The pain she carried was always with her, it could be triggered by a song on the radio, as she remembered how Sergio would sing to her, no matter how off key he was. When Yulisa saw children skipping home from school, she'd remember how her little Rosita would skip on the way inside the house. Yulisa threw herself into her job because at night she'd come home and lay on the couch and cry over her losses. Other nights she'd fight with God, and still other nights she'd wish that she'd never had met Sergio. That would have meant that there would have been no Rosita, and she would not have known heartbreak. But she quickly rejected those thoughts because as sad as Yulisa was, she knew if she had never met Sergio, she wouldn't be the person she was today. As time wore on, she began to accept her fate of having lost everything in the world on that goddamn fucking Friday morning.

At work she always took the initiative and was always busy, going from one task to another. The hours certainly flew by which not only helped Yulisa cope, but also taught her valuable skills as she was being mentored by the office manager. And that's how it went for the next ten months until the company was acquired by a corporation that put profits ahead of people including the office staff. The hire-ups treated the staff like dirt all while trying to run a business. Yulisa understood the different mentality, but it brought down office morale, and Yulisa changed jobs before it was too late.

As Yulisa adjusted to life as a widow, she no longer dwelled in what was once a great life. Instead of crying on the couch after work, she came home and learned the ins and outs of the company software used in the office which she used to line up an Office Manager's position for a realty start-up company. She was the same Yulisa, still feeling the loss of life, but she understood that life had to go on. However, it did not alleviate those painful memories that would flood back from time to time. Still, Yulisa knew that when those moments hit, the best way to deal with it was to let the sadness come out until those memories faded just enough to allow her to maintain her sanity.

By the time Yulisa started working for Diana as an office manager, she'd been widowed for eight years. She was a professional who cared for the office staff. They were the real workers in any company, and she had a good rapport with them. She learned this when she was a newbie many years before from the different managing styles she had encountered, both good and bad, and she realized that for a company to work well, there had to be trust between employer and employee. Yulisa was particular in who she hired, and there were many probationary employees let go at their ninety-day review based on Yulisa's recommendations. Diana trusted her judgement and that's why she was the office manager.

If there's a label for a functioning alcoholic, then there must be a name for a person who functions despite their depression. This was Yulisa. She'd be on her game at work and while cleaning her house in the early evenings, only to become a crying wreck as the evening turned into night. But the tears wouldn't last long as she'd draw a bath, to let the day's worries and grief dissipate into the water. Later, since she'd been on her feet since seven in the morning, sleep always came quickly.

# # #

Yulisa enjoyed her evening at Diana's. Perhaps that's what she needed because being a homebody wasn't doing her any good even though it guaranteed her house was always immaculate. She needed to get out more. She enjoyed a drink or two, but never more because she didn't want to be the stereotypical Mexican crying drunkenly about the pain in their lives. She also recognized that she needed a purpose in life because all she was doing emotionally was treading through the water of life, and every day she was filled with the same feelings of loneliness, emptiness, and sorrow.

That weekend, Yulisa called Diana and thanked her for inviting her over. Diana enjoyed it as well, and told her she'd like to do it again, only girl time, no politics or shop talk. That made Yulisa happy.

Chapter 9

Diana sat at her desk skimming organization reports. If she was going to get out of the business, she had to start making deadlines and quick. Ricardo Resendez had been replaced as Head of the Transportation Division. Ricardo was still in Transportation but was reassigned to a slot in Special Projects. It was rotten luck that Ricardo stepped away from the office to run errands only to find out his decision cost him his job. It was a fluke. Everyone knew it, but someone had to pay, and that someone was Ricardo.

The Transportation Division was part of an umbrella group that consisted of vehicle crews and mechanics. Each followed the Chain of Command, and they worked as a cohesive unit. The best part of the organization was that each member believed in the mission and were focused on doing their job. Each represented a cog in the system, and all were expected to do their part. Each member was paid a living wage and treated with dignity, so there was hardly any turnover.

Diana shook her head at the enormity of the organization. She would never have thought that her running a few Mexican nationals into the United States could have led to this, but here she was, trying to come up with a capable replacement.

Through all the operations conducted over the years, the blunder in Transportation that cost Ricardo his job was the most serious snafu. Other than that, the Transportation Division was run like a teenage boy with an unlimited budget to soup up their muscle car. When a mission called for an old city bus to ferry groups from place to place, there were always two other buses spread twenty minutes apart, just in case the first bus developed mechanical issues. The second bus carried two mechanics with belts, hoses, and parts in case they were needed. Transportation was run efficiently and in detail.

The next department that Diana inspected was Recruiting, which operated in both the United States and in Mexico. Between these two international departments, the recruiters in the US were far more valuable because missions could not proceed without contracts being signed with employers on the US side of the border. While it was a challenge to find sponsors, many people who had been brought over would often step up and sponsor new people when circumstances allowed because these people understood the anxiety one feels in a strange and new land, and they wanted to return the favor as a thank you for the prosperity they were now living in. Other times, large ranch owners were cajoled into offering jobs because they knew they'd be assigned a workhorse. It wasn't only farms, many Latino businesses also sponsored new people coming over. They offered to help to pay it forward because they were grateful for their success and felt it a moral duty to help their fellow brethren.

Vanessa Villamontes was the person in charge of recruiting in the United States. She was a fifty-year-old college educated Latina from Chicago, Illinois. She travelled the country looking for sponsors for the organization all the while working her day job as a headhunter for a Fortune 500 company. Anytime she was scheduled to go to the Northwest part of the country, she always made it a point to stop and say hello to Reynaldo and Rocio Jimenez, one of the most successful families brought over by the organization. Reynaldo and Rocio had been sponsors many times due to Reynaldo's need for people to become part of his boat crew. Wherever Vanessa was sent, she scheduled a meeting or two with potential sponsors. She kept track of the meetings she had, and those who could not afford to sponsor a person or declined to assist had their businesses financially scrutinized. When Vanessa flew back eight months later, she'd schedule a follow up meeting with those that were fiscally thriving, and hand over the results of her analysis to persuade them into sponsoring and remove the excuse that money was tight. Vanessa was also Catholic and had learned the art of making people feel guilty. She often signed those companies on the second try after reminding them how the Lord had blessed them over the past year. When that didn't work, Vanessa had an innocent way of making holdouts feel more inclined to help by suggesting that Karma works both ways, it could bless a person as well as being a curse. She had excellent communication skills and possessed a high degree of the art of persuasion, which she used to the organization's full advantage.

Vanessa liked doing her part for the organization, and all she asked was for her meals to be paid for when dining with potential sponsors as all the other expenses were paid for by her regular job's expense account. Was she moonlighting? Not really, because her organization job was always intertwined with wherever she was sent in search of the company's next hotshot wonder person. The dinner meetings always occurred after business hours, and Vanessa learned that these two jobs were similar. Each job, either from her Fortune 500 Company or Diana's organization, provided her opportunities to hone her skills to get some favorable decisions. She was good at her job and enjoyed the challenge of producing for her employers. She learned early in life that if you pretend that everything is a game, time will fly by quickly, and she set self-imposed quotas that she pushed herself to meet. She enjoyed the thrill of the recruiting game, and the ultimate high was when she had that signature and secured another job that would lead to someone building their own American Dream.

However, Vanessa Villamontes was not a one woman show. She was known as The Closer, but she was also in charge of all recruiting efforts in the United States for the organization. She had a staff that did all the leg work of finding businesses who were open to their Cause. The staff consisted of youngsters straight out of college who wanted to see how businesses work from within as they cut their teeth learning how to interact in the business world that supported what they did. It was a true lens into the machinations of business. They certainly didn't teach that in a college business class.

Diana looked up from her desk and wrote Vanessa Villamontes' name in her notebook as Diana was impressed with her work. She looked at the recruiting organizational chart and saw the pictures of the people and their initial first date of service. Diana noticed that Vanessa oversaw a young workforce, yet her success rate was over eighty percent, and to Diana, that showed leadership.

The Mexican Recruiting group was led by fifty-four-year-old Margarito Magaña. He was a rotund figure with a kind and trusting face that could disarm even the most hateful enemy. Margarito's job was easier than Vanessa's because all he had to do was identify possible candidates to be selected to go North. He had less pressure. He personally visited potential candidates, and from that perspective he made his decision. The candidate's hard work had already been verified, and Margarito made the final judgment on who made the cut. Every two weeks Margarito made his decisions as to which nominees was chosen. There were also times that some groups had to wait up to six weeks before being notified they had been chosen because specific sponsors needed to sign a contract before the next group was sent into the United States.

Diana looked at Margarito's photo closely, he did have a kind face. She put his name in her notebook, then looked at the top person on the organizational chart. It was a picture of her face, taken back in 2013. The hair was a little different now, but those were the same eyes that had seen so much, and she still had that same toothy smile. Under her were the four people who ran the day-to-day operations within the organization. Three men and one woman, who operated the organization like a finely tuned engine. Diana only became involved when pertinent information needed to be passed on to her.

These four people, called The Four, had an average age of fifty-three, only a few years younger than Diana. They had run operations since the founding of the organization, and they all knew each other. Two of the four members of the Administrative team provided support that fateful day when Diana took a life. She respected each one because she understood what it took to run the organization on a day-to-day basis with all the hassles, the near misses with law enforcement, and the stress of trying to deliver what had been promised to the people selected to come to the United States.

The Four, all possible candidates to the ultimate promotion, knew everything about the organization, even more than Diana, but that was by design. There were things that Diana did not care to know, like where the organization obtained their documents. There had never been a problem with documents, so Diana suspected that someone in a government office was involved, and that thought made Diana anxious. Hence, there were some things better left unknown.

The Four understood Diana's predicament because all were growing older and were trying to enjoy other aspects of their lives. All had grandchildren and longed to spend more time with family. In the last six months, Diana asked if they would consider taking over for her, but each declined because they didn't want any added responsibility. They were as tired as Diana, and a life outside of the constant stress of keeping schedules, arranging pickups, and the feeling of dread every time they saw law enforcement had gotten old for all of them. Diana didn't blame anyone, as she was trying to do the same thing. So the top tier of the organization were not vying to be named Diana's successor.

Because The Four declined the job, Diana's hope of hiring someone younger to take over was still alive. Vanessa Villamontes would be a great candidate, but she was already a top earner at her company, so Diana doubted she'd take the job. But she would ask. Diana closed the plastic-coated organizational chart, folded it like a map, and placed it in her black leather satchel.

Diana returned to her desk and sat down. She smiled realizing that today, she had made progress towards finding a solution to her problem. Diana was big on looking at things in a positive light because the world was always ready to pounce on people. Diana could never understand how people could be their own harshest critic. She had been that way once, but after her life-changing experience out in the desert, she vowed to be more positive, because there was more than enough negativity in the world.

Diana swore to herself that she would find a way out so she could start a new life. But how? Some of the questions inside her head excited her. She was mentally tired of leading the Organization, but she wanted it left in capable hands and not have it turn to shit the minute she left. The thought of freeing herself from this personal vocation cleaned a spot in her heart because this is what she deserved. She'd been doing this since 1994, and it was time that she got to put her feet up, rest her body and mind and decompress from all her responsibilities. Diana came back to reality as her cellphone rang, it was her comadre Elizabeth.

## Chapter 10

"Hello," said Diana, as she picked up her cellphone.

"Hi, Diana, ¿qué haces? Hey, tú sabes como soy de metiche, your office manager, I Googled her name today. Do you know anything about her?" asked Elizabeth, trying to read Diana's response.

The question perked Diana up. "She came highly recommended, and does a hell of a job, why?" asked Diana with a farrowed forehead, wondering what she was about to hear.

Elizabeth continued, "Her name sounded familiar, so I did an Internet search on her. Pobrecita, did you know she lost her daughter and husband in a fiery crash six years ago in Northwest El Paso?"

"Oh my God, that was her? I remember reading about that in the paper," replied Diana, sighing sadly, as she imagined the pain Yulisa must live through.

"Yeah, I couldn't handle that heavy shit in my life. Has she ever talked about it or hinted about it?" asked Elizabeth.

"She's strictly professional," stated Diana. She went through her employee records and took out Yulisa Bermudez's application. There was nothing special written on the application.

"We'll I just wanted to let you know about Yulisa. Man, I couldn't function if that shit had happened to me," said Elizabeth.

Diana nodded her head in agreement with her friend. She looked out the window of her office and took in all this new information. A dull pain developed in her gut at the thought of having to live through such a painful experience sent by fate. "I'll ask how she's doing, but only a little at a time, because maybe she doesn't want to remember the tragedy, but I'll probe and see if she's up to talking," announced Diana.

"Okay girl, I just wanted you to be aware of the news I learned. See, sometimes it pays to be nosey," joked Elizabeth.

Diana smiled and replied, "Thanks, I'll call you later." She hung up the phone and was alone in her thoughts. She was floored by the news, and thought it cruel to be happy one day, then the next day a person's whole world is gone, no good-byes, no last hugs, no last words, nothing but pain. She shook her head to try and stop thinking about Yulisa's tragedy and wondered how she carried on.

Diana tried to think of something else, but failed, and she started to cry at the pain Yulisa had to endure. Diana understood how life sometimes puts obstacles in a person's way to teach them to persevere, but in Yulisa's case, life had kicked her in the groin and punched her in the stomach. Diana shook her head thinking about how Yulisa suffered a double whammy, as the lives of her precious daughter and husband were gone in an instant. She sighed deeply, then reached for some tissue from her desk and dabbed her eyes from the sadness she had just learned about.

Diana kept shaking her head at what she had learned about her office manager, and then she tried to calculate when this tragedy occurred. Yulisa must have been twenty-five or twenty-six, when it happened. It made Diana think back at her own life at twenty-six, and then she cried again because she would have been so lost. She wondered how someone goes through dealing with such catastrophic events, especially at such a young age. She didn't know what to say to Yulisa, but she had time to formulate her approach to her because she had scheduled a conference call with The Four. Diana would once again offer the top job to one of them, but she already knew their answers. Yet perhaps someone would change their mind and take the job. Nonetheless, this provided an opportunity for Diana to pick The Fours' brain, run ideas past them, and ask if they had any recommendations to promote from within. Diana slipped out of her office through the back door because she did not know how she would react if she saw Yulisa. She had an hour to prep for her meeting.

# # #

Diana went home for the meeting and quickly prepared a salad from half a cucumber, a tomato and the last of the Romaine lettuce from the crisper. She also took out some Italian dressing and scooped up five fat juicy pepperoncini peppers by the stem with her fork. She took a bowl and placed it on the coffee table next to her laptop. She had fifteen minutes to eat before the conference call. The upcoming meetings were with friends who had help found the Organization, and there was mutual respect. Diana appreciated that The Four stepped up to run things full time when Diana wanted to lessen her load. She rushed through her lunch so fast, that when she looked down at her bowl, all she had left was exactly one sliced cucumber, one sliced tomato, and one leaf of lettuce. She made it into a salad sandwich then got up from the sofa. She placed the now empty bowl into the sink and walked back to the sofa. Diana opened her phone and turned it to camera mode to make sure she didn't have lettuce stuck in her teeth, and with that checked off, she was ready for the video conference.

The conference started at two. The Four, starting with Fátima Fuentes, Esteban Estrada, Gabino Galvez and finally Isidro Infante. The Four were all near Diana's age of fifty-nine. They all knew each other and had great rapport. Diana addressed Fátima Fuentes first. "Fátima, you look fabulous like always," said Diana with a smile. Fátima Fuentes was fifty-five years old. She had black greying hair that was pulled back, and she wore hoop earrings that dangled from her ears. Her Native American features were complete with a skin tone that reminded Diana of a black cup of coffee with a splash of creamer mixed in. Fátima was thin and tiny, but her voice carried authority.

"Good afternoon, Diana, ¿Cómo estás?" asked the female member of The Four.

Diana was all business. "Muy bien, and thank you all for coming to this meeting. I'd like to run a few things by all of you, and I'd like to get some feedback on your thoughts," Diana told them. The Four nodded their heads in understanding, then Diana continued, "First, you all know that I am looking to leave the organization, I love the work, the mission, but I have missed out on part of my life. I've sacrificed many things, and I need to leave. It'd be so easy to walk away, but I want someone competent to take over. I'd be happy if one of you agreed to do it."

Fátima shook her head and then said, "I understand that you want to leave, but personally speaking, I'm tired too. I'm looking forward to not carrying the burden of these responsibilities, so I say the decision is yours on naming a replacement." She picked up her coffee cup and took a sip, reached for a sugar-coated concha, and took a small bite. Daintily, she pressed a napkin to her mouth to remove any remaining sugar that was on her lips.

Gabino Galvaz cleared his throat and said, "Diana, we all know how tired you feel. We've all been on a long journey and have helped many people. We have made sure that when Americans sees our cohorts work, they can't lie and say Mexicans are lazy. I agree with Fátima, since you founded this organization, you are the one to make the final decision." He was the oldest in the group at fifty-seven. Gabino was thin, and he wore an avocado colored Guayabera shirt that made his silver mustache stand out. His salt and paper hair was combed back and contrasted with his dark brown skin. He reached for his iced tea on the table and took a drink, his thick gold rings glinted in the light.

"My problem is that if people are promoted from within the organization, we will have the same dilemma in five years or so," explained Diana, as she looked at the faces on her laptop, trying the read The Four's thoughts.

Esteban Estrada raised one eyebrow, then farrowed his forehead and said, "If you are planning on leaving, the future turnover in the organization should no longer be your concern." Esteban was fifty-four years with a thick build. He was nearly bald except for what he called his whitewalls, as his remaining hair was more salt than pepper. He was strong but also fat. Diana looked at the screen and saw he was drinking beer from a cold frosty mug.

Diana smiled at the comment and explained that she saw his point. "Look, once a person leaves a company, they never think about it again. But when you are the founder, well, it's different, because you want the best for the company. You know, this is my baby," explained Diana as she twisted her napkin due to anxiety, hoping to have made her point.

Fátima cleared her throat and then said, "Diana, I understand you founded the organization, but you either need to keep going or step away completely."

The three others nodded their heads in agreement. "Do you have any idea on who you'd like to promote from within?" asked Isidro Infante, speaking for the first time. Isidro was fifty-six years old with grey hair combed back and a grey beard. His green eyes penetrated through the video call, forcing Diana to reply.

"Well, I was hoping one of you would have a change of heart and accept the job," joked Diana.

"Do you have any ideas?" asked Isidro, as he fidgeted with his white cowboy he had put on the table.

"As I've said before, promoting someone within the organization will be good for five years or so, and then we will be having this same conversation again," replied Diana, as she pleaded her case to The Four.

Then Gabino chimed in, "You said promoting from within. Do you have any plans of bringing in someone from the outside?" His question perked everyone up, and Diana could see The Four move closer to their video cameras.

Diana had been expecting the question and replied quickly. "I'm currently looking into that. I have no one in mind right now, and I know it's a risk to bring an outsider in. But please understand, if I do bring in someone from the outside, remember that I would trust them with my life. There is too much at risk, so I promise they would be fully vetted if we go that route." No one spoke and Diana added, "Look, if you have a person already in mind, please let me know."

"Diana, tranquila, tranquila," replied Gabino. His hand could be seen through the screen giving the universal sign for 'easy, easy,' as his palms went up. "We have complete trust in you, and I know I'm not alone when I say this: we will support any decision you make." His ring clanked on the now empty glass of iced tea.

"Thank you for the support, Gabino. Look everyone," as Diana stared into the camera with a sincere face. "I know finding someone from the outside is hard to believe, and I think almost impossible, but it would be good if we could find a young person who could learn the ropes and take over for the next twenty years." Diana looked at the faces on video, trying to read their reactions, but their stares didn't reveal anything. Diana wondered if The Four ever played poker. "Again, if you have any recommendations, I'd be happy to accept them and move on. Do you know of any recent college graduates in the organization that could do the job?"

"Este es tu bebé Diana, y tu vas a hacer la decisión, y vas a tener todo el apoyo de nosotros," replied Isidro, as the other three nodded their heads in agreement.

"Bueno, I'll start the process of finding someone from the outside, but if I can't find anyone, then we'll promote from within," informed Diana. "Gracias por su tiempo. I'll keep you abreast of this situation." She then waved goodbye before the screen went blank.

With the meeting over, she closed her laptop then sat on the sofa and pulled her feet up. She was finally feeling the nerves from the meeting as her hands trembled. She took in shallow breaths to calm herself and slowly the uneasiness dissipated and was replaced with happiness. She explained her thought process to The Four, and they had given her their support. Diana was also happy because she had started the ball rolling on the final chapter of her organizational duties. For over a year she had thought of leaving, but those were just thoughts. Now her plan of action was set in motion, as she sought a resolution to her quandary.

Chapter 11

Diana woke up at six in the morning and slowly stretched her fifty-nine-year-old body. First her arms, then she slowly stretched her lower back. She was still in bed when she started to think of yesterday's news, from both the meeting with The Four and the revelation about her office manager. Finally, she pulled the sheets away and brought her knees up. She slowly worked her left shoulder in small circular motions, which she had to do every day since she'd been shot through the shoulder by Rodrigo Flores before he met his demise. At last, she pulled her legs away from the bed and got onto her feet. The daily ritual was a reminder to her that she wasn't getting any younger, and things would eventually get worse.

After showering and dressing, Diana thought more about the meeting with The Four. She thought the meeting had been productive and enjoyed their unanimous support. She smiled because she was following through on finding her successor, and this was the first step. It made Diana feel productive, and mentally, it made her feel good that she was making some headway in sorting out the details so she could finally enjoy the rest of her life. The smile she had disappeared when she thought of the news that she had learned about Yulisa. There was no way around it, she'd have a talk with her sometime today.

# # #

"Thank you for calling Solis Realty, this is Yulisa, how may I help you," answered Diana's office manager.

"Hi Yulisa, I'm glad I caught you. I want to take you to lunch today," announced Diana, her knuckles white with the stress of what she would say to her.

"Lunch, sure, where do you want to meet?" Yulisa asked.

"We can go from the office, and I'll drive," replied Diana. Her heart raced from the nervousness of the call. She exhaled as she hung up the phone, but she wasn't looking forward to the talk, though she felt it needed to be done.

When Diana got to the office, she caught up on all the paperwork she had been neglecting. The effort she invested in finding her replacement had taken time away from her regular job. She was grateful Yulisa had put all the pressing work into a pile on her desk along with five envelopes on top of her keyboard. Diana got up and peeked out from behind the window blinds. The office was busy with two clients signing papers, and Yulisa everywhere, taking care of copies, finding contracts, and keeping everything running smoothly. Now that was the Yulisa Bermudez that Diana knew.

# # #

"I hope you brought your appetite, and just a warning, the portions are enormous," said Diana, as she opened the door to don Daniel's Steakhouse. The aroma of tasty food permeated in the air.

"I've never been here," replied Yulisa as she looked at the restaurant's interior and decorations.

They were seated quickly and sat in a booth. "I hope you like steak," Diana expressed.

"I love how they decorated this place plus the delicious smell is making my mouth water," announced Yulisa. She noticed an old branding iron logo burned into the wood next to their table with the initials ADM and wondered what it stood for. She picked up the menu as their server placed a bowl of butter rolls on the table.

"Some people think they have to drive out of El Paso for a good steak, but this place has never disappointed me," said Diana, putting extra butter on her roll. Both women stopped what they were doing when a server brought a tray full of steaks to the table next to them. There was a fillet mignon and two ribeye plates, with the meat still sizzling on the cast iron skillets The aroma made both women salivate. A short while later, their order was taken. They both chose the ribeye with the loaded baked potato and a small green salad along with ice teas.

The garden salad came first with iceberg lettuce, cherry tomatoes and one big fat yellow pepperoncini, served in a wooden bowl. They were halfway through the salad when the main course arrived. Both ribeyes where cooked medium well but retained their savory and juicy flavor. Diana cut and dipped her steak into a silver container of au jus sauce, while Yulisa dabbed hers with steak sauce. They smiled at each other while they shared this food experience. Diana reached for her napkin to clean the sauce off her face. The lunch was delicious, but there was a knot in Diana's stomach from her apprehension about bringing up Yulisa's painful memory. Yulisa noticed the farrows on Diana's forehead and asked if she was okay. Diana replied she was, then got the attention of their server and ordered Red Velvet cake for dessert. She vacillated between talking to Yulisa or just forgetting the whole thing. They enjoyed dessert and were on their second cup of coffee when Diana broached the subject.

Diana cleared her throat and began. "Yulisa, I found out about the tragedy that happened to you. I'm very sorry, no one deserves to have to go through what you have had to endure." She had tears in her eyes and quickly reached for her coffee to keep the rest of her emotions from coming out. Yulisa had a frown on her face, recalling that horrible Friday morning.

"Thanks for the kind words, Diana," replied Yulisa, as the sad statement sent her back to the darkest period of her life. Yulisa sighed, nodded her head, and then said, "It was a nightmare that I hoped to wake from, only it really happened." She looked just past Diana's right shoulder and focused on a window etched with blue and red stained-glass, and she smiled because those were her little Rosita's favorite colors.

Diana reached her hands across the table and patted the top of Yulisa's hand and said, "I'm sorry to have brought it up, but I want you to know that if I can help you in anyway, please let me know."

Yulisa smiled then her eyes welled up in tears, and she brought her napkin to her face before her mascara could run. "Thank you. I appreciate it." There was a long awkward pause and then Yulisa opened up. She shared the events of the day, and while Diana listened, it was like a dark shadow had been cast over them. Yulisa described the events in a monotone voice because she had gone through them at least a million times in her head. But her loved ones would always live through her. "My daughter would have been twelve years old now," she explained. She looked out into the distance and a smile came to her face, as she pictured what her little Rosita would look like now. "Diana, this is some heavy shit, and you're not obligated to have to hear the whole sad tale. It happened, but life must go on."

Diana shook her head and said, "I don't know how you got past this horrible tragedy."

"Got past?" Yulisa sighed heavily then regained her composure and added, "My loved ones were taken from me, but survivors need to continue, so my husband and daughter will always live here," as she thumped her right index finger into her chest. "But have I gotten past it? I don't know. I probably overcompensate in other ways in dealing with this loss."

"All I see is professionalism in the office," replied Diana with a smile on her face, trying to bring some humor on such a heavy topic.

"See, I know I overcompensate at work," laughed Yulisa. She continued to share her pain with Diana. She admitted that her mother was ready to have her committed for depression. "I was alright, but I didn't want to be rushed out of my mourning period just because three weeks had passed. I did it in my own time, it was my pain, so it was my fucking decision," she said, as she looked Diana in the eye. Diana nodded her head in agreement. Yulisa continued, "I went back to work just to keep busy, and so my family didn't think I'd go off the deep end and hang myself." She put her left hand on her throat, stuck out her tongue to the side, and rolled her eyes back, then said, "You know how Latino families are, they always start with the worst-case scenario and work their way back." Diana let out a chuckle and nodded her head in agreement. "So, I went back to work mainly to take my mind off my two angels in Heaven. I've worked for a few companies before I came to you, and now you know my story," she said, as she paused to take a sip of her coffee. She smiled at Diana and then said, "You are the first person that I have ever talked about this that wasn't my family or therapist."

Diana replied, "I'm honored that you told me." She put her hand up to get their server's attention.

"It feels nice to let others into my darkness that I carry around with me," admitted Yulisa. She took out her wallet when the server approached with the check.

"No, no, I invited you so put your money away," announced Diana. She pulled out the company credit card and put it inside the checkbook and handed it to the server.

They didn't rush back to the office as Yulisa wanted to show Diana the scene of the tragedy. "The gas station and store were never rebuilt. It just became a burned-out pile of wood. The city finally bulldozed it because people began writing letters to the Mayor with a suggestion to sanitize the area of such a sad tragedy. There's nothing left but my memories," explained Yulisa. Nothing else was said on the way back to the office. Diana had gotten to see another side of her office manager and friend. Yulisa reminded Diana of herself when she was her age, both in looks and in determination.

Diana drove into the parking garage, then parked her silver 2017 BMW 5 Series right in front of her personal office entrance. Before entering the office, Diana gave her a hug then said, "Yulisa, thank you for allowing me to know your story. If I can help you in anyway, please don't hesitate to ask." Then they stepped back into the office.

As Yulisa closed Diana's door on the way out of her office, Diana sat down on her chair and looked at the work she had left to do. She opened the top right-hand door of her desk and pulled out a heavy gold-plated letter opener and quickly opened the five envelopes in succession. Three of the envelopes contained checks from clients, and the other two were construction companies who wanted to introduce themselves to the El Paso Real Estate Community. Diana caught a glimpse of Yulisa through her office window as she helped the receptionist catch up on some of her work. Diana felt sad that Yulisa had to carry such heartbreak and loss with her ever day of her life.

Diana knew something about death, only the opposite of Yulisa's case, and while traumatic, could never rival Yulisa's horrific experience. Yulisa's work ethic was a coping mechanism for all the anguish she felt, at least that was Diana's guess. But whatever it was, it made her a valuable and important part of her company.

Chapter 12

"¡A la chingada!" said the father as he and his wife raised their hands to the US Border Patrol Officer who was pointing to their group, their five-year-old daughter did the same. The officer pointed gruffly to line up by the rocks, expecting everyone to understand what he meant. The group of nine finally lined up with their wrists facing down, as each person was zip tied, including children. The fathers quickly shushed the tears and cries from their children, as there was no need to make matters worse. "Todo va estar bien mijita, no llores," said the father, trying to silence the crying that disturbed his thought process.

The dream of bringing his family to America had blown up in his face. His vision of what could have been didn't last long. He, his wife, daughter, and the others had been in the United States for less than an hour before they were captured. It was like owning a winning lottery ticket, only to find out that it was worthless. What hurt him most was the fear in his daughter's eyes and the blank look she gave to her mother. He was angry with the authorities for tying up children despite the fear on their faces as they tried to process what was happening to their family.

His wife looked over at him, standing with their hands

zipped tied while trying to read her husband's face. She never truly believed that they would make it. The coyote never made eye contact with people, and she had learned long ago to be wary of people who couldn't look you in the eye. It was no surprise to her when she, her husband, and child were detained, but the damn coyote fell back into the shadows and retreated to the safety of the desert floor, waiting to prey on the next group of immigrants seeking a new life in the United States. They were led to a dirt road next to the dried riverbed. They walked for about ten minutes, in single file: her husband, then her child, and then her. The terrain was uneven, causing the people in front of her to appear like they were bobbing up and down. The wife was angry at giving her blessing for her husband's risky move. They were told nothing but where the assembly point would be, and the coyote was a young teenager wearing a black Snapback cap to the side. The wife didn't have a good feeling about it, but she was tired and prayed they'd be lucky enough to make it without getting caught. When they were apprehended, the wife was at least grateful that the family was still safe and intact.

The families were composed until they got to the makeshift detention facility. The usual protocol called for families to be detained together, but here the migrants were lined up by sex, males sixteen and above went to the left while the females were sent to the right. The children were instructed to line up in the middle. The entire point of entry sounded of heartbreak, with cries from the children trying to reach out to their parents while mothers tried to put on a brave face to reassure their children. The fathers on the left side of the entrance could hear their children crying, as their wives tried to calm the children. The men shouted their promise to their children that soon everyone would be together again, and they would see each other in a few hours before being herded through the heavy metal door painted in gas chamber green.

The men walked through an entrance just five feet wide,

both walls were chain link fencing, and the electricity buzzed from the ceiling. It was stuffy in the tunnel, and the men walked as fast as they could to escape the menacing noise, which was just the way the Border Patrol wanted. The men crossed through the tunnel and were tossed a silver emergency blanket packed in a small box while a fat white officer gestured with his stubby fingers towards the open gate, sneering at each man as they walked past him. Apparently, their new living quarters would be a cement floor with a few picnic tables to eat on or to lay under, depending on the hour. The chain link fence was topped with spools of razor-sharp concertina wire for those entertaining thoughts of escape. The makeshift cell was seventy feet by one hundred, and it was only a third full at present time. Once the men got their bearing of their new environment, they marched over to those who were already in the cage and asked how long they had been there.

Some fathers would not look up and most of their eyes were bloodshot red from obvious heartbreak. One of the single men who'd been rounded up with the families spoke and explained that they had been put in this place three days ago without a word from anyone since. The father's despondent looks sent a chill up every man's spine. This was not the normal practice to be kept for more than a day. He'd been told that if they were caught, they'd be released after they promised to make the required court appearance. Plus families were always kept together. The man was even more disturbed seeing one of the father's probably pushing forty, crying out as others tried to console him. It made the man think of how his wishes for a better life in the United States had led him to this cell. Not knowing how his daughter and wife were doing, it finally hit him, and he broke down sobbing. He tried to stop by punching himself in the chest, as he was filled with sadness for what his wife and daughter were being put through. He was filled with rage at the cruelty of being separated from his family, and angry at himself because there was nothing he could do about it. He found an empty table and sat down with his legs facing the outside and put his head in his hands and wondered about his options. All he could think about was the blank look on his daughter's face as they were being taken away.

After the women were taken to their cell, the new prisoners asked the other inmates where their children were being kept. There was hate in many of the voices as they heard from a Latina Border Patrol Officer say their children were safe and happy. Nobody believed her, and others asked when they would be reunited with their children, but the officer repeated the same line as the other mothers hissed her away. The mother prayed her daughter would be safe, and she hoped there would be no long-term trauma. She was also angry at the United States for having such an inhuman human rights policy that would separate children from their parents, and she seethed with rage that anyone would find this acceptable. She also felt sadness for her husband because she knew that he would put this all on himself. He was probably already beating himself up mentally for putting them in danger. But she made the final decision to go. If she had objected to the trip, her husband would have canceled it. Her husband always did the best he could, and when he told her about the trip, there was excitement in his voice. She wanted to support him. So even though she had a sick feeling in her stomach, she kept it to herself. She looked at her surroundings and shook her head at the bad decision that lead to the family's current situation.

Cries came from a group of mothers, the youngest was eighteen and distraught at having to relinquish her one-year-old son to authorities. She shrieked horribly at the thought of the confusion her son would have. The mothers took turns hugging and encouraging the young mother to have faith that God would keep all the children safe. The mother waited her turn and then she gave the crying mother a tight hug with three pats on the back that she hoped would signal that soon, all families would be together again. They could all hope and pray that everyone would be back together, but the mother picked up on the guard's body language. It was like they knew a secret the detainees didn't, and that same sick feeling returned.

The children had been in their cages for two days now. They were instructed to help take care of and cheer up the new children being brought in. When someone balked, the Latina Border Patrol officer sneeringly reminded the children how scared they were when they first arrived. Many of the children nodded their heads and looked down. The daughter looked at the cage that she would be going in. She went through the box she'd been given and was met by a girl a little older, who told her it held her blanket that would keep her warm. The daughter started to cry from the newness of it all. First, she was arrested along with her family, then separated from her parents, and now she was put in this cage like a wild animal. She wondered why anyone would do this to children and babies. She missed her parents so much that her vision became obscured with the nonstop tears running down her face. While the mother and the father prayed for their daughter's safety, all she could do was cry because she was as confused and scared as the other children. The sound of misery and fear permeated thorough the cage. The daughter was lost in her thoughts of a time when her family was together, back before the big trip, and back to a time when they were in their small village. It had been a time when everything was perfect for her. Not like it was now.

# # #

Two weeks later, the deportations began. Those pending release were called out at three in the morning and told that they would be leaving at dawn. When the people asked questions about when the families would be reunited, they were met with silence. For these remaining in custody, there was no way to find out when families would become whole again. With the outside world completely cut off, these people had to trust the agencies who separated their families. Would the US government be able to bring them back together? What was the purpose of this brutal policy? If it was being used as a deterrent, as a tale of 'this is what awaits you if you are apprehended, so don't attempt it,' that wouldn't work. Clearly, the architects of this horrible system had based their actions on unreal assumptions. The same people who couldn't fathom why families would risk imprisonment or death to have a better life in America were the same people who have never faced a lifetime of poverty or lived in areas that are comparable to warzones. It was during these trying times that families rolled the dice, not because they wanted to break US law, but so they could raise their children in safe areas where kids could play outside and not have to worry about violence from warring cartels. They also longed to come to the United States because they had heard if a person worked hard in America, that anything was possible.

Chapter 13

Diana got home from work at six in the evening. It was Thursday night and the start of her weekend—the fringe benefits of owning her own business. She went to her bedroom and changed from her business attire to comfortable jeans and a UTEP Miner orange and blue tee shirt. She went into the kitchen, took out a wine glass, opened a bottle of Merlot, and brought it to the coffee table. Diana then went back to the kitchen to retrieve an antipasto platter from the refrigerator and placed baguettes on a tray. Next, she chose her music therapy, nothing with too much of a beat and soft enough to reflect on the day's events, to put her into a tranquil state of mind. She started this relaxation method at the suggestion of a friend, then continued to use it after she went for her annual physical when the doctor commented on how her blood pressure had never been better. The music came from the television speaker bar. Diana swirled the wine in the glass and smiled as she saw the wine's legs slowly walk back down into the glass before taking a drink. She closed her eyes and relaxed. This was the start of a long weekend. There was plenty of work to be done, but tonight, Diana would decompress and tackle the work tomorrow.

Diana was so relaxed that she took a short twenty-minute catnap, without spilling the wine that she had placed on her lap secured only by her fingers. She put the glass on the table, then propped up her pillow and stretched herself out on the sofa in her relaxed state. Her thoughts went back to Yulisa, and the horrible experience she had to live through every day of her life. Diana's forehead furrowed thinking of Yulisa having a family one day, then the next day, they were gone. Nothing could prepare people for the cruel fate that awaited some, and Yulisa had been one of those unfortunate souls chosen for grief. Diana got up and refilled her glass., She changed the music, selecting the Texas Tornados and then shuffled the music on her phone.

She was haunted by Yulisa's comment that had this tragedy never occurred, her daughter would have been twelve years old. Diana frowned, thinking of all those missed years, all those memories that families collect through the years, but that none of those would be for Yulisa. Fate had given her friend a short supply of time, so memories were all Yulisa had of her previous life. Diana felt for her friend, and she could see why Yulisa threw herself into her job, but that was only part of her friend, for Diana knew Yulisa's work ethic didn't develop after her tragedy—she had always had it. She was glad that she talked with the woman she now considered a friend and wanted to get to know her better.

Diana knew that everyone had their own crosses to bear and that life was not perfect. People had to cope the best way they knew how, whether they were well off professionals or down at their luck homeless. It was the human condition to try to understand and make sense of events and thus continue with life all while trying to find the answers to, 'what the hell happened?' There was no reset button in life like in video games. In real life, if a person got the shit end of the deal, well, they could be pissed, but sooner or later they'd have to accept their fate and come to grips with their life situation. People had to continue. It was like being diagnosed with cancer but then remembering that the mortgage and others bills still needed to be paid, and the family still needed to eat. So even though the disease could kill them, people continued to go to work, go to school, and care for their children because few people had the luxury of having their problems solved by others.

Diana brought her glass of wine to her lips while still being propped up on the couch which made the sip awkward as she drank from the side of her mouth. Luckily, she didn't spill any wine on her nor on the white carpet. The wine had a self-reflection effect on Diana as she started to inspect her own crosses. Her second cross was directly related to the first, and that first cross went by the name of Rodrigo Flores. They had met about three months after Diana moved in with her sister Lupe. She was still eighteen and enjoyed being spoiled by him. But what had been an initially good relationship transformed into an life and death struggle. Diana would never forget those three long weeks she spent fearing for her life. She even had international assistance from a Russian friend as the threats increased. Finally, one afternoon on a Sonoran Desert sand dune, Diana killed Rodrigo with a shot through the chest. She'd been winged in the shoulder and was scared, but alive. She could still feel the electrical pulse that ran through her body that day, her ears ringing from Rodrigo's blast to her shoulder, but she had survived. After Rodrigo was gone, Diana still had to contend with the morality of having taken a life, easier said than done. Killing someone, be it in self-defense or in cold blood, would always present a problem for those who pulled the trigger and their life would never be the same. Diana was an example of that.

Diana moved from the image of her taking her life back in the Sonoran Desert, to her present situation. Her wine consumption forced her to confront the choices she had made in life, mainly her decision to start the organization. Who would have known that Diana, speaking with a Mexican National and being advised about the ins and outs of smuggling people across the border, would have helped launch this endeavor that had lasted all these years. She smiled at all the good the organization had done for people, and for the happy outcomes, but at the same time, she realized she'd sacrificed part of her life to run it. Diana moved from her prone position back to sitting on the sofa. She reached for more wine and continued down memory lane.

Diana was a fifty-nine-year-old Latina without children, a rarity in Latino culture. To some she was viewed as an old spinster who one day would die alone. She blamed Rodrigo for mentally abusing her in the short time they were together. What some people fail to consider is that trauma of any kind will take its toll on the body both physically and mentally. When Diana's ordeal with Rodrigo was finally over, she rested for three months and then threw herself in her studies at UTEP. She had been too busy helping others to realize that she could be more effective with a business degree where she could maximize her knowledge to help others. After being liberated from her death sentence, she felt she had to make up for lost time. Rodrigo's death had been traumatic for Diana, but it's not like she could she speak with a therapist, so her only audience for solace were her friends who'd participated in the operation. But they weren't mental health professionals. Soon the responsibilities of life came calling for them and as well as her, and trauma or not, Diana had to navigate the roads of life alone while still dealing with emotional wounds.

In following the chain of causation, Diana understood she missed out on motherhood because of her work. But for Diana, her life's work was always about keeping the operation going to help more people. This was Diana's way of coping with issues. Many people follow a similar pattern of understanding, but life's pressing issues always seem to win out and they give up their optimism that they can save the world. The alcohol made Diana emotional as she thought of what she had lost in life because of her job. She understood her regret, but she'd be the first to admit that her dilemma was twofold and self-created. Those life decisions compounded over the years, is what she stared at when reviewing her life. No use in reliving things that could not be changed. What was done was done, and there was no time machine that Diana could hop into that would change the current facts.

Part two of her regret was that she was unmarried. She was single in part because of the Post Traumatic Stress Disorder caused by Rodrigo and in part because she was head of an organization that was bringing in people from Mexico. How could she find a husband and expose him to criminal charges and mortal danger? Diana's mother had taught her that marriage consisted of honesty and a whole lot of forgiveness; however, running this kind of organization didn't go hand in hand with full transparency so Diana missed out on potential suitors because of her business. She had been one of those people who believed that everything happened for a reason. She was a firm believer that people's experiences throughout life were a trial of life, as some people are rewarded for their perseverance while others who were light on work ethic were doomed to struggle their way through life until they learned the rules.

The regrets Diana had of never raising a child of her own: the love, the trust, the hugs, the baby kisses, and the smell of newborn infants, hurt her down to her soul. She looked out at her bookshelf and frowned at having missed out on those experiences. But as sad as Diana was about this, the coping side of her let her acknowledge her loss. She quickly returned her eye on her goal of finding a replacement. The time that she'd lost in life could never be replaced, but leaving the organization now would allow her to do the things that she wanted with no responsibility.

The thought of what she would do once free of the organization brought a smile to her face. After she named her replacement, she would be free to indulge on her every whim, travel anywhere, and not have to read the daily emails dealing with logistics and meetings. She had served well and deserved to enjoy life after sacrificing so much for others. Diana had been the head of the Organization since the beginning, and she had put her time in and then some, but nothing lasts forever. Hundreds of people had prospered in the United States because of her vision. The organization would continue without her because there were a lot of people involved who believed in what they were doing, plus the organization was getting enormous financial support from ordinary people, those that Diana realized had a conscious and were troubled by the current state of the world. These unsolicited donations enabled Diana's group to increase recruitment on both sides of the border. Diana's proudest moment was the foundation of The Organization, but she had never planned on something as gargantuan as what it had become, and no one could have predicted that Diana would still be running it after all these years. She got up from the sofa and put the platter back in the refrigerator, then she rinsed the wine glass and left it in the sink before turning off the light and heading off to bed. Tomorrow would be a workday from home.

Chapter 14

Yulisa was up at five-thirty, watching the local news while she walked on her treadmill. She used the treadmill three times a week while she walked around the campus of El Paso Community College, the home of the Tejanos, two other days a week. If there was one thing that Yulisa was neurotic about, it was her early morning cardio workouts. She grabbed the towel that she'd put on the side railing, then cleaned the beads of sweat that had gathered on her face. She was just about done with her hour workout and was now in the warm down period. One lesson that Yulisa had taken from her tragedy was the importance of exercise. It helped to train the heart physically as it helped the body to cope with stress, and she felt a personal connection to her heart because that was where her daughter and husband resided. Thus, her workout time was truly personal to her as she kept her temple healthy, so that her Rosita and Sergio could continue to live through her.

With the warm down period over, Yulisa again reached

for her towel, wiped off the sweat from her face, and walked over to the laundry room. She tossed the towel into the washer with a flick of her left wrist. Then Yulisa walked to the kitchen and poured herself a cup of coffee just in time to greet the sun coming up over the Franklin Mountains. Yulisa welcomed the morning sun by stretching her arms over her shoulders and giving herself the same motivational speech, she always gave herself every workday, about working time to death. She'd always been a morning person, alert early, but as the evening wore on, she'd be a little tired and a lot less sharp. Similarly, her bedtime had always been early—that's just who she was. Yulisa had always had a good temperament, but since she told Diana about her tragedy, things seemed to have cleared up for her, like a dark cloud had just moved away from her, and the sun was breaking through.

This newfound mental clearing in Yulisa's mind allowed her to see that maybe she needed a new perspective on life. She'd been serious and stoic since the day of the tragedy and all she got out of it were excellent job reviews and an immaculately clean home. There had to be more to life than work and housekeeping. Yulisa smiled as she thought of finding something to become involved in, some project that would take her out of her house and into the world. She knew she needed to get out more than she had been, and she definitely needed more joy in her life. If she was to enjoy her life, she'd need to find a true purpose.

Yulisa was dressed for work, happy it was Friday. Some people looked forward to the weekend to enjoy their family while others viewed the weekend as party time. For Yulisa Bermudez, the weekend always started with an early morning five-mile walk around the Valle Verde Campus of El Paso Community College, but to get to the weekend, Yulisa first had to work the day away. She had grown so used to her job that many times she'd go on autopilot, taking care of the duties at hand so that soon it was lunchtime. She knew how to keep busy, how to provide support to the realtors, and what tasks to take care of, if say, there were only twenty minutes until closing. She ran the office with ease because she was a stickler for detail. The last three receptionists before Diana hired Bea had a hard time paying attention, and Yulisa let them go when their ninety-day probationary period was up. Yulisa had learned at a young age to pay attention, learn quickly, and to take initiative.

# # #

Yulisa walked into the office carrying two large white bags filled with an assortment of pan dulce. There were big fluffy sugar encrusted conchas which went well with coffee, and a couple of pieces of yellow cake with pink icing on top. Yulisa also got a couple of thick oversized cookies with blue, yellow, and red sprinkles on top, as well as regular donuts for those not wanting a cultural food experience. She turned on the coffee pot, then placed the Mexican bread on a tray. It was a professional looking display, one of her many skills. She placed the bread near the receptionist desk, and went to her first task of the day. The weekend couldn't start until the work was done.

# # #

Diana had slept in until seven. She awoke well rested and was already thinking of her to-do list for the day. She had some realty business to take care of in the morning, and the rest of the day would consist of phone calls to or from various organization members. After breakfast and showering, Diana dressed in blue sweats, donned an orange UTEP hoodie, and put her black hair in a ponytail. She looked at herself in the mirror and smiled. She was still an attractive woman with smooth soft skin that other women would swear belonged to a thirty-year-old. Diana knew she was one of the lucky women who looked good with or without makeup. She sat on the sofa, opened her laptop, and reached for her cellphone to call the first person on her list. "Mr. Frank Moreno, please, this is Diana Solis."

"Hello, Diana, this is Frank, ¿cómo estás?"

"I'm good, Frankie. Hey! I read about your son's game last week, damn, three touchdown passes in the fourth quarter to win the game. Bet he's ready for tonight's game too."

"Yes, he had the fourth quarter of his life. Thank you for your kind words, Diana."

"How's the building coming along? Will your model homes be ready to be shown in the next two months?"

"They'll be ready within ten days. Just waiting on some touchups, and then I'll call you to schedule a special tour for your realtors."

"Okay, sounds good, Frankie. I look forward to hearing from you. Have a great weekend."

Diana hung up her cell and reached for the writing tablet to cross off the first number off her list. She got up and poured herself some coffee, then opened the sliding glass window leading to her patio. She carried her laptop and phone to the blue tiled table and tilted the umbrella so the sun would not shine on her. She then retrieved her coffee from the living room table and sat down. Only one task remained from her realty job, a meeting scheduled for two in the afternoon, so the rest of the morning was spent looking into the organization business. She looked at her watch and realized it was still early, so she surfed the web until she received a phone call.

"Hello," answered Diana.

"Diana, this is Vanessa Villamontes, how are you?

"Hi Vanessa, I'm doing well. Listen, I'll be traveling to the Seattle area in a few days. Would you happen to be in the neighborhood? I'd like to do lunch and talk over a few things."

"Perfect, I'll be flying to Seattle tomorrow. I wanted to run a few things by you, too, to see what you think," explained Vanessa.

Diana said, "Sounds good, look for an email in the next few days, and we'll connect then. Have a good day, Vanessa." She was impressed with the work that Vanessa did for the organization. Without her ability to sign contracts with future employers, Diana's organization would not have a purpose other than contributing to economic unrest in the United States. Many employers who agreed to work with the organization were immigrants themselves who had a personal connection and realized the challenges to people wanting to achieve their dreams. The employers knew they were going to get hard-working people who appreciated the opportunity to demonstrate their work ethic, but this endeavor wouldn't be nearly as successful without the help of Vanessa Villamontes. It was easy to renew a contract once an employer knew what kind of employees they were getting, and Vanessa was relentless in her search for that initial sponsor agreement. She'd been known to plant the seed to potential sponsors to at least contemplate what she'd proposed, then a few months later she'd reappear again to gauge their interest.

Diana went back to her laptop and checked up on organization email. There were the mundane reports on operations in the planning stages and other ventures in progress. She'd be happy when these reports were sent to someone else. But in the meantime, it was her business so she plowed through the information, writing notes on questions that needed to be answered. This would be her life until she named her successor, but she was laying the groundwork for part two of her life or as she liked to think: Diana Solis, the sequel. Diana pressed on because while she was tired and wanted her own life, she knew what it took to finish strong. She didn't want people talking about her wanting to leave and then letting things turn to shit on her way out. No, not on her watch.

She'd leave this organization in good hands. Every day was a day closer to her departure date, but there was still a lot of work to do. The biggest was appointing the new leader. That decision was coming up soon, and Diana's stress was made worse by her self-imposed, fast approaching deadline. She knew that once the final decision was made, her life would change immediately for the better. But until then, it was back to work. She moved her work area to the patio table.

Diana sat back in her patio chair and stretched her arms and back. She guessed that the tightness came from stress, just another overt reminder from Father Time that she wasn't a youngster anymore. She picked up the phone and called Margarito Magaña, the recruiter in Mexico. "Margarito, soy yo, Diana Solis."

"Ah, Diana, ¿cómo estás?"

"Muy bien. Listen Margarito, quería decirte que nosotros tenemos mucho dinero, can you increase the vetting of people?"

"Ah ¿sí? ¿Cómo pasó éso?"

Diana smiled then explained to Margarito the influx of cash from strangers; they'd been averaging almost forty thousand dollars in donations per month for the last two years. When Margarito heard the news, he whistled continuously for almost five seconds. That was his signature move when he was amazed at something.

"Okay Diana, I'll let people know that we should expand recruiting operations. La gente se va a poner feliz con esas noticias," replied Margarito. This news made him happy because he knew that people in every village wished that more people could be chosen to come North, and now that extra funds would become available, it would open opportunities for others. Margarito took great pride in choosing the best workers whether they were from cities, towns, or villages. Often it was a tossup between three or four candidates for the one coveted spot. Now that problem had been solved. "Okay

Diana, voy a tiener que cambiar unas cosas, pero está bien."

"Let me know como te puedo ayudar, adiós Margarito," said Diana, before hanging up. She still had an hour and a half before her realty meeting, so she got up, went inside, and began to prepare lunch. She would continue to make this a productive day.

Chapter 15

Diana's realty meeting ended at three forty-five. Afterward she reviewed her day and thought she'd been productive. Lately her mantra had been any day she worked on organization business was a day closer to beginning the next chapter of her life. She was pleased with her progress today and called Elizabeth and Yulisa and invited them over for tri-tip and wine. She stopped at Aniceto's Carniceria and picked up meat, then walked next door to Chan's Liquor Store for three bottles of Merlot. Diana drove home and cleaned up the house before she began prepping her famous hot salsa.

Diana waited until the sun went down to prepare the grill as it was still hot in El Paso in the first weeks of October. She liked to grill and host small gatherings, especially with close friends, such as Elizabeth, and now hopefully, Yulisa. Diana was impressed with the way Yulisa carried herself, not only professionally, but she had a calming presence about her despite the tragedy she had endured. She was looking forward to a relaxing evening of eating, having some wine, and some comadreando with friends.

The girls were scheduled to arrive just before dusk hit the El Paso area. The evening was still warm, but a breeze came through the opening between Diana's home and the house next door that created a convenient and refreshing wind tunnel. Diana was surprised that she didn't hear the neighbor's girls dribbling the basketball because they were always hooping in the backyard. The tri-tip sizzled as soon as it hit the grill, and as in many Latino homes anytime something was on the grill it was treated as a special occasion. Elizabeth was the first one to show. She brought a large garden salad in the huge glass bowl wrapped up as tight as a drum with plastic wrap. She walked straight to kitchen and placed the salad in the refrigerator, looking around the fridge to scope out the snacks she would eat later. Then she opened a cabinet and pulled out three glasses for the wine that would be consumed this evening.

Yulisa was five minutes behind Elizabeth, arriving with a tres leches cakes and a bottle of wine. She smiled and greeted each woman as she looked forward to the camaraderie that the evening had to offer. Yulisa wanted to expand her life and end the days of being a recluse, and she hoped this could be a start. Diana went inside and turned up her stereo. When she came back outside, she saw Yulisa dancing to the beat of Santana's Milagro with her eyes closed and her body in rhythm with the music. It made Diana happy to see Yulisa enjoying herself. She was a good person and deserved some joy.

"Hey, thanks for the invite," Yulisa said, as she continued to groove to the music.

Diana waved her hand and replied, "No, thank you for coming." She walked to the side of the patio and flicked the switch on the beige colored stucco wall that lighted her patio into a crisscross pattern of red, green, and white Christmas light strands. The symmetrical design gave a glow to the women, and making their beauty stand out even more.

Elizabeth had been looking forward to this get-together as she had had a tough week at school. She was looking forward to her retirement from teaching so she and her husband could finally get to travel on their clock. Yes, she would miss working with her students, seeing their successes, and cajoling work out of the least motivated students. These students only did the work because they knew how much she cared for them. Other than that, she was ready to finally stop teaching. It seemed weird to her that a year from now, she would be out of the classroom and in uncharted waters after thirty years in education. Elizabeth made herself the sommelier, pouring wine for the evening.

Elizabeth Elizando had been Diana's first friend when Diana moved to El Paso. When Elizabeth thought of all their time together, the early smuggling missions that were difficult and dangerous, a smile would appear on her face at their courage to do something that imperiled their own liberty to grant freedom for others. Those memories from the early days of the organization when she was a balls-out radical not caring that what she was engaging in was illegal. She'd always loved that point of her life, when she was young and followed her conscious, but time changes people. That gung-ho shit lost its appeal, and while Elizabeth continued in the organization, she was much more cautious, thinking of what she could lose if she were arrested and how it would affect others who were innocent.

"So how was your day, Bethy?" asked Diana, as she tilted her glass towards Elizabeth for another refill.

Elizabeth smiled widely, showing off her dimples and white teeth, and said, "The week flew by, thankfully."

"Who did you get to be in charge of selling burritos at the football game for the MEChA Club tonight?" asked Diana, happy that her friend chose to spend a Friday night with friends.

"I asked the newbie history teacher named Maldonado if he could fill in for me. You know how first year teachers are, always eager to volunteer, but I can tell he's a good man. And his students love him," replied Elizabeth, with a smile on her face.

Yulisa walked over to listen in on their conversation. She could see the bond between them. There was lots of history together, she thought. "We're lucky to get that gentle breeze, just enough to be refreshing, but not strong enough to kick up those damn sandstorms," stated Yulisa. Elizabeth smiled and agreed, then stepped back to the table and brought the bottle of Merlot to replenished Yulisa's glass. "Thank you, and what a way to start the weekend, right?"

"Yes, good food, good wine, and good company," responded Elizabeth, returning Yulisa's smile. Both women walked to the table to take seat.

Diana walked to the patio and opened the grill to check on the tri-tip, then turned to her right and said, "Sorry, Yulisa, but you're going to hear music from when Bethy and I were in high school, though not at the same one." She flicked her wrist and switched the music with her remote control to Peaches & Herb's Reunited. Yulisa looked at both Diana and Elizabeth, as they had smiles on their faces and swayed to the music. "Bet that song was played at many Latino weddings from 1979 to 1990," stated Diana. She smirked because she knew what was coming.

"Yeah, to play that song at your wedding was like the kiss of death," announced Elizabeth, shaking her head, then continued, "I went to a lot of weddings in the eighties and nineties, and there were some marriages that didn't last a year. Like I've said in the past, play that song, and you're just tempting fate," as she gestured with her hands in an upward movement.

Yulisa nodded her head emphatically, then added, "Yes, I remember my tiás always played that song during family parties." Then everyone listened to the music, taking in the rhythm. Kiss of death or not, Yulisa could see that each woman was lost in their own world and memories of the time. Their smiles made Yulisa wonder what these two Latinas were like in high school. To Yulisa, both women were beautiful, graceful, and unpretentious, the perfect trifecta. "So how was high school for you two?"

"Oh, I can confirm I was a heartbreaker but can't vouch for Diana because I didn't know her then," replied Elizabeth with a rueful smile. Then looked towards Diana as one of the red Christmas lights dangled over her head giving her a glowing appearance.

"What? Why are you two looking at me like that?" asked Diana with a farrowed forehead but a smile on her face. "I only had one boyfriend in high school."

"Come on, tell the truth," demanded Elizabeth, jokingly mocking her answer with a smile. Diana wagged her index finger with the international sign for no, and then repeated her answer—the red glow still perfectly centered on her face. Then Elizabeth and Diana turned to Yulisa and posed the same question. Yes, she had suffered an unimaginable tragedy, but she was still part of the girls' club, so she got the business from the two until she answered.

"I'm like Diana, I only had one boyfriend in high school, it was with my Sergio," replied Yulisa, with a smile on her face and a gleam in her eye. She took the bottle from Elizabeth and refilled the glasses, then proposed a toast. "To our high school selves, when we didn't know shit, and thought we were going to change the world." The glasses clanked together, and a chorus of groans could be heard all around.

The evening was festive with good food, good company, and a variety of subjects to debate. The tri-tip was cooked medium well and charred in all the right places. Diana brought out a big bowl of potato salad along with Elizabeth's green salad. The meal was savory, not only from the food but for the company of women who worked hard and were enjoying a night of decompression along with some wine. Just like men love their Friday nights to have their beer and talk shit about the week, women do the same thing, only much less crudely.

Eventually the talk turned to the current situation in politics and the enormous cruelty by the current presidential administration regarding the child separations at the Texas border. All three women had the same opinion: that when the administration said it was using child separation as a deterrent, it was just cover for their own bias against people seeking a better life or those who didn't look like them. This was the playbook that had been used since the beginning of time. Find a scapegoat to blame for their own misery. "Yeah, that's some racist shit going on there," said Yulisa, with her jaw clenched. She took some deep breathes so she could keep her composure, then continued, "Separating children from their parents is barbaric—that's some Nazi type of shit." She shook her head in disgust as Diana and Elizabeth nodded their heads in agreement. "And if you have to lock them up, let them all be together. It's safer for everyone and there would be less anxiety for all involved."

"That's their plan, they want to cause as much pain, worry, and fear as possible," said Elizabeth, with a sneer on her face.

Yulisa took a drink from her glass, then said, "Yeah, I got fed up. You know when that was? When those fuckers didn't provide feminine products to the girls and let them bleed through their pants. Like what the fuck is that? Where is dignity for all? How could people, workers, or guards allow that kind of shit to happen? I wanted to try and do my part, so I stopped tithing at church and instead started sending my ten percent to La Lady Fund." Diana almost spit up her wine hearing that and gave a knowing look to Elizabeth. "I'd rather my money go to try and help with the problem, so that one day there could be the solution." The two women nodded their heads.

At the end of the night, the women cleaned up the patio and put the food away. Diana made sure that everyone had a to-go plate of food for later. She was shocked her friend and office manager was one of those people who were donating money to her cause. It was a small world after all.

Chapter 16

Diana expected Elizabeth's call as soon as she'd left her house, and she didn't disappoint, calling her within ten minutes. "Jesus Christ, can you believe that? Your very own employee donates to the Cause," said Elizabeth. "What do you think Yulisa would say if she knew it was you, her employer, who was the actual La Lady?" Elizabeth never even gave Diana a chance to say hello.

Diana sighed deeply and shook her head, then said, "Yeah, I can't believe. Like how did that even come up?" She took her wine glass that was on the counter and carried it to her sofa.

"See that just goes to show that there are some people who have a conscious," replied her friend, but both still felt the shock of the news.

This made Diana think, then she said, "What a coincidence, right? But is it, really?" Diana, with her hand on her chin, tried to understand this breaking news.

Elizabeth heard Diana's response. "What do you mean by that?" She was interested in her theory.

Diana sighed again and said, "I don't have any proof, but what if this is a sting operation?" Diana's voice seemed to grow weaker.

"Sting operation? No way. Why would you even bring that up?" replied her friend.

"I have no proof, but you never know," Diana's voice was now flat. Elizabeth knew that voice meant that her friend was stressing.

"Calm down Diana, I think you're overreacting, why do you want to think negatively for?"

"I know you're right, it's just the shock, and so unexpected. Look, let me sleep on this and I'll call you after I process it. Good night." Diana hung up the phone. She got her universal remote and dimmed the living room. She played some soothing jazz to try to calm herself down and took deep breaths to return to her center. This was the last thing she expected when she invited the two friends over for the weekend kickoff. This was part of the job that she always feared. The idea of getting caught terrified her, especially this close to retirement. She could almost taste her freedom, but until she left, Diana would be in danger.

She got up from the sofa then closed the house down. She checked the doors, set the alarm, then she dragged herself to the bedroom and undressed. The news about Yulisa had a draining effect on her, and she felt extra tired. She replayed the events back in her head, but soon the wine put her into a deep slumber.

# # #

Diana awoke at six in the morning. Her first thought of the day was about Yulisa. She always rose early the morning after drinking the night before, so she got up, brushed her teeth, and hopped into the shower. After dressing, she tied her hair into a ponytail, then put on her blue and orange UTEP hoodie. Her thoughts were still of the news from last night, but it was Saturday morning, and she was in the mood for pan dulce. So she got into her silver BMW 3 Series and drove to Guerra's Panadería just off Woodrow Bean. She entered the parking lot as she mentally tried to come up with any clues or proof that would reveal Yulisa to be an informant for the Feds. Diana smiled nervously and shook her head, knowing that she was just being paranoid.

She opened the door to the Mexican bakery and took in a deep breath, savoring the sweet smells of sugar and flour. She picked up a cafeteria-sized blue colored plastic tray, then got the metal tongs to pick up the bread. She replayed Yulisa's announcement from last night in her head, to try to catch anything she'd missed, all the while she had absentmindedly clicked the metal tongs together long enough for another customer to give her a concerned look. Diana stopped and smiled as she looked at all the fresh bread that had been baked just minutes earlier. She opened the sliding glass door and grabbed two cookies with red, green, and yellow sprinkles. The other cookies she'd chosen had the same colors, only they were shaped like tiny multicolored BB's. They had always been her favorite. She then picked up the obligatory concha, which was a bread bun coated with sugar on top, in honor of her grandfather.

Diana put the bag next to her as she waited to pull out of the parking lot. While a car approached, she opened the bag and pulled out half of the cookie with the big sprinkles by breaking it in half, then took a bite. She got on the road and was headed home, already on her second bite, when she noticed she was being followed. Then all the crazy scenarios in Diana's head started firing off in her synapses, and she threw the cookie onto the passenger seat. She turned right, going into a residential area. As dawn approached, she could see that the vehicle in question, a dark colored SUV, had also made a right. Her pulse quickened, her mouth grew dry, and she held on to the steering wheel tightly. She made a left and then got back on the same street she had made a right on, only this time she went left, leaving the new residential neighborhood. The SUV was about a quarter mile behind her. Diana's breath was shallow from the thought that it was all over. She knew this day might come, and as she thought about it, cold shivers went up her spine. They turned to nausea, and Diana pulled to the curb, opened the car door, moved her body out of the car and vomited the half-eaten cookie plus a lot of yellow stomach bile that had been percolating in her gut. As the nausea left her body, she felt drained. She closed the car door and looked into her rearview mirror, the SUV had stopped at a house and was still a quarter mile behind her. The street where she parked was barren except for tumbleweeds, as this part of the neighborhood had yet to be developed, but that allowed Diana to have a prefect view of the traffic to the east and west. She saw two flashing police cars coming in her direction and began to cry. This was the last bit of freedom for her. She was pissed off, shaking her head in disgust. Then the flashing police cars failed to make a left to intercept her, but kept on going straight. She couldn't believe it. She looked back from her rear-view mirror, and the SUV in question passed her, then quickly made a right turn onto the main street. Diana felt like a condemned prisoner who'd received a last second reprieve from the Governor.

Diana sat in her car for ten minutes, crying first from fear and then finally, relief. The fear made her tired and drained, and she drove home driving well under the speed limit. There was always a chance that she could be arrested at any time, but the news about Yulisa had really shaken her. Perhaps it was because she was finally getting out of the business that made this near miss so terrifying. This was just another reason to get the hell out before it was too late, she realized. When Diana got home, she cleaned the crumbs from the cookie off her car seat, then grabbed the bakery bag and went inside. She threw the bag on her kitchen table, went straight to her bedroom, and laid down fully clothed. She still felt weak, shaky, and all she wanted to do was sleep.

# # #

Diana was awoken by Elizabeth's phone call, and as soon as Diana was conscious, her thoughts went back to that the scary encounter with the SUV. She recapped her morning to her friend, and Elizabeth could hear the stress in her voice. "I thought, that's it, it's all fucking over, as I saw that SUV following me. Then I freaked when I saw the sirens and lights; I thought they were coming for me," Diana recalled. Her friend consoled her. Elizabeth could tell her friend was shaken.

"If you're up to it, I'll come over, and you can tell me about it. Also, I have something that came to me this morning for you to consider, but only after you get over your susto," replied her friend.

Elizabeth stopped at Zubiran's Kitchen and brought two Cobb salads for lunch, then made her way to her friend's house. Diana opened the door and her friend stepped in. Diana gave her a heartfelt hug, as she was still emotional from her scare. She hoped that by having company, her anxiety would wane. Diana sighed deeply and shook her head, and said, "I hate this shit, I want to get the fuck out, the sooner the better. My God, I thought, ¡chingada madre! ya mi pescaron, then the police passed by, and the SUV took off." Diana was still trying to grasp what happened.

"Well, you worried for nothing," said Elizabeth and regretted it as soon as it came out of her mouth. Diana looked at her friend, and breathing hard, her tears erupted again, and her friend could see the stream of tears roll down Diana's face. "I'm sorry Diana, you know how I like to stick my foot in my mouth. I'm sorry that you were terrified, but I'm glad that it turned out fine."

When Diana finally calmed herself, she said, "I know Bethy, I know. Ya, ya me quiero ir. I'm done with this shit," replied Diana, with an exasperated look on her face. She explained her wish to retire from the organization because she had done her time, and now wanted something else. After twenty-seven years of doing this, she had earned her gold watch and a peaceful retirement. Elizabeth agreed and said that she would support any decision that her friend made. "So, what did you want to run by me?" Diana's voice was strong again. Elizabeth hesitated telling Diana because she was just getting over a frightening situation. "Well, what is it?" Elizabeth fidgeted, then cracked her knuckles, not looking at Diana. "Hello?" She snapped her fingers to get her friend's attention.

"Okay," blurted Elizabeth, putting a hand in front of her face to get Diana to stop snapping her fingers. "If you are considering a person outside of the organization, I think Yulisa could be an excellent candidate."

Diana's eyes grew wide hearing Yulisa's name, as the same emotions continued to brew inside of her. She took several deep breaths and asked, "And how did you come up with such a lovely idea?" She rolled her eyes.

"Well, she's single, she has no husband and kids. She'd be good. You said she was a good worker, and she donates to the Cause. You don't think she'd say yes if you offered her the job?"

Diana laughed then retorted, "Last night I thought she could be an informant for the Feds. Then this morning, I thought I was going to be arrested. And now, you my friend, suggest that she could be a perfect replacement for me?" Diana pointed to Elizabeth like a gameshow host. "I want you to explain this to me."

Chapter 17

Diana napped on her sofa until seven in the evening, because that's how long it took for her to feel normal again. Diana was mentally drained from running the events through her head since the moment Yulisa announced she donated to their organization. She tried to shake off the bad vibe, because after all, she was still lying on her couch and not sitting on a wooden bench at the El Paso County Jail, or in Federal custody. She looked at the white bakery bag that she had tossed on the kitchen table after coming home from her early morning harrowing experience. Life is fragile, thought Diana. One minute you can be starting off a Saturday morning getting pan dulce, taking a bite from your favorite cookie, then the next minute you think you're going to be arrested and everything that you have would be gone—like poof! Only to find out it was more Diana's paranoia than actual events. She shook her head in disgust; she was too damn old to have to sweat this shit on a daily basis. No wonder The Four didn't want her job, they wanted to get the hell out, too.

Diana got up and poured herself a cup of coffee and warmed it in the microwave, then walked to the kitchen table to take the sweet bread from the bag and put the bread and cookies in a Ziploc bag. She frowned because the concha she was going to eat in her honor of her grandfather would be a little stale tomorrow. She broke a sprinkle cookie in half and had it with her coffee. Despite the fright she experienced, the reality was that nothing had changed, she hadn't been arrested, and life continued. Diana had to put this episode past her and continue to follow through on leaving the Organization. She looked around her living room and peered into the kitchen and laughed, then smiled, and pumped her arms up and down in triumph because she was still at home—she was still free. She felt her strength return, but to be truly free, she'd have to find her replacement quickly.

Diana began thinking about what Elizabeth had suggested, about the possibility of considering Yulisa for her job. Every time she thought of Yulisa now, her heart would race, and she'd have to do breathing exercises to calm her nerves. In reality, all Yulisa did was acknowledge that she donated money. When Yulisa announced that, Diana didn't detect any difference in her voice, it was just a matter of fact. It made sense, because many people were sending checks, and Yulisa was one of hundreds who donated monthly. Diana wanted to know when Yulisa's first donation had been. She'd give that job to Elizabeth because she was good at getting to the bottom of things. If there was something to found, Elizabeth could dig it up, and that's why Diana's private nickname for Elizabeth was 'La Metiche.'

Diana trusted Elizabeth and if she suggested to her that Yulisa would be a good candidate to replace her, then there had to be some merit to it. She thought of Yulisa's situation, and she agreed with Elizabeth's assessment that Yulisa had no real attachments, just like her when she founded the organization. Not having a spouse and children was a plus when running an illegal organization because the only person you have to worry about was yourself. Even Diana wasn't sure she would have stayed on as the Head of the Organization if she had had a husband and children. While there is always individual risk taking, having a family and risk imprisonment would be selfish on her part, so Diana could see where Elizabeth's thought process was coming from.

Because Diana knew Yulisa's work ethic firsthand as office manager, she was certain that Yulisa would be more than capable of taking over, and the only obstruction, if there were any, would be resentment for hiring outside the organization. Diana pondered this and then touched her forehead trying to uncrease the farrows that she always got when she was in deep thought. First on her agenda was the full vetting of Yulisa Bermudez to make sure that everything matched up, verify that she had no ties to law enforcement, and to see if she had a criminal record. Her finances would be scrutinized as well as any real estate records in her name. Diana had a slew of people who could pry deep into a person's history, and such scrutiny was warranted because the risks to the organization and Diana were so great that extraordinary and intrusive measures needed to be employed. She'd start the process on Monday.

Diana was in a reflective mood as she assessed her time in the Organization. It was rewarding to help people towards their American Dream, but it didn't come without risks. Diana could count at least five different times that she could have been arrested, but by the grace of God, was she spared. She felt guilty about putting anyone in such a risky situation, but this was the best-case scenario—find a new leader with no attachments, with nothing to worry about but running a smooth operation. Diana's guilt crept up, and she asked herself if Yulisa hadn't already suffered enough in her life. It really was not fair to ask her, but perhaps she wouldn't have to if Yulisa didn't pass her security check. Diana would never have deemed Yulisa worthy of the top position if she hadn't disclosed her monthly donation to the organization.

At the same time, Diana was excited at the prospect of Yulisa passing her security check because she would be the only outside person she would have considered. In truth, where else could she go to seek a replacement from outside of the organization? The more Diana analyzed the benefits of having Yulisa takeover, the more it made sense. If she were in charge, she would run the Organization like she ran her job as Diana's office manager—smoothly, efficiently, and with a keen eye on the details. She smiled because Yulisa would be perfect, and the turnover at the top would not have any effect on the day-to-day operations. But her Office Manager still had to pass the vetting process.

Diana was in a good mood because even though things were not yet finalized, she now was able to picture life after leaving the Organization in good hands. If Yulisa could not pass muster, then she would promote from within, and quickly, because she was tired of this shit, especially with what happened in the morning. She had earned her retirement, and had a good run and thankfully, had never been arrested. She shook her head as she recalled how she led missions across the Sonoran Desert and other parts North. She got up and rearranged the cushions for more back support, then sat on the sofa again. This was the first time that she allowed herself think about life post organization. Her imagination started working on what her life would look like. Would she leave El Paso and go back home to the San Joaquin Valley, and if she did, what would she do with Solis Realty? There were still so many unknowns at present time.

Diana's sleeping schedule was going to be off because she had spent the entire day trying to get her heartrate back to normal. This entailed a long four-hour nap, so she turned on the television and put on an old cop show just to have background noise. She heard the wind chimes from the patio, so she got up and opened the patio door. Then she turned on her decorative lights jos and stepped outside. The wind felt good, and she walked over to the table and sat down. She took deep breaths and raised her arms over her head to get as much oxygen as possible. She wanted to return to her center. People can tell when their body is off, so she tried to focus to find her center for optimal efficiency. Diana was trying to bring positive vibes back into her orbit. Her mother would have called what she experienced in the morning as 'el susto,' and she smiled at the thought of her mother filling up a glass of water and mixing in sugar then having her drink it like she did when Diana was scared as a child.

Diana kept breathing deeply, accepting the desert air into her lungs, and thinking nothing but positive thoughts. She put her chin down and relaxed her breathing. Soon she was sleeping in the chair with her arms crossed. Her slumber lasted twenty minutes, but during that time, Diana was transported back to her favorite beach to hear and watch the waves crash onto the shore. She could smell the salt in the air. The beach had always been Diana's safe haven. In her dream she walked barefoot, the sand between her toes and the water a little cold when the waves came in. Diana's mental state was reenergized—buttressed with positive thoughts.

The dream also contained places she'd long to see. She saw images of herself on the Eiffel Tower in Paris, the Colosseum in Rome, and Checkpoint Charlie in Berlin. All while still hearing the waves hitting the sand on the beach. Her heart felt full and happy. There was no worry, only enjoyment, contentment, and a feeling that everything would turn out well. It was as if a spell had been put on Diana because when she awoke from her dream, she felt well rested and finally felt one hundred percent herself. The El Paso wind had subsided, and as she stepped back into the house, she turned off the backyard lights and locked the door. It was a quarter past eleven in the evening now, but Diana felt refreshed. She turned off the television, secured the house, set the alarm, and ambled into her bedroom. She turned on the ceiling fan without the light and undressed.

There was no more worry for Diana because she knew

what she had to do. The best-case scenario was that Yulisa would pass the security check, and that she would accept the job. That's all Diana thought about because she was on a natural high from the moment of clarity brought on from the dream that still swam in her head. She reached across to the nightstand and plugged her phone in, then set up a rain app that helped her to sleep. She lay down on the bed. Her mind was still focused and alert, so she figured that she could call Elizabeth in the morning to ask her to help her come up with a way to recruit Yulisa. She knew Elizabeth's husband Antonio would be up early for his Sunday morning menudo breakfast with his friends at Adrian's Tacos before he plastered his ass on the couch and got drunk watching the Cowboys play—win or lose. Diana figured she'd call Bethy around nine, when she'd have time to talk. She was going to ask her best friend to explain her reasoning for thinking that Yulisa was a good candidate to take over. Diana was already sold on her, but she wanted her friend to explain the plan to see if there were any holes in her strategy. She had learned to do this from her old Russian friend, Alexander Tupov, who employed this kind of planning that helped to save Diana's life. She stretched out on the bed, concentrated on the sound of rain coming from the phone, and finally fell asleep.

## Chapter 18

Diana called Elizabeth at nine twenty in the morning. Elizabeth could hear excitement in her friend's voice, and she could tell that Diana was stronger today because her voice was not flat. "So, what time did Antonio leave for menudo this morning?" asked Diana.

Elizabeth laughed and replied, "Eight forty-five, y bien crudo también."

Diana paused before speaking, then replied, "Déjalo, he works hard, Bethy."

"Yeah, I know, but I worry about his health, you know, no se cuida, come pura grasa y bebe sus cervezas or worse when he hits the pisto," explained Elizabeth. "But what's up, you seem to be feeling better, at least compared to yesterday."

Diana sat on the sofa and smiled, then said, "I want your help in recruiting Yulisa to take over for me." She waited to hear her friends reply.

Elizabeth was confused, then said, "I thought you said she was a Fed?" Diana laughed and explained that she went on a roller coaster of emotions yesterday, but after having some time to reflect, it made a lot of sense. "Oh, so now she's not a Fed?" Elizabeth was enjoying getting the upper hand on her friend.

"Okay, okay, I was a fucking basket case yesterday, but now I feel like I have more clarity, and you know what they say about hindsight, so sell me on your plan," asked Diana. Elizabeth had hoped to be able to pitch her plan to name Yulisa as Diana's successor, and she was ready with key points that might persuade her. She explained that Diana could ask her to contribute full time to the Latino Cause. Another enticement would be that she would be the head of the organization—she would be the boss, the leader, and have all the responsibility and authority it entailed. Third on Elizabeth's list was that Yulisa could bring in some innovative ideas, because, in truth, she would have to keep up on the latest technology and need to find safer ways of running the operation. Last on Elizabeth's list was Yulisa would never have to worry about money again, but in the short amount of time Elizabeth had known Yulisa, she could tell she wasn't the type of person driven by money. Diana was busy writing all this down, and managed an "Umm," between flipping pages on the writing tablet. Finally, she stopped writing and replied, "Those are all good reasons, but the question is, will she take it? What if she says no? Then she'd know everything, putting the whole operation in danger."

Elizabeth sighed loudly and replied, "Yeah, there's always a chance she could turn you down, but she's sending money to us, so I think she'd keep quiet." Diana ran that through her head, and hoped Elizabeth was correct with her assessment.

"Well, either way, I got the ball rolling on this. I emailed Yulisa's résumé and application to Tito. All this talk could be academic if she can't pass the vetting process," explained Diana. "Thank you for your ear and tell Antonio I said he could have an extra beer if the Cowboys win."

"Shit, win or lose, va estar three sheets to the wind. Okay, talk to you later chica, bye," replied Elizabeth before she hung up the phone.

Diana put her cell down, reached in her satchel, and

pulled out an organization chart that was laminated and folded into thirds. It was well worn and starting to tear at the edges. Her picture was at the top, followed by The Four, then branched out even more. It was from this section of the tree that Diana would select from if Yulisa didn't work out. They were mostly men in their mid-forties, all capable of doing the job, or else they would not have risen to where they were today. It would be a hard choice, but Diana needed to have another plan in place. Shit goes wrong all the time, so Diana was a true believer in having options.

Diana was still working on the possible candidates when her cell rang. She answered and learned that Yulisa was more than three quarters of the way cleared, the only thing left was to verify if any of her relatives were in law enforcement. If all went well, she would be fully vetted, and the only thing in question would be if she'd be open to the idea of taking over for her. But that would be for later, for now, she continued working on contingency plans should Yulisa decline her offer. Diana identified four candidates to choose from. She'd ask The Four for guidance if Diana's original plan didn't come to fruition.

After another two hours, the four possible successors were cut to two. Diana was happy to stop there, she had done enough today, and it had been another productive day. It was late in the afternoon, so she poured herself some Chianti and sat at her patio table, her hair blowing around her face. She took a sip of the wine and felt refreshed, probably more from the good news on Yulisa. She felt happy her time was coming to an end, and now she had to contemplate how she was going to offer Yulisa the job.

# # #

The vetting of Diana's hoped for successor was complete on Monday just before eleven in the morning, and Diana was ecstatic. She got off the phone and did a little dance around her desk, her hips swayed in jubilation, as she pumped both fists into the air. Then she put her palms together and thanked God for answering her prayers. She opened her office door and walked to Yulisa's desk and asked her to have lunch with her.

Yulisa chose Vietnamese for lunch, so they went to Saigon One. Diana felt tense as they sat down, and her heartrate was working overtime—she hoped her friend did not notice. Diana tried to relax her breathing because this lunch was just a probing mission. She hoped to get roundabout answers on subjects, like a pitcher nibbling at the plate ahead on a 0-2 count. They both ordered the shrimp pho and iced tea with lemon. "So, what are your thoughts on the state of the world," asked Diana, as she put sugar into her tea.

Yulisa frowned, sighed, and then said, "It's all fucked up."

Diana smiled and nodded her head in agreement, then replied, "Yep, all we can do is try to make things better than they are now." The waitress came to the table and delivered two plates of condiments, which contained brussels sprouts, sliced jalapeños, cilantro, and assorted sauces to mix into the soup.

Yulisa smiled at Diana's comment and replied, "Yes, in our own way." Just then, their bowls of steaming hot pho came to the table. Diana watched as Yulisa put both sauces into the soup, giving the soup a dark tint, then added the cilantro and brussels sprouts, and mixed them as she tried to bury the sprouts and bring the shrimp up to the surface. Diana did the same but left one of the sauces unused. Yulisa took a spoonful of soup into her mouth, smiled, nodded, then said, "Yes, perfect like always."

Diana took a spoonful and agreed with Yulisa's assessment. She used chopsticks to take a bite from her shrimp and washed it down with her iced tea. Then she began to probe. "The other night, you said you donated to La Lady Fund, may

I ask you why? I hope that doesn't come off as being nosey."

Yulisa listened, then wiped her mouth with a napkin and replied, "Because I want to do my part to help these children who are forcefully separated from their families. Why?" Her eyes slowly narrowed.

"No reason, I was just wondering."

"Well, what do you think about all this madness going on? Personally, I think God is going to punish us all if we don't try and do our part. This child separation is cruel and makes this damn Administration look like the second coming of Hitler," explained Yulisa, as she savored the healthy lunch.

"Yes, I agree, Yulisa. There's so much hate I get the feeling those in charge of these horrific policies are rubbing their hands together, smiling with glee. They say this will work as a deterrent, but we all know the joy they get from traumatizing brown children," added Diana. Yulisa nodded, taking a few sprouts in her mouth. Despite being in the hot soup, they still had a crunch when she bit into them.

"That's why I stopped tithing at church, I wanted to do my part to help with this human catastrophe," replied Yulisa. Diana looked her straight in the eye and wanted to tell Yulisa the truth about her, but it wasn't time yet.

"Yeah, I hear that lots of people are doing that, do you think the churches are wondering why the till isn't at its usual peak?" chuckled Diana.

Yulisa looked up from her bowl, raised one eyebrow in thought then said, "Yeah, no shit, I never thought of that," nodding her head in agreement. They both laughed and continued to enjoy their meal. "So, what do you think of La Lady Fund?"

"Me?" said Diana, pointing a finger at her own chest as she ate noodles with the chopsticks.

"Yes, you," replied Yulisa.

She wiped her mouth with a napkin, then Diana stated,

"I think if it helps our people improve their lives, well, what's wrong with that?"

"I agree."

"What about it being illegal to do it?" asked Diana, waiting to hear her answer.

"Pissh," responded Yulisa, her lips curled in annoyance every time she heard that question. Diana observed her disdain, as Yulisa's forehead farrowed in disgust, then she added, "Look, our people, Latinos, are hard workers. If you see our gente in the streets, they are always selling something, fruit, flowers, hell, even pillows. When I come off the freeway all I ever see are güeros begging, always with their hand out asking for money. Now those are the real takers of the world. Our people bust their ass." Diana agreed, and now that she knew Yulisa's politics, she felt the odds of Yulisa taking over had gone up. They enjoyed lunch and the conversation, then they went back to the office.

Diana now felt more confident in the plan. It could still fall apart along the way, but she took this as real progress. Diana had learned the importance of taking one step at a time and paying attention to detail, picking up those skills from her twenty-seven plus years of leading the organization. Slowly but surely, she would soon take the next step to see if Yulisa would take over. The key was making it sound as appealing and as important as possible, but part of her heart grew heavy as she reminded herself that she had to let Yulisa know the personal risks involved in such a job, not to mention the continuous stress. There was a reason why she had to touch up her greys every two weeks. Tomorrow would be step two, with Thursday being the day she'd officially ask Yulisa to take over.

Chapter 19

Diana left work early, then called Elizabeth at three thirty in the afternoon—the exact time that school let out. Elizabeth was still in her classroom when she took the call. Diana gave her the rundown of her lunch with Yulisa and told her that everything was going well. They agreed that Diana would call her at seven-thirty in the evening.

Diana worked on some realty paperwork that had been neglected. She stopped what she was doing and wondered how long she'd still own her realty company when she finally retired from the organization. Diana was happy with the progress she made. She was glad to take care of business, and she smiled because like always, she was going to see it through.

Now her mind wandered to the thought of selling her realty business. Diana was always getting offers, but she always threw the letters away. Perhaps now she should start opening them. She got up from her home desk, walked into the kitchen and poured herself another cup of coffee. She contemplated where her first trip would be? Would it be going back home to visit her family in California, or would she visit Europe? The way things were breaking for her, she could do both and then travel even more. Saturday's morning drama seemed like a long time ago, and Diana was feeling more at peace. Her breathing was relaxed, and she felt contentment in her heart. She was still aware things could quickly go to hell, so she viewed all this good news with cautious optimism. Because she knew how the world worked and there was always a new problem to overcome, Diana would be ready if the wheels started to come off of her planning—she had plenty of experience fixing messes on the fly, and she considered herself an expert at making quick adjustments, and keeping her eyes on the goals at hand.

# # #

Diana called Elizabeth. "Hello Bethy, ¿cómo estás?" asked Diana, as she sat on her sofa with her feet up.

"Good, so tell me, are you going to ask her tomorrow?" inquired Elizabeth.

"No, if everything goes according to pla…" Diana was interrupted.

"Ha," replied Elizabeth, louder than she intended.

"Yeah, I know, there's always at least one problem that comes up. But easy on the negativity, Bethy," replied Diana.

"Negativity? ¿Qué? I'm just reminding you that shit never goes according to plan."

"I know, Bethy, but I need all the positive energy I can get. I need positive vibes, and lots of prayers."

"I know what you mean, yeah. But I think everything sounds like Yulisa will be open to at least hear about the job offer."

"Let's hope. I'm going to take her on a trip tomorrow, and plan on asking her about the job on Thursday," replied Diana.

"Trip? What kind of trip?"

"I'm going to show her an operation while it's happening, only she won't know, nor will she ever know, if she declines the offer. But I think her seeing an operation in action is the best way to gauge her thought process," explained Diana.

"Well, it sounds like you have everything under control, chica," stated Elizabeth.

The rest of the phone call was just girl talk, and Diana asked if Antonio drank that extra beer she suggested if the Cowboys won, which they did. Diana laughed at the story her friend told her about her husband's happy Sunday. Elizabeth also shared with Diana that she turned in her paperwork for retirement effective at the end of the current school year. Diana knew Elizabeth would miss the classroom, but nothing lasts forever, and change is always inevitable. She let her friend vent, listening until she was through. Diana knew the game because she did the same. It helped both women, and this is what friends did for each other. Later, Diana called the temp agency and requested a person for Yulisa tomorrow because both would be out of the office. To top off her evening, Diana took a long relaxing bath. She had to be at work early in the morning and baths always helped sleep to come quickly.

# # #

Diana got to work at six forty in the morning. She wanted to be the first one there so she could explain to Yulisa that they were both going to be out of the office. She even had time to stop and pick up donuts. She turned the key and flicked the lights on. The lights gave off a buzzing sound; this would be the quietest the office would be before it turned into the usual madhouse. Diana greeted the temp worker at the door when she arrive at seven thirty. She offered her a donut and told her to relax until her office manager arrived. Diana went back in her office and looked over the agenda she had written down.

Yulisa arrived at seven thirty-five and was shocked that Diana was already in the office. "Good morning, Diana, what are you doing here so early?" she inquired as she picked up a powered white donut.

"Good morning, Yulisa. Hey, today is special. Brief the temp over at the table because you are with me today. We're taking a road trip," explained Diana in a deep voice trying to sound like an MC. Yulisa had a puzzled look on her face as Diana patted her on the shoulder and said, "It's okay, I just want to show you a few things."

"Okay, let me brief my replacement on what she'll be doing. Wait, I'll be on the clock, right?" replied Yulisa, with one eye closed for dramatic purposes, then she smiled.

# # #

Diana and Yulisa were on the road by eight twenty. Diana explained she wanted her as company for this road trip to give her a break from the day-to-day routine, plus it would be fun to have someone to talk to. She explained they would be going to New Mexico in the morning, then make their way to Arizona in the afternoon. Diana looked at Yulisa and saw her furrowing forehead, then she patted Yulisa's arm and said, "Sit back and enjoy the view."

They took I-10 and then went north on I-25. They headed for Truth or Consequences, New Mexico for a ten-thirty meeting with Basilio, who had knowledge of the current operation going on in Arizona. During the drive up north, they listened to some old school music, and both nodded their heads to the beat. Yulisa enjoyed the trip because this was better than running around the office, taking care of everyone's problems. It was a good break from her routine, and she looked out the window and enjoyed the desert scene which was nothing but small hills surrounded by desert. It was a soothing view for Yulisa, one she never had the time to enjoy. But today she would because she was in excellent company.

They got to Gutierrez's Bar in Truth or Consequences just as it opened. Diana explained that she had a meeting with a client, and that Yulisa could go to the bar section and order a drink. Yulisa saw an older man come through the door. He was five foot nine and weighed about one hundred and seventy-five pounds. His hair was white and parted in the middle. Yulisa saw him give Diana a friendly hug, then she walked into the bar section, sat down, and ordered a strawberry margarita. She looked around the bar and liked its dark and mysterious décor—having a drink here certainly felt mysterious. Diana was finished with her meeting right when Yulisa ordered another drink. They stayed until she finished it. This would be a leisurely day for Yulisa.

"So how did your meeting go," asked Yulisa as they got back on the road.

"It went well. He wanted me to look over some new ideas he had. How were the margaritas?"

Yulisa smiled because she was already feeling the buzz from her drinks. They stopped one time to gas up and pee since their destination was almost four hours away. Throughout the drive there was banter between the women on what they thought were the best fashions, the best music, and their taste in men. It was a good time with each learning more about the other. They were on Interstate 25 going south, then took I-10 heading towards Arizona. The brown sand combined with the dark brown shale provided beautiful scenery. Diana looked at the clock in her car, and the blue numbers registered 1:17 PM. She got off the freeway and drove down a country highway for about thirty minutes, then made a right onto a dirt road. Yulisa saw a luxury recreational vehicle parked on the side of the road, open its door. A group of eight people in various stages of dishevelment appeared out of the bushes, ran straight into the RV, and disappeared into its interior. Diana watched Yulisa's expression. It did not register shock. A minute later the RV drove down the dirt road and headed north. "I guess we saw some migrants coming in," stated Diana, as she drove down the same dirt road then headed south.

"Poor people, I hope they make it all the way and don't get caught," replied Yulisa.

"Yeah, I'm sure that happens more than people realize,"

"Go with God," said Yulisa, shaking her fist in the air as she turned and smiled at Diana. Then they both had a laugh.

They got back to El Paso just before five in the afternoon. Diana dropped Yulisa off at the office. Just before getting out of the car, Diana said, "Hey, I'm throwing a midweek party tomorrow night, just some old friends getting together since everyone is in town all at the same time. That happens like once every ten years, so that's the reason for the midweek party, I want you to come."

"Sure, sounds good to me. I'll see you at work tomorrow. I'm beat from the trip," replied Yulisa. She waved goodbye, then got in her car, and drove away.

Diana headed home as she recalled her day. She wondered what Yulisa thought of driving down a dirt road and witnessing immigrants being saved. She had a good feeling about Yulisa, and by the end of the party tomorrow, she would know if she was going to offer the job to Yulisa. Thursday was the day she officially planned to ask her. Diana knew not to rule out any last-minute snafus because most times things never worked out as planned, but she would remain hopeful. She drove to her house and parked her car in the garage. It had been a long day, and she was tired.

Chapter 20

Diana was at work finishing up the last of the paperwork that she had left on the pile of tasks to be completed. When that was done, she returned a few phone calls. Before leaving she walked up to Yulisa and to hear how excited she was for the upcoming party, then left the office through her private door. Diana was greatly anticipating the night because this could be a preview of introducing the new boss to the group. They would get to see Yulisa's character and mannerisms without her knowing about it. This party would solidify support from her choice to take over. Observing Yulisa, Diana was sure they would like her. On the other hand, if Yulisa declined her offer, then this party would be nothing more than a good time to be had. Diana felt exhilarated about her plan, but by no means was this a slam dunk. It would be Yulisa's choice since she'd have to understand all the risks that the job entailed.

As Diana pulled into her driveway, Elizabeth's blue Ford F-150 was already in the driveway. Elizabeth had taken half a day off and had already taken a personal day for tomorrow, so she was primed to get her drink on with close friends that she had met over the years while working for the Organization. Elizabeth hugged Diana just outside the door. They didn't hug all the time, but Diana's best friend knew how important the next two days were to her friend, so she hoped her hug would bring her friend good luck and positive vibes. They began decorating the backyard with streamers, then Diana opened a bottle of wine so they would not get dehydrated. She turned on the outside speakers and they danced on the side of the patio that needed work. Both were excited to see old friends from the organization, friends who served in operations together, working in tandem with one goal in mind—to give others an opportunity as they went after their American Dream.

# # #

The first guests arrived together at five fifty in the afternoon. It was The Four, and they had come together. The lone woman, Fátima Fuentes was wearing a grey colored cotton pantsuit made from breathable material because she was ready for the El Paso heat should it make an appearance. Her black greying hair was braided and parted in the middle. She wore turquoise earrings along with a matching broach. She hugged Diana and Elizabeth, then walked through the open sliding door and out onto the patio. The men of The Four, Esteban Estrada, Gabino Galvez and Isidro Infante, all wore casual attire, though each one had a different color Guayabera shirt. Esteban sported a teal-colored shirt which made his greying beard stand out. Gabino wore a white shirt and had a thick grey mustache; his hair was combed towards the back, and he hoped that others could see he was going for the Mafiosi look. Isidro finished the Guayabera fashion show with what he liked to call his Bruin blue shirt. His grey beard was closely cropped and his green eyes were penetrating. They hugged both women then explored the patio as other guests arrived.

Yulisa showed up at six twenty and was introduced to everyone there. She met two attorneys, a couple of software engineers, two college professors, a school administrator, and two teachers along with one doctor and two nurses. Everyone was welcoming and polite. Diana had a Southern style dinner catered, which consisted of either fried or baked chicken, chicken fried steak and gravy, or meatloaf. The sides consisted of four cheese macaroni, collard greens, garlic mashed potatoes, and green beans along with jalapeño cheddar cornbread. There was a colorful Southwestern salad especially prepared for the non-meat eaters of the party. For dessert, there were two freshly baked pies, one apple the other peach. The caterer promised to serve at exactly seven in the evening, and that's what she did. Everyone sat and enjoyed the scrumptious meal along with the flowing wine and beer.

After dinner, Yulisa heard stories from their past, and how this day was special because it was the first time in ten years that they were all together for a party. Diana walked up to her and said, "Drink up Yuli, I have a temp coming in for you tomorrow, just so you know," as she held an imaginary cup in her hand and tilted it up, the universal sign for a free night of drinking with no repercussions, "And before you ask, yes, you're getting paid for tomorrow, so drink up."

"Why am I out of the office again tomorrow?" she asked.

"Solis Realty business," said Diana with a smile. She patted Yulisa on the back and told her to enjoy herself, then she introduced her to her old friends, Basilio, Monica, Leonardo, Sandra and Beto. They were around the same age as Diana. Yulisa could see that Diana was telling a story to Gabino, because her hands were gesturing wildly, and then heard a hearty laugh come from him. Yulisa looked around and saw Elizabeth talking with Basilio and Monica. She could see the joy these people had for each other as they intermingled.

The music changed from Vicente Fernández to disco and Diana's patio became a crowed dancefloor. Gabino was dancing with Monica, and he shimmied around the dancefloor while still holding his Modelo beer with a sincere smile on his face. Isidro walked over to Yulisa and asked her to dance. He took her hand and led the way. Even though he was old, he still had charisma. Yulisa couldn't tell if it was because of his beard or those penetrating green eyes. They danced four straight songs before Isidro said, "Come with me, I need another beer." They walked to the ice chest for a can. Yulisa went to her table, picked up her wine glass, then rejoined Isidro near the ice chest. "I hear you donate to La Lady Fund," he said. Yulisa nodded her head. "We all donate, too. That's what binds us together."

"That's why you're so close?"

Isidro smiled and said, 'Yes, that's why we are all brothers and sisters, and since you donate, you are one of us."

"Seems like a good club to be in," replied Yulisa, as she took a drink of her wine.

He smiled for a long time like he was thinking about what she had said, and announced, "Yes, it is." His cell rang and he said, "Excuse me." He walked into Diana's house to take the call.

"So how do you like my friends," asked Diana as she clinked her glass with Yulisa's.

"They all seem pretty cool."

"They like you too, Yuli. Hey, Fátima would like to have a word with you, she's sitting in the living room on the sofa. Diana led her inside the house.

"Doña Fátima, soy, Yulisa Bermudez." She shook the hand of the lone female member of The Four. Her hand offered warmth.

"Yulisa, sit down please." She patted the cushion next to her. She kept holding Yulisa's hand looking at her palm even when Yulisa sat down. "Diana told me about your tragedy. I am very sorry for you. Your palm shows you to be a strong person." Fátima looked her right in the eye.

"Thank you Doña Fátima," shaking her hand again, as

Fátima released her grip.

Fátima shifted her legs to the left side, allowing her to place her hands on Yulisa's face to bring it close to hers. "Child, you have strength, and God would not have put you through this hell if he knew you couldn't handle it. So take that pain and turn it into something positive." She kissed Yulisa on the forehead and let her head go.

"Thank you Doña Fátima," she said, taking Fátima's hand again. Then Yulisa excused herself and stepped out to the patio again. She walked to the table and poured herself another glass of wine. Then she walked around until she found Diana.

"So how was it?" asked Diana with a wry smile on her face.

"She's a nice lady. I like her, very Native American-ish," replied Yulisa. "All your friends are cool, lots of class in this group." She looked to the other side of the patio, where two different groups were talking and telling stories. Each person got to tell a story, and about two minutes later, there would be a chorus of laughter at different times. Yulisa could feel the camaraderie of the group, and the love they had for each other—now she understood why this midweek party was special to them.

Yulisa was a lightweight and excused herself at midnight. But before she left, every one of Diana's friends lined up to give her a hug. They were warm and caring, and she felt some sadness leaving such amazing company, but it was time to call it a night.

"I called you an Uber about a minute ago. We'll see each other tomorrow, so I'll drive to your house and pick you up. Thank you for coming amiga," stated Diana, as they gave each other a hug.

Yulisa smiled, still buzzing from the wine. "Thank you for the invite, all these people were so amazing, so authentic."

Diana smiled, then she looked down the street and saw the Uber approach. "Your ride's here. Yeah, these are what are called good people. Perhaps you'll meet them again." She opened the back door for her friend and then helped Yulisa in before closing the door.

Yulisa was a complete hit with Diana's friends. The Four had nothing but praise and they complimented her on her poise and grace. Even those in the lower ranks in the organization were impressed with her demeanor. Diana's plan to offer Yulisa the job was still a go. If she accepted the job, she could jump in and have everyone's support, but Diana understood the significance of her job offer. The job had its perks, but along with the benefits came the unnerving stress that never truly went away, and liked to hide in the dark corners of her mind. The job was the ultimate commitment, and the consequences brutal and life altering. All Diana could do was ask her friend to take over and try to convince her that she could do the job, but she'd understand if her friend said no because this type of life was not for everyone. Diana felt guilty even offering this job to someone who had already suffered more than her share. Diana's choice was a longshot, but the good thing was this would be played out in several days. Tomorrow would be the offer. She'd give Yulisa twenty-four hours to think about it. If Yulisa declined the offer, Diana was ready to name her replacement from inside the organization, and one way or another she would be out of the immigrant smuggling business once and for all.

Chapter 21

The next morning Yulisa slept in, knowing that she didn't have to get up for work. She finally got out of bed a little after nine in the morning, brushed her teeth, and showered. She wasn't hung over, and the warm water felt refreshing as she let it massage her skull. After the revitalizing shower, she dressed and then walked into the kitchen to make coffee. She then strolled to the living room and turned the television on. Her thoughts went back to last night and all the good people she'd met. She was still thinking about the party when the phone rang. She saw it was Diana and picked it up. "Hello, Diana, ¿cómo estas?"

"Hi Yulisa, I hope you're not cruda. Let's go to don Daniel's for some steaks at around eleven thirty. I'll pick you up."

"Sure, I can eat some carne today. I'll be ready, see you then," replied Yulisa, with her hand still on her phone as she walked back into the kitchen for her first cup of coffee.

# # #

Don Daniel's was more crowded than Diana expected. Perhaps everyone had the same idea of trying to beat the noon rush. Yulisa was in a good mood and smiling, the effects from the night before. Their server took their order, they both chose the New York steak with a loaded baked potato, a side salad, and iced tea. Don Daniel's was noisy with conversation and laughter. Diana told Yulisa a story she'd heard from doña Fátima and they both laughed. Yulisa was as relaxed as she'd ever been, perhaps it was good to take a personal day every now and then because she was having a relaxing day.

When their lunch arrived, there was no talking as both went straight to eating. The only noise that could be heard was when steak knives met plates. The loaded baked potato was just that, accompanied by two scoops of sour cream and two scoops of butter. The New York steak was tender, and Yulisa dunked each piece into the silver container of steak sauce. Diana finally had to remove one of the two scoops of sour cream, which allowed her to sprinkle the potato with salt. She looked over at Yulisa eating and was starting to get nervous about asking her friend to replace her as the head of an immigrant smuggling organization. She looked at her friend, who was happy and smiling, and a sadness came over Diana, because she knew that happiness and smile would soon be replaced by apprehension, stress, and fear. Diana dreaded bringing it up, but soon it would be time to know if Yulisa would be the new organization boss.

They shared a chocolate cake with ice cream for dessert. Don Daniel's certainly knew the art of presentation. They ordered coffee with dessert and enjoyed each other's company as the lunchtime crowd dissipated and the noise level returned to normal. They waited another five minutes while the server ran her credit card, which gave them enough time to finish their coffee.

After lunch they got into Diana's silver BMW. Diana merged onto the I-10 West, then connected to State Highway Twenty heading North. They passed Sunland Park, Canutillo, and Vinton then crossed the border into Anthony, New Mexico. She took Anthony Drive, then made a right on Ohara Road, also known as State Highway 404, and soon they connected to the I-10 West again. Diana was in no rush, and she took the long way to their destination because she was feeling sentimental by retracing the route her grandfather used to take when driving to Las Cruces, but she was also prolonging the drive to build up her courage. As Diana drove, she engaged in political talk about the cruelty of separating children from their parents, and she brought up valid points, but it was the passion in her voice that made people want to agree with her. Yulisa nodded her head. It was time for Diana to ask Yulisa and she took a few deep breaths, then began. "Yulisa, I'm going to take a risk and tell you something, but you can't tell anyone, ever." She glanced at Yulisa and made eye contact.

Yulisa looked concerned, "What, what is it?"

Diana could feel her heart racing and her cheeks blush. She felt warm all over and reminded herself to breathe deeply to regain her calm. She said a silent prayer, then blurted out, "I am the lady in La Lady Fund. I oversee the whole organization. Remember that RV that picked up immigrants?" Yulisa nodded her head in the affirmative. "That was us," as Diana pointed to her chest.

Yulisa turned towards Diana and replied, "What? How long have you been La Lady?'

Diana smiled, then confessed, "I founded this organization in the 90's, and now I'm looking to leave."

Yulisa looked shocked and then said, "Why are you telling me this?"

"I'm telling you because you're my friend and I trust you. I see that trust in your eyes. I would like to offer you the top position in the organization. I want you to continue running the operations."

Yulisa looked at Diana as her forehead farrowed, trying to decipher what she had just heard. "Why me? Why did you choose me?"

"Yulisa, I have seen your work ethic, and your leadership skills. Your attention to detail makes you an ideal candidate." They were now on the outskirts of Las Cruces. "I normally would have promoted someone within the organization, but your age is ideal. You know I was around your age when I started this."

"My age? What do you mean by that?" inquired Yulisa.

Diana sighed loudly, not out of frustration, but because she had said the same thing to different people. First it was to The Four, then she ran her theory by Elizabeth, and now once again, she'd have to explain. "By your age Yulisa, I mean that if you took the job, you could run it for many years, and the organization would not have as much turnover." Diana explained, "Look, if I promoted from within, there would be a new boss, for what, five or six years before they'd retire. While you my friend, are still a spring chicken."

Yulisa put her hands to her face trying to understand what she'd just heard. Her head was reeling from all this new information, and then she smiled and laughed and said, "Jesus Christ, waking up this morning, I had no idea what I'd be hearing today." She put her hand in her hair and ran her fingers through it. She did this every time she was nervous.

Diana took the off ramp to the New Mexico State University campus, then drove to the football stadium parking lot, turned her car off, and faced her friend. "I know this is a lot of information at one time but allow me a chance to explain how we operate." Diana shed light on how her operations ran on both sides of the border. She explained the recruiting process of those brought across. She also went into detail about the nominating process in Mexico, and the work contracts signed by employers in the United States. Diana explained that the people brought across the border were given support even after they were in the US because the organization wanted them to be successful.

Diana eased Yulisa into the operations of the organization. The day Yulisa saw the RV picking up people was a trial balloon to see what Yulisa's reaction would be. Had she been appalled by what she saw, Diana knew that she'd have to promote from within, but Yulisa showed no signs of disgust at what she observed. Hence, the job offer that Yulisa was now receiving. "So, tell me, what are your thoughts?" asked Diana.

Yulisa sighed then stated, "It's a lot to take in right now. I'll have to think about this, but I want you to know that I think what you do is amazing. You give people opportunities."

Diana smiled then added, "All we do is give them an opportunity, but it's their work ethic that keeps them employed. I get tired of that goddamn fucking moron, Trump, accusing Mexicans of only being drug dealers and rapists."

"I get it, this Administration is downright mean. They want to cause as much personal grief as possible and call it a deterrent when really those white supremacist bastards are laughing at their own cruelty," added Yulisa with disgust on her face.

"Yes, and that's why we are getting so many donations for La Lady Fund. Many people are not happy with the child separation, and there is a lot of support against this policy," stated Diana. She parked her car in the stall and continued. "I think you'd be perfect to take over for me. You are the kind of person who can excel at this job because of your work ethic, and I've noticed, you're very detailed oriented, which is a plus for this job." Diana patted Yulisa's left knee and added, "Look, take the weekend to think this through. There's a lot of fringe benefits to the job, but I won't sugar coat it. It's a risky job, and I want you to be aware of the dangers, but I also want you to know that we have been doing this for twenty-seven years, and our operations have not been detected. One last thing, I don't want you to feel obligated to take this offer, if you feel the risks are not worth it, I'll understand." Diana left the university parking lot and got back on I-10 back towards El Paso.

On the forty-five-minute drive back home, few words were spoken, each woman alone in her thoughts. Diana hoped that Yulisa would take the offer, which would be the perfect scenario for her. Yulisa was running the offer through her head. She felt excitement, but also fear, so she knew that she was going to write out the pros and cons of accepting the job offer. "I can't believe that I am in the same car as the lady who helps the Mexicans. You know you're famous, and immigrants love you, because they know you are trying to help them, and that's why they hold you in such reverence," stated Yulisa.

Diana looked over to her, smiled then nodded her head. She knew she was loved in the immigrant community, and she was grateful for being able to do her part in helping people find their American Dream. She had set the foundation, and if Yulisa accepted the job, the odds would be excellent that it would continue.

Chapter 22

Yulisa awoke at a quarter till nine on Friday morning. Her first thought went back to Diana's job offer, and she felt exhilaration as well as fear. She took a deep breath, trying to relax, but she felt nervous energy, so she knew she could skip the coffee for today. Eventually, she got out of bed and got ready for her day. It felt unusual to be off two consecutive days during the week, but here she was at home with Diana's job offer running through her mind. Her day was as open as a tight end on hot route near the end zone with an all-out blitz, and she was contemplating a few places to visit. Then an idea came to her. She remembered that she and her husband's only vice when married was visiting the Native American casinos on a quarterly basis. She made reservations for a night's stay at the Casino Del Sol Resort in Tucson, Arizona. It was a four-and-a-half-hour drive one way, but she had to entertain Diana's offer and hitting the slots was always relaxing to her.

The closer she got to Tucson, the more emotional she became because she recalled her last time here with her Sergio and all the little stories he'd tell her to kill the long half day trip. She drove up to valet, then carried her blue sports bag around her shoulder and walked straight to the Registration Desk. She was assigned a room on the ninth floor, and when she swiped her key card and opened the door, she was rewarded with a fantastic view of the Tucson Mountains. She took off her shoes, got on the bed, set her alarm clock to ring in an hour and a half, and napped in comfort. As soon as the alarm woke her, her first thought was of Diana's job offer. Yulisa went to the sink, washed her face, brushed her teeth, and tied her hair into a ponytail. She wore faded Levis and put on her blue and orange UTEP hoodie because the casino was always on the cold side. She hoped those U of A people wouldn't give her any shit for her choice in hoodies.

Yulisa took the elevator down to the Player's Booth, then gave the attendant her driver's license. In less than a minute she had her player's card complete with a black looping clip that she connected to her belt. Now ready, she cased the casino, trying to find a good machine to play. Yulisa wasn't after a jackpot because she was set for life due to Sergio's and Rosita's fatal accident, but she wanted to stretch out her money. She was one of the few slot players to understand that the true game in gambling was to make your money last as long as possible. Yulisa would consider playing four to five hours to be a good gambling day regarding the amount of time spent. If she dropped a hundred on slots, she was okay with if it lasted two hours. She viewed it as the price for entertainment, just as if she had paid for a ticket to see the Blue Man Group in Vegas.

Yulisa surveyed the casino floor and looked for Sergio's favorite slot machine to see if it was still there—she turned the corner and found the Wolf Run penny slot with a three dollar maximum bet per throw. She sat down on the red cushioned chair, took out a crisp hundred-dollar bill, inserted it into the machine, and placed her purse around her left shoulder, securing the shoulder bag with her arms like if she were carrying a football. She adjusted the screen for maximum volume, just like how Sergio liked. She played a three-dollar bet, and won a dollar of that back, the background sounds made the game more enticing. She hit the max bet button and got lost in her task. Yulisa ran Diana's offer in her head. She would be the Head of the Organization that brought immigrants over which could bring immense risk, especially for her freedom. But at the same time, this would be a way to save immigrants from the cruel family separations that had been shown in the media. She cashed out with a ninety-six-dollar ticket and walked to find another machine.

She ambled around past a thin elderly looking Native American woman talking to her machine. The lady had placed three trolls on top of her slot machine to entice the gambling Gods. Yulisa made her way to the bar, sat down, and ordered a beer. The only time she drank beer was when she came to the casino, and sadly this would be her first beer since her husband and daughter were taken from her. She squeezed some lime juice into the Modelo bottle then took a drink. It was perfect like always, and the only thing missing was her husband. Yulisa sat at the bar looking up at a college football game on the television, then contemplated the job offer again. There was still a lot of things she needed to know before she could make up her mind, but this trip was for her to see if she would even consider the job. She did like the idea of helping immigrants, especially with this current sadistic administration. So that was a plus.

She got up from the bar and trekked around the perimeter of the entire casino, lost in her thoughts. Yes, she thought, it would be excellent to help immigrants, but by assisting them, she was putting herself in peril. If she took the job and then was discovered, life as she knew it would be over. She would rot away in jail and be an embarrassment to her family, the latter concerned her more than the former. She knew that when it came time to decide, the family aspect would play a huge role in whether she accepted or not. Yulisa stopped dead in her tracks when she found Sergio's second favorite machine called Bier Haus, or as Sergio liked to call it, 'La Chichona,' for the blonde with the big boobs holding a beer mug that appeared for a chance at a bonus. This was one of the only times that he allowed himself to be macho, and Yulisa used to laugh because it always came out so forced, as if he didn't want to hurt his wife's feelings. Thinking of him, she sat down, put her ticket into the machine and yelled, "Come on Chichona!

Yulisa played the slot and was quickly down twelve dollars. She smiled, took a drink of her beer, cashed her ticket out, and then put it back in. After each loss, she would hit the ticket button, then immediately put it back in. She had learned this from her Sergio when he used to play slots and began losing. He would always print his ticket, then reinserted the same ticket. She asked him what he was doing and explained that if he was going to lose money, then he was going to make the casino use its resources of paper and ink. It was silly, but that's just the way her Sergio was; so in his honor, she did the same.

She grew bored of the slot as her ticket dwindled to sixty dollars. Yulisa was enjoying her time at the casino. She was relaxed as she evaluated Diana's job offer. She liked that she was not losing herself in the gambling even with a major life decision ahead. She had always been efficient. She finished her beer, ordered another one, then headed upstairs to her room. She propped up the pillows, took her shoes off, then lay on the bed. She grabbed the remote and quickly found the Lifetime Channel. She used it as background noise as she ran more questions in her head.

Most people would run away from a job opportunity that Diana presented to Yulisa, but not her. Had she not been widowed and still had her Rosita, she would have said no, but the trauma she'd experienced had changed her mindset. Through all the therapy to cope with the loss, she knew that these were just Band-Aids to throw at her issues. What people don't realize when people suffer tragedies is it can affect them in ways that could change a person's outlook on life. They could get some assistance, but people handled their misfortunes in their own way either through pity, anger, hate, jealousy, or acceptance. The latter was Yulisa's approach because no matter how much therapy and family support there was, nothing was going to bring little Rosita and her Sergio back to her. So she learned to keep busy. This is how she coped with her loss, but she felt like a hamster, just spinning the wheel of activity, as she went through life.

Yulisa looked within herself and asked if she really needed Diana's job offer. Monetarily she did not, but she was missing a purpose in life and this opportunity could be beneficial to her. She knew what she was—she was fucked up emotionally from her loss, but everyone had their own issues. Some people dealt with them while others ignored their problems, praying they would go away by themselves. That's why the world had a plethora of people, some good, some bad, some assholes, while others who were just plain mean. Yes, this opportunity could be good for her. She felt at peace, and she had come here to get clarity, to ask herself if she could even consider such a career move, and the more she analyzed it, the more she saw how it could give her a true purpose in life now that her family had been taken away.

She took a short nap and woke up refreshed and relaxed. The task that she had given herself had been accomplished, and now she was going to enjoy herself. She called room service and ordered a ribeye steak, medium, with a loaded baked potato and a garden salad with Italian dressing. She looked out of her hotel window and saw the Sonoran Desert, remembering how Sergio loved the desert with its colorful rock formations. She felt a closeness to her husband here, and in her head, she asked him if she was making a mistake by accepting Diana's offer, but instead, she only felt bliss, contentment, and peace. She felt he would think it would be a good idea, or else she figured she'd feel some apprehension, and there was none. She sat on the sofa, with the remote in her hand and flipped through the channels. She left it on a Friday night college football game, as she waited for room service to deliver her dinner.

Chapter 23

Yulisa slept in until almost ten—there was just something about a hotel bed that brought the most comfortable night's sleep. She was happy with her decision and would call Diana when she got back home, but for now, it was a quick shower, followed by breakfast before a late morning gambling session. She wanted to be on the road by noon, so she could be back in El Paso by six in the evening.

# # #

"Thank you very much," said Yulisa, as she gave the valet a ten-dollar tip, then got into her blue 2016 Honda CR-V. She had just cashed out her winnings; she'd made a twenty-six-dollar profit from her gambling. She liked this casino because she felt Sergio's presence in it. It was like she'd been talking and discussing Diana's offer with him. That was the reason why she would tell Diana that she'd accept her offer. She felt with full confidence that Sergio would have supported her decision. Her heart felt happy, and she was relaxed, content that she had set out to make a decison and had followed through. She drove down East Valencia Road and stopped at the ARCO to fill up her gas tank and got more coffee. Soon she was on Interstate 10 heading east and looking forward to a new life.

After she had made her decision about Diana's job offer, Yulisa was in a tranquil state. She was in no rush to get home, and as she leisurely drove back to El Paso, she enjoyed the desert scenery. She hit the drive-thru, before Yulisa got home at a quarter past six in the evening. She walked through her foyer, placed her car keys in an old Native American wooden bowl, and threw her travel bag into the laundry room. She was glad to be home, and dying to inform Diana of her acceptance, but she'd call her tomorrow. For now, she opened a kitchen cabinet for a plate and then placed four soft tacos in a neat display before throwing the Styrofoam box into the garbage can. The tacos were delicious as always, and she topped off the evening with a candlelit bubble bath. In the past, Yulisa would soak in the tub and cry tears of despair, mourning the loss of her daughter and husband, but now, the bath had been transformed into an emotional cleanse, the washing off of tragedy, and turning that pain into a life mission of helping others.

# # #

It was ten in the morning when Yulisa phoned Diana, the phone rang three times before it was answered. "Diana, it's me, Yulisa, when can we meet so we can chat in person?"

"Good to hear from you Yulisa. I can meet you wherever you want. Just name the time and place," replied Diana as her heartrate increased with anticipation.

"Can I pick you up at noon?"

"Yes, I'll be ready. See you then, bye," said Diana as her brain went a mile a minute trying to figure out if her friend was going to take the job. Diana smiled because either way she was going to get out of the immigrant smuggling business. Either her friend was going to be her successor, or she'd hire from within the organization. It was a win-win situation for Diana because either way she was going to start her new life It was just a matter of who would be taking over. Things were moving fast, and Diana looked forward to something new where her only problem would be is if she still had coffee creamer left in the refrigerator instead of being notified that the transportation never arrived for the waiting group of immigrants. Now that was some straight up stress, so Diana was happy that she was making progress and soon she would be free to do anything, go anywhere, and be whoever the hell she wanted to be.

Yulisa was precise in her time, and she arrived at Diana's right at straight up noon. Diana saw her friend's blue Honda CR-V coming up the street and smiled and waved. She opened the door and got in. Nothing was said, as Yulisa drove out of Diana's neighborhood. "Do you mind, I'm on a Mexican food kick for the last two days so I want to have some menudo from Jesusita's, if you don't mind."

"That sounds good," replied Diana, trying to get a feel of where the conversation was going—and she didn't have to wait long.

"So, tell me about this job?" enquired Yulisa.

"If you take the job, you'll be the head of the organization. Just keep things as they are right now, you don't have to do much," said Diana, as she pointed to an empty parking spot right by the front of the door.

"What do you mean I don't have to do much?"

Diana explained to her that everyone in the organization had a job to do, and they were all professionals. "Everyone knows they are just a cog in the system, and everyone is responsible for their own tasks."

"But I don't know anyone," replied Yulisa, with a farrowed forehead announcing her uncertainty.

They got out of Yulisa's vehicle and entered the restaurant. It wasn't too crowded for this time of day. "But you have, my dear," said Diana, looking Yulisa in the eye.

"Who?" Was her shocked reply.

"You met a lot of the members at the party the other night. Everyone at the party works for the organization. You even met The Four," Diana announced, and before her friend could speak, she continued, "Remember doña Fátima? She's one of The Four, as well as Gabino, Esteban, and Isidro. Even my friend Elizabeth works with the Organization." She put her arm around Yulisa so her friend wouldn't feel overwhelmed.

Yulisa moved her eyes upward, as she recalled the party. "Oh, no wonder she put her hands on my head. I thought it was pretty weird at the time, but now it all makes sense." A smile crept onto her face at the recognition of events.

"So, I take it that you have interest in the job?" Diana said with a smile on her face. Inside she was dancing with joy because she was going to be able to move on and start a new life and was happy that Yulisa would be her replacement. She was getting the exact kind of successor she wanted.

"Well, I still don't know what I'll be doing," Yulisa replied as they were led to a table. The server handed them a menu, then quickly returned with some salsa and chips.

Diana put her hand up to lower Yulisa's anxiety and replied, "We're going to be traveling starting on Tuesday. I want to introduce you to our recruiter in the U.S. We'll be going to Seattle for a day and a half, then we're going to fly into Burbank and then go down to the San Joaquin Valley near Bakersfield. Don't worry, I'll show you everything, I wouldn't throw you to the wolves."

"Well, I would hope not. Do you mind?" asked Yulisa, before putting some salt into the salsa. Diana nodded her head, and Yulisa salted the red sauce that contained tomatoes and onions before dipping a crisp chip into the bowl.

Yulisa went for the menudo while Diana chose the three-chicken soft taco combo and both ordered diet sodas. "Yulisa, thank you for accepting this job. There is nothing to compare it to. It's fun, exciting, rewarding, but it can be dangerous. More from the law enforcement standpoint than dangerous people."

Yulisa smiled, then nodded her head. She explained to Diana the reasons she agreed to take her up on the offer. The first was the Cause. Yulisa thought that too many people were under the impression that Latinos in general where lazy people who leeched off Government Programs, but most Latinos Yulisa knew were hard workers and provided for their families. The second reason she chose to accept the job was it provided a way to keep her busy so she could not dwell on the past. Yulisa would be the first to admit that the tragedy that befell her was traumatic and thus changed her view on life. But everyone had their own crosses to bear and confronted their demons in their own way. Lastly, her view of her new endeavor was if she could keep the operation alive on her watch, in her own way, the memory of her Rosita and husband would live on. It was twisted logic, but Yulisa would use it as motivation to do her job.

Their lunch was served just as Yulisa finished giving Diana her reasons for accepting. Diana reached for some salsa and spread it on her chicken tacos. The server brought Yulisa corn tortillas along with the condiments for her menudo. She flipped the container of chopped onions into her bowl, then she added some chili flakes before squeezing three lemon slices into her soup. The tripe was perfectly cut in uniform square patterns that were just the right bite size. On the other side of the table, Diana was going to work on her food, squeezing lemon on her tacos, then adding a little salt before taking a bite, followed by a small bite from a jalapeño pepper. After about three minutes of silence, they both laughed because they had been lost in the food.

After they finished eating, Diana gave her the quick rundown of how the operations worked. Before any group could be brought in, there had to be jobs waiting for them. She explained to Yulisa that they had someone who would arrange jobs and signed contracts with employers. She informed her friend of the support the groups received so they wouldn't feel like they had to fend for themselves. She said the goal of this was two-fold, one was to help the people get into the United States, and the people's work ethic would take care of the rest. Many businesses had signed various employment contracts because they knew they would get employees who busted their asses. The second part was to show Americans that the myth of the lazy Mexican was created to distort the truth and the organization had proof of that success.

After lunch they drove to Diana's house where she shared some files with Yulisa. "I guess we'll have to update this," announced Diana, as she handed the organizational chart that had Diana at the top of the page.

Yulisa looked at the chart and recognized many faces from Wednesday's party. Then it hit her that she was going to be doing something that would be risky but also important—she would be responsible for the continued success of organizational operations. She was ready for a job like this; it was exactly what she needed. She would take care of organization business as if it was her child because in a sense it would be. She looked forward to helping people not have to risk being brought onto American soil by coyotés. Yulisa looked over the chart one more time, smiled broadly then said, "So when do I take my picture?"

Chapter 24

Yulisa was at the office by seven-fifteen in the morning because she wanted to meet her replacement when she came in. It gave her time to collect her things and put them in a box. She studied the family photo of Rosita, Sergio, and herself, then put it in the box. She cleaned out her desk and wondered what her new office would look like. She was still in shock at the turn of events. It had been six days since Diana threw the Wednesday night party, and now she was going to start a new job, one where she would be at the helm. She still had a hard time believing it herself, but here she was removing her possessions and loading them into her vehicle.

Yulisa briefed her replacement about the daily tasks, and gave her tips on some of the idiosyncrasies of the realtors so she could anticipate their wants and make a good impression. Diana came in just before eight and asked Yulisa to step into her office. Diana walked to her desk and sat down. She had a serious look on her face. "Again, thank you for accepting this job," said Diana, as she opened her laptop. "Listen, I need you to understand that by accepting this job, you are opening yourself up to possible imprisonment. I'm not going to bullshit you. You'll have constant stress, and each time you eat food, you'll wonder if that was your last meal as a free person." Diana looked Yulisa in the eye and put the palms of her hands on her desk and continued, "Yulisa, you're my friend, and I don't want to sugarcoat this job and blow smoke up your butt. This job is risky. Just over ten days ago, I thought I was busted. I thought I was being followed, then I saw two police cars coming my way, and I thought it was all over," she explained. Tears welled up in her eyes before they fell down her brown face.

Yulisa reached out to hold her hand, then replied, "Listen, thank you for the warning, but I need this job, more for my sanity than anything else. This gives me a purpose, but I do appreciate you being honest with me."

Diana got up from her desk and walked around to give Yulisa a heartfelt hug. "Thank you for accepting my offer. By taking over for me, you've allowed me to get on with my own life. I'm tired, and I think I've done my part for the Cause." She went back to her desk and took out a writing tablet, then turned it so Yulisa could read it. It was an itinerary for the next few days. They'd be flying to Seattle to meet with Vanessa Villamontes, the Head of the US Recruitment for the Organization, followed by a trip to the Bakersfield area. "I'm going to need your driver's license to make plane reservations," added Diana.

Yulisa fished out her driver's license and gave it to Diana. The wheels were now set in motion, and Yulisa was really going to do this. A smile crept onto her face because she knew this was exactly what she needed. She would have a true purpose in her life other than going to work and coming home. With the new job, she felt that she would be too focused to dwell on the past. She knew her little Rosita and Sergio would never be forgotten because they would always live in her heart. In her way of thinking, they would help her to be successful because this was not just any job, but one where people's lives could be vastly improved. She was looking forward to starting her new purpose in life.

# # #

Diana picked Yulisa up at five-forty-five in the morning for a six-fifty-five Southwest Airlines flight to Seattle. "I hope you like planes because you're going to be in the air a lot," said Diana as they drove to El Paso International Airport.

"It beats driving, I guess, but there is something about being in a metal tube that is so weird to me," Yulisa replied. Diana parked and popped the trunk as the two ladies gathered their luggage. They took a short walk to the pickup stop, then the airport shuttle bus dropped them off at the Southwest Airlines terminal.

"Flying gets old after a while, but it sure cuts down on travel time. This is one part of the job I won't miss," admitted Diana. The driver unloaded their bags, and they walked into the airport.

Their flight left at nine in the morning with an hour and a half layover in Las Vegas. They arrived at the Seattle-Tacoma Airport just before four in the afternoon, and walked over to rent a silver 2017 Ford Explorer. Yulisa had never been to Seattle before and by the expressions on her face, she was impressed with the Emerald City. They drove to the Seattle Marriott Waterfront and checked into a suite. "Do you always stay at such nice places?" asked Yulisa, entirely impressed with the Marriott as she looked at the boat docks from their hotel window.

Diana smiled and laughed as she thought how far they had come from the organization's foundation. "When I first started out, I was happy to secure a room at a Motel Six. We've grown immensely, especially with all the checks being sent to La Lady Fund," Diana explained. Yulisa listened to her, but her eyes were on the boats moored on the water as she watched the boats bob up and down with the chop. "Yulisa, this is all yours now. You are going to run the ship, and I know this organization will be in good hands because

I know you truly care right here." She lightly touched the top of Yulisa's chest, "Right here," repeated Diana. Yulisa smiled and thanked her. She gauged Diana was comfortable with her decision, and Yulisa knew she was ready for such a commitment. "We'll have dinner tonight, and then tomorrow you're going to meet our main US Recruiter," Diana informed.

"For the jobs?" inquired Yulisa.

"See, you're a fast learner. Part of this whole process is getting jobs for the people coming over. It would make no sense to bring people in without jobs, so signing contracts with employers is a win-win situation," explained Diana. Yulisa saw a yacht pulling out of the harbor and a smile crossed her face. She nodded to herself and put the image of the boat into her memory bank. "Don't worry, everything will make more sense tomorrow; it's a learning process. Every day you'll get a little more clarity. Come on, let's go be tourists."

# # #

The two explored Seattle as it began to get dark. They went to Pike Place Market, one of the most photographed scenes from the Emerald City. Diana reminded Yulisa that there wasn't any rush to see all the sights because she'd be back in ten days. They viewed fish being tossed from hand to hand and into the display case. Everyone behind the counter knew it was show-time as they displayed pride in their work by demonstrating their professionalism at its best. After the sun went down, they went up to the Space Needle and saw the three-hundred-and-sixty-degree view of the Seattle skyline at night. Both now understood why Seattle was known as the Emerald City because that's what it appeared from this amazing view as the lights twinkled in the breeze. Eventually they ended up at their hotel bar and had a glass of wine as Diana briefed Yulisa on their upcoming meeting.

"Do you know our US Recruiter doesn't even work for

us?" admitted Diana, as she took a drink from her wine.

Yulisa's face was in a half frown trying to decipher what Diana had told her. "What? How is that even possible?"

Diana laughed, "I know how it sounds, but she has her own job, and wherever they send her, she works trying to finalize contracts with future employers for the organization."

Yulisa was still confused, "But she doesn't work for you?"

"Well, not in an official capacity or on our payroll. We comp her lunches and dinners. Lots of times she'll have evening meetings to finalize contracts. She goes all over, to Seattle, San Francisco, Los Angeles, Las Vegas, Chicago, St. Louis, Miami, Austin, Atlanta, and New York City, almost anywhere."

Yulisa's eyes grew big as she processed the news. "You mean the people that you bring in go to all these places? It's not just a Southwestern thing?"

Diana smiled and replied, "No, we're not just a Southwestern thing."

"Humm, well, I'm going to get another drink then," Yulisa announced, trying to understand the enormity of the organization's footprint. Diana laughed and told her she'd join her for another glass.

Diana reached into her purse and took out her wallet, slid the company credit card out, and handed it to her friend. "Here, this belongs to you now—you'll get another one in your name in a few weeks." She swiveled her chair towards Yulisa and gave her a hug. Up until that moment, nothing had been spoken regarding a salary. But now it was time. "You know why I know I've made the correct decision in naming you as my successor?" Yulisa shrugged. "Because you never brought up money. Never once did you ask about the pay." She looked her friend in the eye. "To me that shows that you understand that this job is a mission. Not everyone is like you, too many people think about what's in it for them. But not you, and that's how I know I've made the perfect choice."

Yulisa acknowledged Diana with a smile. Diana continued. "Your annual salary is going to be four hundred thousand. The reason it's so high is that you're taking the most risk. You know what they say: the reward better exceed the risk. You will have a health plan which also includes dental and vision. Sorry, no stock options," Diana said with a smirk. "Oh, and we're going to be together for the next thirty days or so. I'll be showing you around the Mexican side of the operation, and I'll introduce you as their new leader."

Yulisa nodded her head, taking everything in. She'd always been a good listener and understood what was being asked of her. She was excited to start a new job, and never in her wildest dreams could she ever conceive of an idea where she would oversee an immigrant smuggling organization. She thanked God for allowing her to be put in this situation and felt fortunate that she would be working with others to help people to improve their lives. This was the exact type of job she needed, one where she'd be so consumed with details that she'd be too busy to dwell on the loss of her family. Yes, this is exactly what she needed, and she was looking forward to it.

## Chapter 25

Diana and Yulisa were already sitting at the table when Vanessa Villamontes came through the door. Vanessa had black curly hair that went down to her shoulders, and wore a blue pantsuit with a white blouse. When she saw Diana, a smile came to her face. After they hugged and exchanged pleasantries, Diana introduced Yulisa to Vanessa. "Vanessa, I present to you the new leader of the organization, Yulisa Bermudez."

Yulisa stuck her right hand out, but Vanessa gave her a hug instead. "Welcome to the club, I guess we're sticking with the girl power," she said, extending her fist in the air with force.

Yulisa smiled and thanked her for the warm welcome. Diana had never really thought of it like that, but it was true, another female was going to oversee an immigrant smuggling organization that she hoped would last forever. Diana's heart was happy because this was the start of her leaving this life and finally starting her own.

Vanessa explained to Yulisa how she became involved in Diana's organization, and it was indeed a small world. Her uncle Basilio was an employee for the organization. One holiday season her family drove from Chicago down to El Paso to spend time with family and to get the hell out before the snowstorms that were due to hit. Vanessa learned about the organization from her uncle and became intrigued. At the time Vanessa was four years at her present company and rising fast. Soon she was the main headhunter for a company that tried to lure top Information Technology talent to her company. This allowed her to travel all over the United States in search of people.

Basilio told Diana about his niece's job and how she wanted to help the organization. Diana contemplated this for a few months before Basilio reminded her again how his niece would like to assist. Eventually they met and Vanessa presented her with what she could do for the organization, explaining that her company sent her all over the country, and how she could do organizational work after hours. Diana gave her a curious look. Vanessa explained that she was very tenacious and wanted to be of help to the Organization. It took Diana a few days to think about it, then realized that there were others like her, who wanted to help people to achieve their American Dream.

When Diana asked Vanessa if she wanted to be on the organization's payroll, she declined. She reminded Diana that her job took her across the country, and Diana could save the money that would have gone for her salary for other operational uses instead. She reminded Diana of her own grandfather with her 'stick to the man' attitude. Vanessa provided a valuable service, and she was excellent at her job. Being raised a Catholic, she learned to use the art of guilt when prospective employers balked at signing contracts. Without Vanessa's persuasion, the operation couldn't work, and the supply side would be overflowing with people without jobs. Diana considered Vanessa an important cog in the system, because without her knocking out contracts, there would be no entry for the Cohorts.

"Congratulations on your promotion," stated Vanessa with a smile. She then picked up the menu.

"Thank you, Vanessa, and I want you to know that I come from the 'if it ain't broke then don't fix it' crowd," Yulisa explained. The server brought a basket of French bread and a plate of butter packets for the table. "I still can't believe it." Diana smiled and looked over the table.

"Yulisa was my office manager at my realty company. This is the only person I would trust outside of the organization. Her work ethic was what brought her to my attention," explained Diana, as she reached for the French bread, then put the butter packet into the palm of her left hand to warm it up before slathering it onto the bread.

"Really?" said Vanessa.

Diana patted Yulisa on the back and said, "I trust this girl completely. She's unique and a strong individual with a heart of gold. Like I said before, she's the only one I'd consider from outside of the organization."

"Well, that's good to know," replied Vanessa.

Vanessa talked about her travel schedule for the next week. She was in Seattle for a day, then would travel to Los Angeles, San Diego, and the Phoenix area before heading to Austin, Houston, and Shreveport, Louisiana.

"How many cities will you sign contracts in for the organization," Yulisa asked.

Diana and Vanessa looked at each other and smiled. "All the cities I'm going to have an organization component to it," replied Vanessa. "I'm hoping to sign contracts in all those cities."

Yulisa was floored by the news. She had no idea how big the organizational footprint was. She smiled when she realized these contracts Vanessa signed were the actual beginnings of people starting their American Dream. The organization opened the door for them, but it was up to the people to work their asses off to achieve their dreams. "Wow, that's amazing."

Diana and Vanessa picked up on what Yulisa had just

said, both were happy she was thinking like a team player. "It's not that hard, once employers find out they are getting quality employees, they jump at the chance. They get tired of hiring people who want to get paid but only produce the minimum amount of work. Our workers focus on doing the job to take care of their families, and that is why we have contracts just about everywhere," explained Vanessa.

The three ladies ordered the Caesar salad as they filled up on bread. They enjoyed their time together, with Yulisa getting to meet others from the organization while having Vanessa meet the new leader. Yulisa listened to Vanessa and Diana discuss what she had planned for the next month. Vanessa would be busy traversing this land helping to find top talent for her company by day while in the evening, she worked hard meeting potential clients that would open doors for immigrants who wanted a better life. As the meeting was about to end, Vanessa extended her right hand and said, "It was great to meet you Yulisa."

"The pleasure was all mine. I look forward to working with you. You do amazing work," replied Yulisa, then she hugged Vanessa.

"Okay, I'll send you an email by the end of the week to let you know how everything is progressing," announced Vanessa. She waved goodbye to the ladies, then she opened the door and stepped out.

"Well, what do you think about our US Recruiter?"

"I think she does a hell of a job. I can't believe you bring people and spread them out across the country. That's just awesome," replied Yulisa. Diana could hear the excitement in her voice.

Diana was happy that the change was going according to plan. The good thing about this job was that everyone had an assignment, they were too busy working to look around to see who wasn't pulling their weight. Diana took pride in the great attitude the members had. "Vanessa works her ass off to bring in contracts, and we're lucky to have her. She has a hard-working staff that sets up all the meetings, and Vanessa comes in to close the deal. Es chingona," said Diana, with pride.

"Yes, she is indeed a bad ass," added Yulisa before taking a drink.

"Girl, you've only seen one side. Wait until we get to Mexico, then you'll really be impressed," replied Diana, with a gleam in her eye and a smile on her face.

Yulisa took a deep breath and smiled. She felt blessed to be asked to run the organization, and even though she had not officially started work as the boss, she knew this was the perfect job for her. She looked forward to the challenge of taking over for Diana, and once she learned all the ropes, she would push herself so there would be no drop off when she officially took over. She was hard on herself, but she knew she possessed the discipline and drive to get the job done. She was a natural born go-getter. "How long will we be in Seattle?" she asked.

"Well, I was going to surprise you, but we'll leave Thursday morning for the San Joaquin Valley in California. Tonight, you are going to meet a family that I helped bring across in 1995. You'll see how much a person can prosper when they work hard and don't complain," announced Diana.

Yulisa's eyes sparkled and her face lit up from the news. This was an organization that she wanted to be a part of and would be proud to be its leader. She understood how hard work helped people have a successful life. For Yulisa, being able to provide an opportunity to hard working immigrants was a dream job. "Well, I look forward to meeting them, and I want to thank you again for asking me to take over for you. I can already see the operation is intricate, with international components, but I'm ready to learn," stated Yulisa, as she hugged her friend.

Diana smiled and returned the hug. She looked at her

friend beaming with elation at her new circumstances, and she knew that she had picked the right person for the job. She knew that Yulisa would work hard, and she also understood the trauma that her friend experienced could be beneficial in a business like this. Most people who suffer painful experiences tend to view the world differently, the depths of it only known to the person experiencing the pain. Many of those out-of-the-box-thinkers of the world probably had a defining moment that changed their world view, often through tragedy. The pain Yulisa experienced would now be put to work for her. The job called for attention to detail and Yulisa would thrive in the organization. Diana knew firsthand about traumatic experiences, like when she killed Rodrigo. She worked her way through her emotions by working on herself. Yulisa was already past that stage, so now this job would keep her busy full-time, and she'd enjoy it. Yes, Diana was happy with her decision.

Chapter 26

Diana and Yulisa had a dinner invitation for six o'clock in the evening. Diana drove south on Interstate Five, then connected to Highway 516 until they got to the town of Kent, Washington. They pulled into a quiet neighborhood and Diana parked on the curb by the front gate. The house was painted light blue and had white shutters. The lawn was lush and green, evidence of the rain that frequently fell in the area. The couple had been waiting for them. A black screen door opened, and an older Latino man came out. His hair was salt and pepper with a matching well-trimmed beard, and behind him was his beautiful wife, her thick long black hair turning grey at the temples. They held hands as they went down the steps. They opened the gate and then walked to the driver's side door to wait for the door to open. When Diana stepped out, she was greeted with shouts of joy as the couple hugged the lady who made their American Dream possible.

After their greeting, Diana walked around the car, opened the passenger door, extended her hand, and helped her successor out of the car. "Reynaldo y Rocio, te presento, Yulisa Bermudez. She's going to be taking over for me. Yulisa, this is Reynaldo and Rocio. We have a lot of history," said Diana with a nod and smile. The couple smiled at her and then gave her a welcoming hug.

"Come on in, Rocio has been in the kitchen since three forty-five," informed Reynaldo, as he opened the heavy black screen door for the ladies. They walked into an immaculately cleaned home with nothing out of place. "Sit down, what can I get you to drink?"

Both ladies smelled a fresh pot of coffee brewing, and soon Reynaldo came with a tray holding two cups of black coffee, a sugar bowl, some coffee creamer, and two spoons.

They sat down to enjoy the coffee, but both ladies kept looking towards the kitchen. When guilt finally won out, Diana and Yulisa walked into the kitchen and asked if they could be of assistance, but Rocio just smiled and asked them to sit down. Rocio was happy for the visit and wanted to make a scrumptious meal as a way of saying thank you to Diana for giving them the opportunity to prosper in the United States.

Reynaldo set the table, smiling like a proud papa, knowing that these two ladies were going to have one of the best food experiences in their lives. Reynaldo could hear the three ladies enjoying themselves and sharing a laugh. He stopped what he was doing and looked around at his house, then at the green grass in his backyard, and felt blessed to have the life that he was given. He thanked God every day for his good fortune. Reynaldo walked into the kitchen and announced that the table had be set, and being the gracious host, he re-filled everyone's coffee. "Reynaldo, I love what you have done to this place," informed Diana.

A huge smile appeared on Reynaldo's face, and he replied, "Thank you Diana, and in more ways than one."

Diana held up her hand then said, "Reynaldo, you need to quit thanking me, you're the one who had to do the hard part, we just helped you to get started. You have what you have because of you and Rocio's hard work, you have all this porque son trabajadores con mucho corazón." She tapped her chest with the palm of her right hand.

"Okay, a comer," replied Rocio, as she picked up the blue

oven mitts and carried the platter with lobster to the kitchen table. Reynaldo carried the platter with the ribeye steaks and then returned for the roasted asparagus.

Rocio's meal was colorful. The ribeyes were topped with sautéed mushrooms, which contrasted with the white and orange lobster, and the colors were complete with the green asparagus. "Rocio, this looks so good," declared Diana.

"Thank you, it's nice to cook something besides Mexican all the time," replied Rocio.

"Rocio and Reynaldo work together, Yulisa. He captains the boat, and Rocio is the chef for the dinner cruises," informed Diana.

"Oh, that must be exciting," exclaimed Yulisa as she used the steak knife to cut into her ribeye.

Rocio smiled and nodded her head. "Yes, we work four days on and then three days off," she explained.

"Next time we're in Seattle, we're going to get on one of your cruises," said Diana.

"We look forward to it," said Reynaldo.

The dinner was fantastic, and Diana thought that whoever booked a cruise on Reynaldo's boat was in for a culinary delight no matter what Rocio made. It was quiet while everyone concentrated on their dinner. Diana always knew the sign of a delicious dinner was when there was silence when people ate, and this was one of those times. After dinner they retreated to the living room and talked about old times. Yulisa sat back and listened to the stories. She was happy she was there because she was getting an inside look at Diana's organization. No, strike that, her organization, from the people that Diana brought in. This was the essence of the vision for the organization. It brought immigrants into the United States, who were hard working and busted their asses to make a better life for their families. Yulisa looked around and could see what their fruits of their work ethic brought them.

After dinner, Rocio brewed more coffee, then removed

the cheesecake from the refrigerator while Diana looked at the pictures on the wall. The Jimenez living room was a shrine to their twenty-eight-year-old daughter, Mari. There were pictures of her from each grade in school, all the way to her graduation from UCLA. As Diana and Yulisa walked to the sofa, Diana saw the photo arrangement. "Is that Mari? My God, she's all grown up now." gushed Diana.

The couple beamed with pride. "Yes, that is our Mari. She's an attorney now," replied Reynaldo as he filled each cup with the freshly brewed coffee.

Diana tapped Yulisa on the elbow to get her attention, then said, "I brought this family in myself, way back in 1995. Mari was just five or six years old, and now look at her—a college graduate and an attorney." Diana smiled because if this wasn't a great example of why she did what she did, then there would be no other, and she hoped that Yulisa felt the same way.

"Aquí está el pastel," said Reynaldo, as he handed Diana and Yulisa a slice of cheesecake with a heavy silver fork on each plate.

"Gracias, Reynaldo," replied Diana. They dug into the cheesecake and only came up for air to have a sip of their coffee. "Rocio, this pastel está muy sabroso, gracias."

"De nada Diana, es un placer," replied Rocio.

After dessert, they sat and talked for another two hours about how they adjusted to their new country and all the support that they had. "Diana told me that she was the one who brought you into the US," stated Yulisa, hoping to hear the story.

"Oh yes, I can still remember ese pinche viento. That was the hardest day of my life, but as you can see," he opened his arms up, "it was well worth it," replied Reynaldo.

"Yes, Reynaldo has helped us many times, as he's always in need of new crew members," said Diana, with a mischievous grin on her face.

"Yes, I am always in need of hard-working people, y Rocio también. We are always here to help," said Reynaldo.

"Reynaldo, Yulisa wants to hear the story of our journey that day," reminded Rocio.

"Oh, sí, el viento. It was a long day. It was very hard, muy físico. Walking todo el día and resting from time to time." Reynaldo looked over to his wife and asked, "¿La derecha o la izquierda? ¿Qué te lastimaste?"

"The left," answered Rocio.

"Yes, Rocio twisted her left ankle around las dos de la tarde, so it made the trip even harder. But Diana was always at the front checking to make sure everyone was doing as well as they could."

Diana heard Reynaldo's comment and smiled. Just hearing that story again took her back to that time. Reynaldo was right about the wind because it blew in their faces for the entire journey.

Reynaldo continued, "By seven that night, even I was feeling débil, but our last rest helped, and just before midnight we entered the United States." Reynaldo smiled remembering how happy they were to have crossed the border. "We saw some shadows and when we got close, we could see that they were a row of cars. We screamed with joy to be on tierra Americana, como babosos, pero todos estábamos alegres."

Yulisa looked at Reynaldo and nodded her head. She had a big smile on her face. This is the kind of work she wanted to be a part of, and she looked forward to learning more from Diana. "Y así es como los sueños nacen," said Yulisa, as she patted Rocio's knee and smiled at their dream making tale.

"We owe all this to Diana. She's the one who brought us in, and she helped us with the support to get started," added Rocio.

"Yes, we would never be where we are today if it wasn't for this lady." Reynaldo pointed to Diana.

"No, we just opened the door for you, and you did not

waste your opportunity. All the success you have had is because son trabajadores," replied Diana.

Rocio looked at Yulisa and said, "That is why we always help Diana, because este trabajo es muy importante. And we know that whoever we help will be hard working."

Yulisa nodded her head in acknowledgment. This evening with the Jimenez family had encapsulated what her organization was all about. Reynaldo apologized to Diana and Yulisa for having missed his nephew, Jacinto and his wife, Mercedes, but they were attending a school function for their daughter right now. Diana and Yulisa thanked Rocio and Reynaldo for their hospitality, the excellent dinner, and the valuable time they gave them so Yulisa could see the organization at its best.

It was quiet on the way back to the hotel, the only noise heard were the raindrops falling and the sound of the wipers. The lights on the Space Needle grew brighter the closer they got to their destination. Then Diana broke the silence with, "Well, what did you think?"

Yulisa turned to her, smiled then said, "Amazing, simply amazing, and you've done this since the early nineties?"

Diana nodded, smiled and then replied, "Yes, and you're in charge now. This is our mission." Yulisa was impressed with the organization, and she looked forward to getting hands-on knowledge, so she could learn everything about her new position. Right now, she felt like she was seeing everything in the dark, hence the mystery of it all, at the present time, but she knew things would look different and hopefully less vague as time went on. Almost as if reading Yulisa's mind, Diana said, "Don't worry, every day you're going to learn more about the organization, your organization. Remember, I won't leave until you are one hundred percent sure you are ready. Until then, I'm going to show you all the ins and outs of what we do. I want to thank you again for taking the job. I think it's a perfect fit for you."

When they arrived at their hotel, Diana reminded Yulisa that they needed to be at airport by eight in the morning. Diana was happy because it had been another productive day.

Chapter 27

"In about a minute, you'll see the Southern End of the San Joaquin Valley, aka, my home," said Diana, as she pointed with her right index finger, as they made their way towards the valley floor from the part of Interstate Five known as the Grapevine.

Yulisa didn't have to wait long, she saw the valley appear in from of her: green squares of agricultural land that resembled a green checkerboard. "Yes, I've heard of it, it feeds most of America. When was the last time you were home?"

"I come home at least once a year now. You know it's our turn to worry about our parents," stated Diana. She looked at the speedometer, then took her foot off the gas to get back into the flow of traffic. It was just past noon, and the sky was cloudy.

They drove in silence, as Yulisa looked out the window at all the farms in the area. Over to her right was an outline of the biggest mountain in the area. "What do they call that?" she asked, pointing with her right thumb.

Diana replied, "That's Bear Mountain. You'll get a closer look tomorrow when we go see the Valaderas's. They just came in about a month ago, and you'll be able to see the support that we provide them. It's the support that helps to facilitate success."

Yulisa nodded her head in acknowledgment, understanding that Diana was showing her the ropes of the operation, the final product. She knew she'd be in Mexico soon to see how the organization worked on the other side of the border. She remained silent thinking about her new job. She appreciated Diana not overwhelming her with everything that she had to learn, and meeting immigrants in their new country allowed her to see the impact the organization had in assisting people towards their American Dream.

Diana turned to her and said, "You know, Yuli, I'm also happy to be home, to see the places where I grew up at. I love the Franklin Mountains in El Paso, but when I picture a mountain, the image of Bear Mountain comes to mind," as she pointed to the peak. "Being home just reminds me of who I've become. My experiences living here have shaped my attitudes of today."

Yulisa nodded her head because it made sense to her. It gave her time to put it in personal terms. She was who she was because of everything she'd experienced. The death of her child and husband further solidified who she was because that horrible pain also gave her inner strength.

"See that sign? It says Bear Mountain Boulevard, aka, the 223, aka, that's how you get to Arvin from the freeway. We'll be there tomorrow," informed Diana. About twenty minutes later, they were on Main Street in Lamont, California, Diana's hometown. It was a small town that reminded Yulisa of Canutillo, a small town outside of El Paso. "Shit, you have to go the speed limit around here, because the chotas are out in full force," informed Diana. "See, what did I tell you." She pointed out a California Highway Patrol, as the officer stepped out of his car holding his ticket book.

"California or Texas Highway Patrols, they sure love the small towns to help them increase their revenue," Yulisa replied.

# # #

As much as Diana begged Yulisa to stay with her at her parent's home, Yulisa convinced her that staying at a hotel would be good practice for her, so Diana drove into Bakersfield and dropped her off at the downtown Marriot. Yulisa won her case with Diana by explaining that time with family was precious, and to bring a stranger on a visit would be considered rude in her book. Yulisa wanted Diana to have an uninterrupted home visit, and she wanted to have a quiet place to go to, so she could process everything that she'd learned so far.

After checking in, Yulisa went up to the sixth floor and found her room. She placed her travel bag on the red covered chair, and tested the firmness of the mattress by sitting on the edge. The mattress was to Yulisa's liking. She got up and opened the curtains and the skyline of downtown Bakersfield came into view. She was a long way from Solis Realty. Yulisa lounged in her room, trying out the sofa as she turned on the television. She was happy with her decision, and now it was just a question of learning everything about her new job. She was hungry and looked at her watch. It was almost five, so she picked up the hotel pamphlets next to the phone and looked at the room service menu.

At five forty there was a knock on her door. It was room service, and her Caesar salad was rolled in on a table with a white tablecloth. The table was perfectly set, with her salad on one side, along with dinner rolls, and a carafe of iced tea which was next to the flowery centerpiece in the middle of the table. She tipped the worker and shut the door. Yulisa rolled the table near the sofa and placed the food on the coffee table. She ate her dinner in silence while watching the local news. The salad was fresh, the dinner rolls heavenly, and she enjoyed a relaxing evening. Then she went down to the hotel bar to explore more than just her room. She sat down and ordered a Merlot. The bar was crowded with travelers as country music played in the background. Yulisa always enjoyed observing people and their mannerisms as she tried to imagine their story. She'd learned that as a kid and some habits die hard.

While Yulisa was enjoying some wine, Diana as having dinner with her parents. Manuel Solis, Diana's father, was in his third year of retirement, enjoying his well-deserved break. Diana had been lucky that this was one of the weeks where her parents were not in Las Vegas. It gave Diana joy that her parents had time to travel now, and when she shared the news that she was retiring for the organization, her parents were happy because they always worried that she would be arrested. The Solis's were not happy with Diana's choice of a career, and were ecstatic that she was getting out of the business. They spent dinner reminiscing, and it made Diana happy to spend time with her parents because she had friends who'd lost theirs at a young age. So she embraced their time together. They talked until midnight, then it was time for bed.

# # #

After two glasses of Merlot, Yulisa went back up to her room, her belly full from the salad. The wine created just enough of a buzz to make her cheeks feel red and flush. The curtains were still open, and she watched the traffic on Truxtun Avenue roll by. Yulisa smiled when she realized this was her new career, and she was getting the feel of the boss's chair. She had confidence that she would do an excellent job because that's what she did. She was a tremendous worker and paid attention to detail. She was happy with the decision to take over for Diana because this was the type of job she needed, busy as hell and always thinking about the next step. Yes, this was a perfect job for Yulisa Bermudez.

# # #

Diana called Yulisa just after ten in the morning. Yulisa had been awake listening to the traffic passing by since eight-thirty and enjoying the comfortable bed that made her feel like she was floating on air. Diana would pick her up at noon, then she'd show her her hometown as they waited for Vicente Valaderas to get home from work. Yulisa would be able to see how his family was adjusting to their new lives. This excited Yulisa because the Jimenez family from Seattle had been in the US for over twenty-five years, and now she was going to see how a newly arrived family was dealing with their new surroundings. Yulisa had many questions for Diana about the support given to the new arrivals, but she wanted to personally ask the Valaderas' what they wished they had when they first arrived so that the organizaation's program could be evaluated and perhaps tweaked to give more support for those coming into the US. That was typical Yulisa, always finding ways to make things run more efficiently. She went to the hotel restaurant to order coffee and a Danish. Then she found a chair in the lobby and read the local newspaper. She reveled in this down time, because she knew she'd soon be busy, but she was looking forward to it and that filled her heart with joy.

# # #

Yulisa was waiting at the curb when Diana drove up. She had her travel bag over her left shoulder and carried her purse in her right hand. "Did you get some rest?" asked Diana, as she looked for oncoming traffic. When there was none, she quickly got into the number two lane.

"Yes, that's a nice hotel, clean, quiet and the bed was amazing," replied Yulisa. "How was your visit with your parents?"

Diana smiled then replied, "It was good to see them, but it reminds me that they aren't getting any younger. It was a nice visit." Diana turned right and followed the road as it curved back around. On one side of the road were train tracks, and the sun shined off the rails creating an amber colored glare. To the right was an old industrial park setting of machine and tire shops mixed with now defunct businesses with broken windows and crumbling walls. Almost as if Yulisa could read her mind, Diana added, "Yes, this place was better back when I was a kid, and the deterioration of the properties makes me feel goddamn old."

Yulisa acknowledged Diana with a smile, and she certainly understood her comment because she saw it in El Paso, too, old neighborhoods being ignored in the name of progress as her city kept expanding. This area of Bakersfield started as the hub of the city until it began to build westward thus making the area seem drab, depressing, and forgotten.

"We have time to kill before Vicente gets off of work and we are going to be treated to another dinner," informed Diana. She made a right from Junction 184 and then straight on the road leading to the Kern River. In less than fifteen minutes they were at the mouth of the Kern Canyon with some amazing views of the Kern River. After ten minutes, Diana pulled her rental onto the shoulder so she could give her friend a closer look at the famous Kern River, made famous by Bakersfield's own country music legend, Merle Haggard. The ladies got out of the vehicle and immediately heard the cascading water as it hit the rocks below. The sound was soothing and put both ladies into a tranquil state. Diana was preparing to leave the organization in capable hands, and life was looking better every day. For Yulisa, this was a brand-new road that she was going to take, but she was sure of herself, trusted her instincts, and was highly confident that she could continue in Diana's footsteps of helping people begin their American Dream.

Chapter 28

Diana and Yulisa found a well-worn trail that led them to the banks of the river. The water was fast moving and dangerous, yet peaceful at the same time. The water flowed off the rocks and was soothing to both women as they thought of their futures. Yulisa looked up over the rocky hills and saw nothing but a clear blue sky, which is what she felt like in her current life situation. She couldn't believe this was her new job, and that she was the leader of an immigrant smuggling operation that would help people to improve their lives. Diana was also thinking about her future, and her unwavering faith that Yulisa would succeed her while the organization would continue to prosper.

"The river's so peaceful," announced Yulisa, but Diana was lost in her own thoughts. Yulisa waved her hand in front of Diana's face. "Hello, earth to Diana, come in, Diana."

Diana snapped out of her thoughts and replied, "Yes, the water has a calming effect on me too. Hey Yuli, I'm thankful that you chose to take over for me. You don't know how happy that has made me. I know that you'll do an outstanding job and I hate to keep thanking you, but I'm very appreciative."

Yulisa smiled then walked over and hugged Diana. "No, thank you. This is the perfect kind of work for me and important, too."

"I think this is what people call a win-win situation. It works out for both of us, and is all part of God's plan," replied Diana. She looked at her watch.

They were at the river for another forty-five minutes before they returned to the car. Yulisa liked that everywhere they went, they got to see local sights while in the area. Yulisa would enjoy the fringe benefits of this job. She looked at the rocks and the dry brush on the mountain as the blue sky gave off a peaceful vibe. Yulisa understood why people visited such a peaceful site. The fresh air had done both women good, clearing their minds as well as getting to enjoy nature's beauty.

They got back on the road heading west before connecting to Highway 223. "We still have time to kill so I'm going to show you more of Kern County's gems," announced Diana, giving a quick toothy grin to Yulisa. "I want you to remember that while Bakersfield has its own country music sound, with Merle Haggard and Buck Owens, my hometown of Lamont produced some pretty good people, too. There's my friend Bobby Martinez, who wrote a book of short stories. He was influenced by reading Leonel Martinez, who had a column in the Lamont Reporter. I hear he still makes his living using words."

"Are they…"

Diana interrupted her friend. "No, no relation." She'd anticipated her friend's question. "Lamont also has a famous musician. Marcos Reyes. He's a percussionist for the musical group WAR. Both of those guys were trailblazers that filled all Lamonsters with pride." Diana said with a smile. "Did you know that Muhammad Ali, 'The Greatest,' came to Lamont? It was even front-page news in the Lamont Reporter. And you know who wrote that story? Our very own Lamontster, Leonel Martinez." Diana smiled as she reminisced.

Yulisa returned the smile as she enjoyed the view. She

turned right to look outside the passenger window and was treated to the spectacular immense view of the Southern San Joaquin Valley. Then Yulisa looked to her left and was blown away by the majestic beauty. Cows were grazing in absolute peace as if they were part of the tapestry of brown fields of grass, along with sycamore trees that provided shade for the cattle. The scene brought Yulisa inner peace, and she subconsciously smiled because this is what she needed in her life. She was going to help people, she now had an actual mission, and she embraced that fact. Her heart was full, and the inner feeling of contentment came to her in the form of her spine tingling—a feeling she always had when she was happy.

# # #

Vicente Valladeres walked into the workshop and straight to the sink to wipe off the grease and oil from his working hands. He lathered up and cleaned his hands all the way to the wrist, then he walked to the time clock. He waved to his boss, who gave him the thumbs up. Vicente had come to work an hour earlier so that he could leave to help his wife with anything she needed. He waved to his boss again before walking to his pickup.

He came through his apartment door holding his lunchbox in one hand and a twenty-pound bag of crushed ice in the other. His daughter Veronica had just finished vacuuming and was rolling up the cord. "Hola mi chicquita, how was school?" he asked. He kissed her on the forehead just as his wife walked in from down the hall. "Hola mi amor, can I help with anything," he said, after putting the bag of ice in the freezer.

"No Vicente, todo ya está listo. Go shower, y no te preocupes de nada," said his wife Oralia, as they kissed.

# # #

Diana and Yulisa rang the doorbell at five thirty and when the door opened the smell of enchiladas was the first thing to greet them, followed by the Valladeres family. Vicente shook both ladies' hands while his wife and daughter shared hugs with the two women. They sat and talked for ten minutes, which was the exact time needed for the Mexican rice to be ready, then retreated to the long brown table with a white tablecloth. There were two large skillets, one contained refried beans with cheese melting on top, while the other had steaming rice with tomatoes and cilantro on top. The main dish was shredded beef enchiladas baked in two glass containers. Vicente went to the kitchen to retrieve a pitcher of iced tea, serving everyone at the table. They began eating and nothing was said as everyone enjoyed dinner. Silence while eating is the highest compliment for a cook. After dinner, they all sat in the living room, and Veronica brought out a tray of pan dulce, Mexican pastries of different varieties. Vicente went into the kitchen and came back with a pot of coffee which he placed on the living room table. "Please enjoy these. I had my friend make these conchas just for you. They came out of the horno not more than two hours ago," beamed Oralia.

"Gracias," replied Diana, "Oh, sí, todavía se siente caliente el pan," as she took a bite from the Mexican sweet bread. After chewing, she wiped the sugar from her mouth, then she took a long drink of coffee and said, "Éso, that's the perfect concha," followed by "este cafecito, está perfecto también." Diana pumped her fist à la Kirk Gibson when he hit his famous World Series game winning pinch-hit home run, to show her appreciation for the perfectly brewed drink.

They talked for over two hours. Diana let them know that Yulisa would be taking over for her but for them not to worry because everything was to carry on as it had before. Nothing would change, and all contracts would still be honored. Yulisa was glad that she could meet the people who had come to the United States, to see their faces, to talk with them, and to break bread with them. It helped Yulisa understand that they weren't much different than her. Both the Valaderes family, and Yulisa, had been taught that hard work was a ticket to a good life, and now both were being rewarded. They learned that Veronica was excelling in school as she even showed them some of her favorite books. The proudest moment for Veronica was when she told them that she was a member of the Haven Drive Middle School Bulldogs Marching Band, and showed them her band picture.

Diana knew that tomorrow was a workday, and they didn't want to overstay their welcome, so they politely excused themselves at seven forty-five. They hugged in the living room, then Oralia walked them to their vehicle. She shared the recipe for the seasonings in her shredded beef with Yulisa.

"Gracias por la visita. I just wanted you to know that Vicente wanted to make the best impression for you," said Oralia, as she looked at the two ladies. "Estuvo muy emotivo. He's eyes were watery because he was so grateful to you for the opportunity that you have given us here."

Diana and Yulisa smiled at being let in on something private, a sort of sisterhood connection, and Diana replied, "No, él está trabajando, y tú cuidas la casa, y Veronica está trabajando en sus estudios. Todos están trabajando por una vida más tranquila con mucho éxito." They hugged once again, then they left the small town of Arvin, California.

"Look, there's the school that Vero goes to," pointed out Diana with her index finger.

"It's awesome that she enjoys school, that's half the battle," chuckled Yulisa. "So far, the two families that I've met seem to have adjusted well to their new lives in the US."

"Yeah, and you know what's interesting, Vanessa, told me that three other ranchers in the area are open to taking on more workers like Vicente," added Diana.

"Of course they are, because they know they will get

hard-working people, instead of all that bullshit that's spouted on Fox News that all immigrants are rapists and drug dealers who just want to suck on the government's teat," announced Yulisa, trying to remain calm.

Diana laughed, "Don't get upset because it affects your health. It's all bullshit from the politicians, all of them. Remember, all we can do is focus on what we can do, if you have no control, then why worry about it?"

"Ha, how long did it take you to learn that?" asked Yulisa as she looked out the window.

"Actually, I'm still learning that, but really, remember this, while others bitch and moan about injustices, we're doing something about it and that's so much more important," Diana explained. Yulisa looked down at the console, contemplating Diana's words, then slowly nodded her head at the realization that she was part of something special. There were enormous risks in their endeavors, but the rewards of seeing people thrive helped to give Yulisa strength to embrace her new job. Diana drove into the left-hand lane then made a U-turn and drove to the Marriot's front door to let Yulisa off. "I'll pick you up at nine, and we have a two-hour drive to Burbank. Have a good night."

Yulisa thanked her then went through the automatic doors. She thought of going directly to her room but made a left for the bar. She sat with her back against the wall so she could see people coming in, an old habit from watching too many mafia movies. She ordered a Merlot and thought of her trips to Seattle, Lamont, and Arvin. In just a short amount of time, she had seen two Mexican families working hard to have successful lives. She picked up her glass and swirled her wine. While looking down at her glass, she thought of how fortunate she was to have the privilege to do a job that was so rewarding, where she would help people to create their dreams. She took a drink and then shook her head as she tried to figure out how lucky she was to have walked into this job. The truth was, Yulisa needed this job more than anyone knew because it gave her a mission to work on and continue to develop. Already, she was thinking of innovation, and how to limit risks for the groups coming in. She took a deep relaxing breath, then finished her drink before going upstairs to her room.

Chapter 29

After landing back in El Paso, Diana drove Yulisa home. Diana entertained thoughts of stopping at her house but knew that work was piling up at the office, so she went straight to work. She was correct, the tray of items that needed her signature called out for her attention. She couldn't wait for the organizational business to be complete, so she could begin the process of selling her realty company. Only then could she truly be free of obligations.

Yulisa was happy to be home. It had only been a four-day trip, but it felt much longer. She'd missed the confines of her home, plus she would be gone another four days beginning on Monday as she and Diana were headed South to meet the organization's contingent based in Mexico. She went to the kitchen to make fresh coffee, then opened her suitcase and dumped the clothes into the washing machine. After relaxing in the living room, she poured herself a fresh cup of coffee. Yulisa looked at her reflection in the mirror and saw a completely different person than the one who had traveled to Seattle then Bakersfield in the last week. She felt that way because the more she knew about the organization, the less stress she'd have when she officially took over. Yulisa was also a realist, and she understood perfectly that if events went south, it would be her ass on the line and she would be incarcerated. That thought scared the hell out of her, yet, she felt, or at least hoped, that God would protect her from danger and or jail. Yes, she knew the risks involved, but the benefits to her mental wellbeing took precedence over the risk of being arrested.

Back at her office, Diana was on the phone returning calls from both vendors and clients. She was happy with Yulisa's replacement office manager because the office didn't seem to miss a beat, and it surprised Diana because she thought there was no one more efficient than Yulisa. She pushed her chair back and put her feet on the desk and sighed. Yes, little by little, things were working out perfectly, then she could leave everything and just focus on herself for once. She was looking forward to that day.

# # #

Yulisa looked at the red blinking light on her answering machine and pushed the button. It was a message from her mother giving her the usual guilt trip about never visiting her. She smiled because that's what she always did upon hearing her mother lambast her for being a stranger to the person who had spent sixteen hours in labor giving birth to her. She reached for the phone and punched in her mom's number, waiting for her to pick up. "Amá, I got your message, and I'm doing well," she said, as she plopped onto the sofa.

"Yuli, how much longer do I have to wait until I see my beautiful daughter's face again?"

"Amá, I'm free all weekend. I can come visit tomorrow," Yulisa replied.

"Pues, ya es tiempo."

"I know mom, I know. Hey, I have a new job. I'll tell you all about it tomorrow."

"What happened to the realty job you had?"

Yulisa noticed the concern in her mother's voice and said,

"No te mortifiques amá, todo está bien. You'll hear all about it tomorrow."

"Your sister will be here tomorrow, and you know how Angel thinks he's the grill master," said her mother, throwing her usual shade at others not there to defend themselves.

"Amá, be nice. Angel treats Alondra like a queen, give him some props, mom. No seas así."

'Yuli, you're right, Angel is a good man, but his constant bragging about his grilling skills me cae gordo," explained her mother. "Okay, I'll see you tomorrow, mija."

"Yes amá, I'll be there tomorrow, and I'll even bring some ribeyes, so we can all hear from Angel," chucked Yulisa.

"Okay, see you tomorrow Yuli," said her mother before hanging up.

Yulisa hung up and laughed to herself. Her mother was certainly a character, but she was also a loving mother who helped her immensely when she lost her Rosita and Sergio. She looked around her living room. Everything seemed to be more in focus, and she was content. It was her new job that helped to elevate her spirits, and she'd have to thank Diana again for such a rewarding promotion. Yes, it seemed that Yulisa was seeing everything with more clarity.

# # #

Diana finally caught up on all her work just before three in the afternoon and stared at the now empty in-box. It had taken her almost three hours to finish all her pressing obligations. She knew when she came back from Mexico that the in-box would once again be overflowing, but what could she do? This was how the world operated.

Diana left the office at three-forty-five and stopped at Adrian's Tacos to pick up dinner. She ordered three carne asada tacos with everything and an asada burrito for tomorrow. After getting home, she carried her travel bag on her left shoulder and the brown paper bag with her food in her right hand. It felt good to be home, and soon things would be different when she stepped away from the organization. She smiled at the thought that one day she'd be free to do whatever she pleased, and when that day came, Diana would make up for lost time.

She placed her food on the counter and walked to her bedroom to throw her travel bag in the corner. Then she walked back into the kitchen. She glanced up at the clock; it was four-thirty-five. She didn't like to eat dinner early, but there was nothing worse than eating cold tacos. So she grabbed a plate from the cabinet and unwrapped her asada tacos to place them neatly on the white plate. She brought out her homemade salsa, cut a lemon into quarters, and took out an ice cold Modelo to wash the food down. She placed everything on the coffee table, then sat down.

The tacos were excellent as always. Diana stretched out and put her feet on top of the table while balancing her plate of food on her lap. She was happy to be home, and she let her mind wonder back to her trip. She thought it was a major success. Yulisa met with important people within the organization who she'd need in her corner. More importantly, Yulisa had met with people who the organization had brought over, and her friend got to see the end results, which was how they were doing in their new country. Diana was confident that Yulisa could take over the head job without any hicups to the organization.

After eating, she looked up at the clock and saw that it was already past five in the afternoon. Surely her friend and educator, Elizabeth, was still not in the classroom. After finishing her beer, she picked up her cell and dialed her friend's number. "Hey, are you still at school?" asked Diana.

"Hey there, stranger. No, I just got home, what's up?" replied Elizabeth.

"Yuli and I just got back from our first trip. I think it went well, and I think I made an excellent choice for my successor," said Diana. She got up from the sofa and put her dish in the sink. "I'm really happy, and all the families liked her."

"Well, you've always had good intuition. I'm glad that everything went well. Where are you two going next?"

"We're going to meet Margarito Magaña in Monterrey on Monday."

"I'm sure it will go well there, too. You were stubborn on choosing your successor, but I'm glad you found a winner."

"Bethy, you should take some time off and join us. I know you have a ton of sick time accrued."

"I'll make time for it, but don't know when. I'll talk with you later; the King just told me he was hungry. See you later," said Elizabeth.

Diana put down her phone and relaxed on the sofa for the rest of the evening. She always did this on the night back from a trip. It gave her time to reflect on all that had transpired.

# # #

"Hi Angel, I brought some ribeye steaks for you to grill. My mom loves your mad grilling skills," Yulisa said with a smile, just loud enough for her mother to overhear. Yulisa knew her mother had heard because she gave her the look of death followed by her squinting her eyes. The family called it her pissed off look.

"Oh, thanks Yuli," replied Angel as he gave her a hug, took the ribeye steaks, and put them on a tray to season. Angel was thirty-five with a medium build and curly black hair and a perfect brown tan. He'd been in the family four years, since he married Yulisa's sister.

"Hi everyone," announced Yulisa, as she saw the family gathered in the backyard. Everyone waved and said hello to her from where they sat.

Despite her mother's early mood, spending the day with her family was very rewarding for Yulisa. These same people in the yard were the ones that came to her aid when she went through her devastating tragedy, so she had a soft spot for them despite each one having their own irritating idiosyncrasies. Yulisa would never forget the help each one of these people gave her in her moment of need. People came over with food or would visit her to keep her company. She also realized at the time that she was a huge manic pain in the ass who needed all the help she could get, so she could put up with these people for the day—that's the least she could do.

"Yuli, these ribeyes are kickass," proclaimed Angel, as he showed her the seasoned tray of steaks ready for the grill.

Yulisa smiled, then said, "Got to have the best for the grill master."

It was a beautiful late October afternoon in El Paso, and the family was having a good time eating, drinking, and catching up. The young children played tag in the backyard, while the adults sat at different tables having conversations about the state of their lives. The one part of family gatherings that Yulisa did not like was the fact that she was alone, with no child or husband. They had been taken from her, and it had changed her DNA about how she viewed life. It made her sad that Rosita and Sergio were not at the gathering. The only thing she could do was close her eyes to picture Rosita joining the other children having fun on a Saturday afternoon, and she imagined Sergio with a Modelo in his hand talking with Angel about the Cowboys around the grill. Yes, there were times that she hated family gatherings, but these were the cards that Yulisa had been dealt. She went through the grief and anger process, and now acceptance, because it's not like she was going to find a time machine to change the events in her life.

Yulisa's mom took a seat next to her which made her come back to reality. "Yuli, dime de tu nuevo trabajo."

Yulisa had been waiting for this question for the last two days. She knew she couldn't tell her mother the whole truth because she'd go off on her, so she decided to tell a white lie, to avoid her mother's wrath.

Chapter 30

"I'm going to work for an immigration organization," said Yulisa as she looked her mother in the eye.

"Will you be making more money?"

"Yes, mom, I'll be making more money," replied Yulisa. She never understood why money was so important to her mother.

"Well, when do you start?"

"I've already attended some training, and I'll be going again on Monday," added Yulisa as she glanced at the children running around in the backyard.

"Well, mija, as long as you don't bring shame to the family, I'm happy for you." Her mother moved to her left and reached to give her daughter a hug.

"Thanks amá," said Yulisa, as she kissed her mother on the cheek.

# # #

Diana was home on a Saturday night. She had a college football game on, but it was more for noise than any interest she had in the game. She was writing a list of what she wanted Margarito to show Yulisa so she could understand the process of how a person became nominated, and how they were chosen to come to America.

Diana stopped what she was doing and smiled as she realized that all the talk of finding her replacement had now become a reality and the training would go fast. Soon she would be free of her current obligation. There were times that it was hard to fathom since she'd been doing the same thing for twenty-seven years. This was her baby, and now it was going to be left in the hands of an intelligent and capable person. Diana knew that Yulisa was perfect for the job.

With Diana's exit plan already in motion, it allowed her time to recall many of the personal sacrifices she'd made during that time. Today's organization looked little like how it began on that fateful day in Juárez, Mexico. In the early days everything was disorganized as Diana was learning the ropes through trial and error, but she learned quickly then the organization took off. While the organization thrived, Diana had to put herself second as she was the leader.

This led to one of the few resentments she had. Because of what she did, she could not be one hundred percent truthful with the men in her life. And her being the moral person that she was, she could not live a lie. So she'd break off relationships because if she didn't, she'd be a fake, and Diana detested dishonest people. There were times that she allowed herself to wonder where she'd be and who she'd be with had she not become the leader of an immigrant smuggling organization. But it was all academic now because she was who she was. There was a part of her, however, who wondered who she would have become had she not chosen this life.

Whenever Diana thought of the 'what ifs' of life and the people she'd met, her thoughts aways returned to her being a fifty-nine-year-old Chicana without children. When she thought of being cheated out of motherhood, it tugged at her heart. She felt like there was a part in her heart that was empty. She sighed and looked around her living room. Then logic took over. She'd been denied being a mother because of circumstances in her life, and while she was sad, it was not filled with loss but of hope for the future.

It was at this moment when Diana realized that while she didn't have an actual newborn, that her organization was her baby. She was with it in its infancy and raised it to what it was today. She was, in fact, a mother and that brought a smile to her face. She got up from the sofa, walked to the dishwasher to pull out her UTEP football coffee mug and then poured the remaining coffee into her cup and warmed it in the microwave. She was still smiling as she looked at her patio through the sliding glass door. The trees swayed softly, and the wind chimes moved just enough for her to hear the audible clank of bells.

When the microwave beeped, she took out her coffee, then put creamer into the cup until the coffee was a perfect shade of brown. Then she opened the sliding glass door and stepped onto her patio, taking a seat in the shade. Diana let her mind wander to picture what her new life would be like. She admitted that she'd miss the friendships, and the aspect of working with a cohesive unit. Working as a team was what she'd miss the most because she was like the head football coach and everyone else had their own department to take care of. Everyone liked her because she was an honest and fair boss, but when someone needed an attitude adjustment, she was there to light a fire under them and remind them of their mission. However, the time had come to put herself first. She'd given many years to the organization and now it was time to step away and be able to do what she wanted. Those would be Yulisa's issues to deal with now.

Diana took a drink of her coffee and remembered when she became the person who she was today. At the time, she had a contract out for her life taken out by her ex-boyfriend for witnessing a murder and she had left El Paso for California to clear her head. She'd been driving up and down the West Coast from Santa Barbara in the north, to Laguna

Beach to the south. It was during this time that she found her resolve. While she was away from Texas, there were many people trying to help her out of her dire situation. They were working night and day, and then it hit her. While she was trying to get her head straight, others were doing their job to protect her. It was at that moment that she knew that she had to take care of her responsibilities. She cut her trip short to take care of her business. This was the turning point in her life which catapulted her into the position she had today, and now after an excellent run, it was time to step away and live the life she always wanted.

# # #

It was Sunday morning just after eleven and Yulisa was packing for her next trip. She folded her clothes, and when she was done, she placed her travel pack by the front door. It had been a long time since she'd been this happy, and she knew it was because of this new opportunity. She thanked God because this was exactly the kind of job she needed. In truth, Yulisa had just been going through the motions of life, like many people do. But this job offer was perfect because it gave her purpose, and she could use the pain she experienced through tragedy to help others.

Her new job opportunity gave her a natural high because she believed in Diana's mission of bringing in hard working immigrants to America for a better life. She knew the work would be hard, intense, dangerous, and risky, but she was ready for it.

It was past noon and Yulisa was hungry. So she reheated the leftovers from last night. After the food was ready, she walked to the living room and put the plate on the coffee table. All she could think about was her next trip. She looked forward to meeting with the Mexican contingent of the organization.

After lunch she took out a writing tablet and wrote the questions that she had for Diana and others. One question she wanted answered was how were the people chosen to come to America? Diana had covered it simplistically, but now she'd speak with Margarito Magaña, the person who ran operations on the Southern side of the border. She also had questions about how contracts were signed with employers, and she was curious to know how many employers sponsored people annually. She figured she could pick Diana's brain on Monday morning for the answer. Almost as if she were a mind reader, Diana's number came up on Yulisa's phone. "Hello."

"Hi Yuli, just calling to remind you that if you have any questions, write them down and either I or Margarito will answer them," informed Diana.

Yulisa laughed out loud, then said, "Funny, I was just jotting down a few questions when you called.

"Good, we'll have plenty of time when we fly into Monterrey tomorrow. I'll pick you up at six in the morning, it's an international flight, so we must be there early," informed Diana.

"Yeah, I figured as much. I'm ready, my bag is packed," replied Yulisa.

"Okay, see you en la manaña," said Diana, before she hung up the phone.

Diana walked back to her sofa and sat down. Yulisa Bermudez's training had gone perfectly. She had been well received within the organization and was a quick study. She was the perfect replacement, and they had developed a close bond. But Diana knew she'd have to talk with her friend about the downside of running an organization like this. She wasn't looking forward to it, but it needed to be done. Diana recalled the times when she'd be driving and a police car would follow behind her. Talk about shitting bricks. It was a feeling Diana hoped she would lose over time, but no, twenty-seven years later, she still felt the same anxiety whenever she saw a police vehicle nearby. The thought put her in a blue mood, but she needed to disclose this to Yulisa so she'd fully understand what she was getting into.

Diana's heart was heavy, as she began to formulate a strategy in which she could emphasize the danger to Yulisa. Up to this point, Diana had highlighted all the support they gave to incoming immigrants, the services provided, but she knew she had to tell Yulisa about the risks of running the organization. All the paranoia, all the fear, all the stress she carried with her every day knowing the organization could end at a moment's notice. She sighed as she struggled to find the best way to approach Yulisa so she could understand the danger and risks that she'd be taking on.

Diana looked out to the backyard and saw the trees gently swaying. She got up, took an ice cold Modelo from the refrigerator, opened the gold foiled cap, and walked out to her patio. She sat down and the breeze was refreshing, but she was still in deep thought recalling all her near misses with law enforcement. The breeze and beer did little to get Diana out of her funk. She reminded herself not to sugarcoat the danger of being the leader of the organization to her friend. Yulisa was going to have to understand that if things went south, it would be her ass on the line. Diana had been lucky enough to have never been caught, but she still felt the stress and agony of the constant worry, and she would make it a point to let Yulisa know exactly what she was getting into.

Chapter 31

Yulisa saw Diana's headlights through her living room window, grabbed her travel bag, placed it on her left shoulder, and opened the front door. She stepped out, then with her right hand, she made sure the front door was secure and walked to Diana's car. She opened the car door and placed her travel bag in the back seat, got into the car, shut the door, and put on her seatbelt.

"Good morning. I stopped at Dunkin Donuts and got a large coffee for you with lots of cream," said Diana. "There's the sugar and a spoon for you," as she pointed to the console.

"Good morning. Perfect, thank you," replied Yulisa. She took two sugar packets and ripped them open, then poured them into her coffee. She placed the trash into the plastic bag that was hanging from the car lighter. Dawn was approaching and the first signs of light were peaking over the Franklin Mountains.

"We're flying to Dallas/Ft. Worth then connecting to our flight to Monterrey. Have you ever been?" asked Diana, as she took a sip of coffee.

"To Dallas yes, but not Monterrey."

We have a three-hour layover, but we'll be in Monterrey before dinner," announced Diana. "We'll meet Margarito

Magaña for a breakfast meeting tomorrow. Anything you need to understand about the Mexican side of the operation, he's the man who would know."

As they boarded their flight, Diana helped Yulisa load their travel bags onto the overhead bin and invited Yulisa to take the window seat. After the flight took off, Diana swiftly fell asleep while Yulisa looked out the window at the vastness of the land. To Yulisa, Diana seemed out of sorts, not her usual talkative self, and she'd picked up on that. The flight felt quicker than the hour and fifty minutes that they were in the air. Diana awoke about ten minutes before landing and stretched her legs out as much as possible, wiped her eyes, and looked like she'd never been asleep.

As they walked out of the concourse, Diana said, "It's almost ten, do you mind if we get something to eat, we have a long layover."

"Yes, I'm game, for whatever.

Diana smiled then said, "Let's go to this overpriced, probably shitty breakfast bar."

"Well, it's our fault for not waking up early and making papa con chorizo burritos, wrapped up in foil and carried in a see-through plastic bag," replied Yulisa.

"Ay, Yuli, you make me laugh, yes we should have planned better, but when in Rome," she said, as she shrugged her shoulders with her palms turned upward to indicate 'ni modo.'

They found the restaurant and were seated quickly. Each ordered a Denver omelet with country fried potatoes, a biscuit with butter, and coffee. The food wasn't bad for airport food, but Diana didn't enjoy her meal because of the talk she had to have with Yulisa. She hated to do it, but it was only fair to Yulisa to know exactly what she was getting into. Diana cut her biscuit in half and buttered both open ends. The coffee went well with the biscuit, but it just contributed to Diana's heartburn. It was now or never. She cleared her throat and began, "Yuli, I need to talk with you about something really important."

"What? What is it?" Yulisa asked, as she felt her anxiety kick into fourth gear.

"Yuli, maybe I haven't been clear enough about how dangerous this job is."

Feeling somewhat relieved that Diana had not had change of heart about the job offer, she replied, "Diana, I know the risks, and I'm okay with it."

"Yuli, I have a fuckin' ulcer from this job, and I have to dye my canas," as Diana pointed to her hair. "This job esta cabrón, it takes its toll on your emotions, your health and mind. It's really a bitch, and I want you to know it's not all fun and games, plus the traveling gets old quick."

Yulisa smiled at her, appreciating her friend's candor about her new endeavor. She took a bite of her biscuit, washed it down with coffee, and cleaned her mouth with her napkin before she said, "Look, I know what I'm getting into."

Diana sighed loudly then replied, "Let me tell you a story. About three years after running this organization, I started to have such serious anxiety that I had to take pills. The stress is enormous." She stopped talking to see if what she was saying was registering with her friend. She couldn't tell so she continued, "The worst part of this job is understanding that it could end at a moment's notice. Straight to jail without the opportunity to collect two hundred dollars." She snapped her finger and pointed with an outstretched index finger for emphasis. Then she looked her friend and said, "It's serious, Yuli."

Yulisa took another sip of coffee and nodded her head to Diana to indicate she was getting her message. "Look, I know the risks involved, but you know what? I don't give a fuck. Right now, my life has a purpose, and I'm living again." She reached for her napkin on the table and folded it in half. "You have no idea how I was before. Thank God that I know how to keep busy because I could have easily been admitted into the booby hatch for depression." She shook her head and then continued, "This is exactly what I need. I need this." She tapped her finger on the table. She stopped and looked at Diana who acknowledged her words with a nod of her head. "You don't know the life I was living trying to deal with tragedy. I was afraid I'd go crazy, so I learned to throw myself into my work so that I was too tired to think about my losses." She turned to her right then the warm tears washed over her eyes. After a while she took a few deep breaths to compose herself, and continued, "When you offered me this job, it felt like a blessing from God because it allowed me to have a mission in life." She smiled and shook her head. "I don't know. It's stupid. But in my head, I have already programmed that by helping immigrants start their American Dream, I can somehow keep the memory of my Rosita and Sergio alive. That's how I feel. Does that make sense?" she said with her nose scrunched up.

Diana smiled, nodded her head, then said, "Yeah, I know what you mean. I can't even imagine the pain you have suffered, but you need to know a few things. All these plans we have for the organization could all go up in smoke quickly, and if it does, you'll be looking at some serious federal time. The government can take your home, all your possessions, everything, and there's nothing anyone could do about it. The shit can hit the fan quickly."

Yulisa smiled at her friend and reached across the table and took Diana's hands into her own. "Thank you, Diana, but I assume all the risks."

Diana was exasperated. She sighed deeply then said, "Okay, Yuli, let me tell you about the paranoia." She caught their server's attention for a refill of coffee. "Over the years, from out of the blue, I've had to fight this feeling that the Feds were closing in on me and that my arrest was imminent. It's a fuckin' horrible feeling. It just sits there deep in my gut. I feel its darkness and the stress drains me. I know you're chingo-na, but it never goes away, and it takes its toll on a person. It's a hard job, Yuli, more mental than anything else, but it aged me. All the goddamn worrying changes your outlook on life."

"Can you give me an example?" asked Yulisa.

Diana looked at Yulisa and said, "Food. You're eating the most perfect meal in the world, perfectly seasoned, and then your mind wonders to—will this be my last meal as a free person? Am I close to getting arrested? It's those little things that take the fun out of the joys of life, and that has always made me less trusting of everything I see. Can you understand? Does that make sense?" Her farrowed forehead showed Yulisa the anguished pain of responsibility.

Yulisa nodded her head. "Listen, I'm sure it's as shitty as you describe, but you must understand where I'm com-ing from. I consider myself chingona, you know, mentally strong, but what I have gone through I wouldn't wish on my own worst enemy. And this opportunity that you have given me is like a new life. I can't describe the utter horror that I had lived through, and when you offered the job, it felt like God was throwing me a lifeline."

Their conversation was interrupted by their server. "Can I get you anything else?" she asked before placing the bill on the table.

Both Diana and Yulisa politely said no, then the dishes were cleared. Diana looked at her watch and noticed they had only burned an hour at breakfast, which meant they still had almost two hours before boarding. They paid the bill, left the restaurant, and walked to the airport newsstand where Diana picked up the Dallas Morning News and a few maga-zines to read on their flight to Monterrey.

As they waited by their gate, both were on their phones checking up on personal business before finally re-laxing with some light reading. Diana was back to normal, talking and smiling, the burden of her talk with Yulisa had been lifted. She had made her point, and Yulisa clearly got the message. Now her conscience was clear, and that made her happy. She opened the paper and took the sports section out, read the top headline, then asked, "Think the Cowboys will win this week?"

With a wry smile, and grinning, Yulisa replied, "Not if Jason Garrett is still our coach."

Diana laughed and agreed with her friend's assessment by nodding her head and sadly acknowledging that the Cowboys were a mess. "Yuli, I'm glad we finally had this talk. It needed to be said, and now we're both on the same page." She neatly put the paper in its proper order, folded it in half, and put it in her purse. "We needed to talk about the real risks of this job. Shit, I'm just glad you didn't get up from the table and run away because then I'd be back to square one."

Yulisa smiled at her as she listened, then rolled her eyes and said, "I thought you had had a change of heart and were going to rescind the job offer. I thought you were going to shit can me."

They both laughed at the same time, then Diana added, "I had to tell you the truth, but I'm certainly glad that I didn't scare you off, either."

Yulisa nodded her head. "Yes, I understand, and believe me, you made some excellent points. But I already told you, I'm all in. I need this, and I'll make it work. You know how I am, if I don't know something, I learn it."

The last thirty minutes before boarding, Yulisa went over some of the questions she had for Margarito with Diana. She was excited that she was learning all aspects of the organization, and she wanted to carry out her new job with the same success and as quietly as Diana had done.

## Chapter 32

Diana had been correct, they were at their hotel ordering dinner by six fifteen, just as she'd promised. It had seemed like a long day, but now they could relax and go over questions Yulisa had for Margarito. "I think I'm going to have another margarita," announced Yulisa as she looked for their waitress. She was enjoying her first trip into Mexico.

Diana smiled and said, "Sure, go ahead, enjoy yourself. Mi pinche úlcera no mi deja tomar como antes."

"I better enjoy it now before all the stress of responsibility takes away all the playtime."

"Yes, trust me, you'd better enjoy it now," replied Diana. She reached for a tortilla chip and dunked it into the red salsa.

"So how many times do you come to Mexico per year?" asked Yulisa.

"About three or four times. It really depends on if anything special is needed. Remember, everyone has their own job to do, and you'll just oversee everything. You're a good troubleshooter. You're a problem solver, Yuli." Diana stopped to look at Yulisa's face, then added, "You're excellent at being able to anticipate things, so please feel to add anything when you see the need."

Yulisa was happy with the complement; it made her

smile. She was glad that others picked up on her fine-tuned intuition. She looked around the crowded restaurant, and she could hear conversations near her as well as the clanking when the utensils encountered plates. Yulisa had a moment of reflection. She still could not believe that she was going to be leading an immigrant smuggling organization. This is what she needed, and she felt like God was walking with her, leading her by the hand. She knew she was a good person and firmly believed that God was providing a plan for her by giving her this opportunity not only to help other people start their American Dream, but also to help her escape her tragedies.

"See, I told you we'd be in Monterrey by dinner time," said Diana, as she sat mesmerized by Monterrey's famed mountain top, the Cerro de la Silla.

"My God this is beautiful. The peaks stand out like sentries guarding their land," replied Yulisa, awed by the sights in front of her.

"It's beautiful alright. Did you know that Monterrey is considered Mexico's most Western city?" informed Diana, as she looked out of their dinner window.

"Yeah, I've been reading up on the city. It's huge, and the suburbs are nice," said Yulisa like she was a tourist on vacation.

"Just wait until tomorrow's meeting with Margarito. We're having breakfast on the roof next to the pool with a gorgeous view of the city," informed Diana with a smile. She was momentarily lost in her thoughts, then Dina came back around. "Sorry. But from time to time, my head finally realizes that I'm moving on with life, and it throws me off." Diana was not embarrassed. She was excited that the pressure would finally be off her.

"No that's cool. I wanna say thank you again for choosing me," replied Yulisa.

"I couldn't leave the job with just anyone. Yuli, your work

ethic spoke for you. Too many people of the younger generation are in their own little world, and it's nice to come across people like you who are not afraid of work. Los trabajadores," responded Diana, as she took a sip of coffee.

# # #

Diana and Yulisa were sitting at their roof top table and enjoying the views of Monterrey. The elevator door opened, and Diana clutched Yulisa's jacket and said, "There he is."

Margarito Magaña was a forty-nine-year-old man born and raised just outside Monterrey, Mexico. He was five foot eight, had a chubby build and dark skin. He was balding, but his silver pencil mustache was on point. He wore a button up white shirt with beige pants, and his houndstooth sports coat fit him perfectly. Both ladies got up from the table and walked to greet him.

"Margarito, te ves muy guapo esta manaña," said Diana before embracing him with a hug.

Margarito smiled broadly, showing off his perfectly white teeth in a smile, then said, "Diana, you look good, and may I say, happier now that you can see the end of the line before you start your blissful retirement."

"Thank you, Margarito. Te presento a mi amiga y la mera mera de la organización, Yulisa Bermudez. The new boss." Diana formally introduced Yulisa to Margarito, and they cordially shook hands.

"Buenos días, y mucho gusto," replied Yulisa with a smile.

"Good morning. I look forward to working with you," replied Maragarito as he placed both hands over Yulisa's.

Their server walked up to the table and smiled at them, then asked, "¿Quieres un café?"

"Sí por favor, ¿y podemos ordenar pan tostado con mantequilla?" asked Diana.

Their server nodded and said, "A sus órdenes." She walked

the ticket into the kitchen.

It was a productive working breakfast. Margarito was impressed with the questions that Yulisa had for him and noticed her attention to detail. He spoke privately to Diana and told her she had made an excellent choice for her replacement. She thanked him and smiled because she was happy that other people saw the same thing in her friend. Arrangements were made to drop Yulisa off at Margarito's office after lunch so she could see how the nominating process worked and understand the criteria for being chosen. Diana looked at her friend throughout the day and could see that Yulisa was perfectly comfortable. She was in her element.

#

"¡Yulisa! Pásale, pásele, ¿quieres un cafecito?" asked Margarito, being the good host that he was.

"Gracias Margarito, pero no," replied Yulisa.

"Siéntate aquí. Here are the files of the people who we will be bringing in soon," he said. He handed her the paperwork.

Yulisa looked at the names and ages of the people on the list. There were two families with young children, and two couples. Yulisa did the math in her head. The average age of adults on the list was thirty-two, the same age as her. Before she could ask a question, Margarito said, "I will take you to the safe house so you can meet the people on the list."

Yulisa was impressed with Margarito's timing, and noticed he was the type of person who paid attention to detail, which went hand in hand in this line of work.

It took forty-five minutes to get to the organization's safe house, which was located outside of Monterrey proper. The building was two stories high and was made from stucco and painted off white. Yulisa could see the organization's security detail as they walked around the perimeter of the compound. Margarito led Yulisa to the heavy black screen door, then fished the keys out of his left pocket. He turned the lock and opened the door. "¡Hola! Soy yo, Margarito, estoy aquí con la nueva jefa de la organización," he announced. It took about two minutes for the people to assemble in the living room.

Yulisa was introduced to the group and was able to ask about their experiences since being chosen to cross the border. She was impressed with their attitude; it was little wonder why they were chosen. Yulisa observed them working hard practicing their English so when they got to the US, they'd be better able to adapt. Margarito was next to Yulisa in case she had any questions.

The man who in charge of the Mexican sector for the organization was impressed with Yulisa because she was calm. Most people learning a new job would have many questions, but Yulisa seemed to understand why things were done a certain way and understood the organization's methods.

"Later on, you'll have time to ask any additional questions you may have to the group. Así sabes que pasa antes de irte al norte," said Margarito.

"Sí, gracias Margarito." Yulisa was happy to get an inner peek of the process of bringing people into the United States. To her, Margarito was a perfect guide for this group. She noticed his directions to the people were precise, and she could see the great rapport he had with them. He was the type of person people didn't want to disappoint. His kind face and proper manners only solidified to Yulisa that he was an asset to the organization—her organization.

Margarito called Yulisa over to him with a hand gesture. "Yulisa, este es Guillermo Guevera."

"¡Hola Guillermo! Mucho gusto," she replied offering her hand.

A tall man in his late twenties smiled back at her before shaking her hand. "Mucho gusto."

"¿Ya están listos para a entrar a los Estados Unidos?" she asked.

"Sí, I mean yes. Tengo que practicar el inglés. Por favor disculpe. Yeees, I am ready to go to America," said Guillermo with a huge smile.

"Do you know cuándo se van a ir?" she asked.

Guillermo was searching for the right word. "How you say…." He grasped to come up with the right phrase. "When they sign the work contracts con las compañías." The man caught himself and said, "When the work contracts are signed in America."

Yulisa nodded her head, knowing how crucial the US contingent part of the immigrant smuggling organization was to the people waiting to start their new lives. "¿Cuántas semanas han estado aquí?"

Guillermo put up two fingers before saying, "Two weeks. Y yo puedo agantar dos meses aquí. All I want is to be able to take care of my familia." Yulisa could see the confidence this man had in his abilities to adapt into a new world. "Yo soy trabajador. I am not afraid of work. I have to take care of my family, y lo voy a hacer, porque Dios me dará, como se dice," as he searched for the right words in English. "God has geeving me an oportunidad, and I will be able to raise my family in a safe area. ¿Qué más queremos, verdad?"

Yulisa smiled at Guillermo and said, "Yes, all we want is an opportunity."

Guillermo smiled because he knew she understood him. "Sí, nada más una oportunidad."

"Bueno Guillermo, nos vemos. I promise to visit you and your family once you get inside los Estados Unidos."

A smile came across his face, and Yulisa could feel his excitement. "Sí, nos vemos," he said, before disappearing.

# # #

Yulisa was back at the Radisson Hotel by six in the evening. She and Diana were again having dinner on the rooftop. The sun had set, and the outline of the Cerro de la Silla, the five thousand, nine-hundred-and-seventy-foot mountain could still be seen, it's two bulging rocks gave quite an intimidating look. It was the perfect backdrop for the beautiful city of Monterrey.

Diana inquired how her day went, and Yulisa could not stop talking about Margarito's efficiency at leading the group. Diana was pleased to hear that her colleague had made a good impression. She wanted her friend to be as comfortable as possible, and everyone she employed brought their own skill set which helped the entire organization. Yulisa's first experience in Mexico galvanized her belief that she could step up and continue Diana's work without missing a beat. Yulisa was looking forward to carrying on for Diana so she worked hard to learn as much as possible. She had full confidence that she was up for the job because she was the type of person who was focused. The tragedy of losing her loved ones was now an asset to her because no matter what, she resolved to be successful. It is who she had become.

Chapter 33

Diana and Yulisa were back in El Paso at ten-thirty in the evening. It had been a jam packed two days of meetings with Margarito and with some of the people who would be brought into the United States within the week. This was an opportunity to show Yulisa the personalized care and support the groups received from the organization to make the transition of living in a new country go a lot smoother. The more Yulisa read about the post-country support, the better she liked it because the people knew that they were cared for. It certainly wasn't like paying a coyoté to bring them over as all they cared about was the cash. No, the organization chose a person, prepped them for the big move, and were right there next to them for support as they tested their legs in their new country. The organization knew that the support inside the new country was crucial in getting the best results, and it made the groups feel like they weren't thrown into a new place to fend for themselves. The organization had a reputation for helping people prosper.

Diana drove Yulisa home and said, "That's all the traveling for this week. But you have a Monday evening meeting with Vanessa Villamontes in Seattle, and I'd also like for you to stop at Reynaldo and Rocio Jimenez's home so you can meet his nephew, Jacinto, his wife and daughter. You'll have to leave Monday morning."

Yulisa nodded her head to show she had heard Diana's instructions, then said, "I'll start doing laundry now," with a smile on her face. She was happy she was busy, and she worked best on a tight schedule. Yulisa found that most people are not happy about attending constant meetings and being on the go, but this is where she thrived because she liked being in constant motion, either physically, mentally, or both. She reached into the back seat to pull out her travel bag.

"And just to let you know, Margarito couldn't stop praising you and your attention to detail. You made quite the impression on him with your leadership skills, too," informed Diana.

Yulisa smiled at her, and it made Diana wonder just how different she was from her friend. "I'm happy that he doesn't think of me as a pendeja," she said before closing the car door. She waved to her friend and then carried her bag to the front door.

It felt good to be home. She was finding her way through her new job and was full of confidence, but she felt her home was a sanctuary. This is where she would build her energy to get the job done. She was a go-getter, but she still felt her home was a shelter which helped her to make good choices. Yulisa sat on the sofa trying to relax. Her mind was still whirling with ideas, and she embraced her view on life because this was her place to re-charge and mentally prepare for the meetings she would have. She got up and threw her laundry into the washing machine, walked to her bedroom, and pulled out some workout clothes for tomorrow to lay them on a chair. She would wake up early, get her cardio in, and prepare for the upcoming meeting with Vanessa.

Diana's future looked bright. Her choice of Yulisa had been a grand slam that made her happy. Everything she'd hoped for had materialized. There hadn't been a hiccup yet. Diana knew that Yulisa was perfect for the job, and the pain she'd suffered through, the fiery deaths of her daughter and husband would serve her well as she focused on the tasks before her. Diana was happy that even though Yulisa's life had been a nightmare, she was using that pain to her advantage. Even when Yulisa was working as her office manager, Diana was aware of how quickly Yulisa could focus on work. She knew how to turn it on when it was needed. Diana figured that was what was happening in her first few weeks on the job. It took a special person to use pain from life and turn it into an asset.

Diana changed into pajamas, took out a soft warm blanket from the linen closet and walked to her sofa to lay down. She wasn't tired, so she turned on the television, then reached for her laptop that was on the coffee table and opened it. She balanced the laptop on her stomach and googled California beaches. It had been a long time since she had been to the beach. As a matter of fact, the last time she was at the beach she'd been trying to find the courage to take on Rodrigo Flores. And she lived to see another day. She smiled, figuring she'd go to the same beaches to come full circle. She looked at the clock. It was ten minutes after eleven, and Diana contemplated calling her friend Elizabeth. Betting she was still up, she grabbed her cell and called her friend. The phone rang once and then a voice answered. "Bethy, it's me Diana, I hope you were still awake."

"You know me, I've been grading papers since a little after eight this evening. What's up?"

"Just letting you know that Yulisa has been a smashing

success. Vanessa met her last week, and Margarito was impressed with her as well." Elizabeth could hear the pride in her friend's voice.

"Well, that's not surprising. You've always had good intuition," replied her friend.

"Thanks. Can you meet up for lunch this weekend?"

Elizabeth thought for a moment and then replied that she could. "Yes. Call me later."

Diana said she would and put her cell down. She went back to surfing the Internet and reading information on specific beaches. She'd have more time for herself now, and she certainly deserved it. To run a business for over twenty-seven years was a milestone, but the fact that Diana had never been arrested for being the leader of an immigrant smuggling organization showed she was both a cautious and shewed businesswoman. She took pride in never having been caught, but there had been some frighteningly close calls. She had to stop thinking about those times before her anxiety kicked in. Through it all, Diana knew she had been fortunate to come out unscathed, and she hoped Yulisa would have the same luck.

Diana was still up, trying to unwind from her trip. She was in a good mood and feeling nostalgic about the early days of the organization. Those days carried the most risk, but Diana remembered the excitement and the rush of having done something illegal without getting caught. They were so young then and didn't know shit at the time. She smiled as she recalled the euphoric feeling of excitement, as it had not yet manifested into the terrifying anxiety of today. Back then, the young group figured if they were caught, they would just stop. Only they were never arrested, and the organization continued to bloom.

Diana smiled again, shaking her head at their lack of understanding of the consequences of being arrested and how they had been playing with fire. She remembered operations where she and others would personally lead groups through Mexico's mountains and deserts. It was always hard with plenty of blisters on their feet as proof. The challenging operations bringing in people needed to change to reduce the risk of apprehension and fortunately, Diana and Elizabeth met some like-minded individuals who shared the same beliefs.

Diana's group morphed into a team of thirty people with Diana at the helm. Not everyone was directly involved with smuggling immigrants. Many provided support in other ways such as transportation, lodging, or as lookouts providing security for the operations. They came from all walks of life. There was a banker, a loan officer, and a couple of teachers along with some blue-collar workers. Each was on a mission and believed in the Cause. That's how this rag-tag group became a cohesive unit of opportunity to help immigrants. Along the way, these people became close, since taking such risks breeds a certain type of person, and each felt a kinship with one another. Being in this line of work made people trust each other, and that in turn, cemented valuable and long-term friendships that lasted to this day. Diana wouldn't miss the stress and anxiety of the operations, but she would miss the connections that she had made with her team. She hoped they could remain close, but that was still a way off.

Diana respected everyone on the team, especially after they came to her aid when Rodrigo Flores was trying to kill her. At first Diana was floored with the team's all hands-on deck attitude. Everyone stepped up to do their part. Diana had never expected that, and looking back, it was probably the incentive that she needed to face Rodrigo in battle. She remembered all too well the vacillating between confronting Rodrigo on her own, or letting the Russian, Alexander Tupov, take care of her 'Rodrigo problem.' Because all her team was on her side, Diana found the courage to face the man who scared the hell out of her, and even thought she was terrified, she felt she needed to be strong because everyone was doing what they could to assist her. This forced her to push herself past her fears and out of her comfort zone because everyone was doing their job, and she had to pull her own weight.

Part of who Diana became was formed out in the Sonoran Desert, and it changed her life for the better. After she handled Rodrigo, she also took care of herself. She grew into the person she was today because she confronted her fears and was mentally stronger for it. Diana believed that fateful day out in the desert had transformed her.

After Rodrigo was killed, Diana had to reevaluate her life. She chose to earn a business degree from UTEP which she hoped would help her run her organization from afar. Many of the things she learned in her coursework, she applied to the organization, and it began to be even more efficient than before.

It wasn't until 2017 that the organization changed in a big way. When the new president was inaugurated on January 20, 2017, nobody within the organization knew how popular they would become. The donated checks soon came in droves, but the Treasurer of the Organization, Louise Macias, was suspicious. After all the checks were counted, the total amount donated was over fifty thousand dollars. The Organizational Leadership thought it was a trap by the Feds, and Diana wanted to rip up the checks, but Louise asked her to wait until she could find out if the checks were genuine.

Louise devised a plan to write a letter to twenty people who donated money. Of those, thirteen replied stating that they were disgusted with the way immigrants were being treated and wanted to do their part. After some strong vetting and arguing within the Leadership, the organization began accepting donations. People were astute as to which business owners supported immigrant rights, and slowly but surely, the money started finding its way to the organization. As 2017 bled into 2018, those donations doubled and then tripled. Diana stopped her musings and shook her head.

Never in her wildest dreams could she have foreseen how big the organization would become.

All her reminiscing made time fly, and when she looked up at her living room clock, it read five minutes till one. It was time to turn off her brain and get some rest. There would be plenty of time for remembrance once this was all complete. Diana got off the couch, folded her blanket, and put it away before retiring for the night.

Chapter 34

Diana was back at her realty office by nine. She had work to catch up on that she let pile up while accompanying Yulisa. Before she tackled the paperwork, she got up, poured herself a cup of coffee and made the rounds greeting the office staff. It turned out Yulisa's replacement was just as productive as she had been.

Diana walked back to her desk. She looked to her left and saw the mountainous stack of papers, contracts, and mail to deal with. She was methodical, opening each envelope, reading through its contents, and signing her name where applicable, then it was on to the next. After about two hours Diana stopped and reached for her laptop. She was happy to have made a dent in her work, but her mind was still on the California beaches from the night before.

She felt restless. Yes, she was leaving the organization, which made her happy, but there was still her realty business that she'd have to contend with. Sure, she could retire from the immigrant smuggling business, but she would never be truly free to do as she pleased until she dealt with her other business. It was just like life to clear something off the plate, only to leave a portion of something else to deal with. But that's how life worked. A person should understand that for everything good in life, there was always another obstacle to deal with. There was no such thing as a perfect fairy tale life because everyone had their own cross to bear. Diana sighed and continued to look at a West Coast map on her laptop.

Eventually she buckled down, and the pile of work dwindled down to half. Diana finished her tasks just before one in the afternoon. After she signed her last document she put the paperwork into the out box for processing, then got online and bought a roundtrip plane ticket to Burbank, California leaving at three-thirty in the afternoon. She quickly went home and packed a small bag. Part of Diana couldn't understand what she was doing, she'd just got home from a trip earlier in the week, and now here she was, going to California out of the blue. But the other part of Diana knew exactly what she was doing.

# # #

Diana opened the sliding glass window of her hotel room and stepped out onto the balcony. She was greeted with the sounds of waves hitting the beach, and the wind in her face. The smell of the sea felt refreshing and brought back memories of when it was life or death for her. She smiled as she saw the waves break down into white foam before receding back into the sea, only to do it again and again. Diana had an amazing view of the beach which brought her instant peace, and the tide coming onto the beach mesmerized her. The view from her hotel was perfect. She saw the sun slowly sinking into the water: going, going, and then the sun was gone.

Diana was hungry and made her way to the elevators, then took a quick right to the hotel restaurant for dinner. Yes, it was just like last time. She was seated by a window that allowed her a view of the beach that was well lit and offered a view of the waves hitting the sand, and it all felt like déjá vu for her. Years earlier at this same hotel, Diana was fighting the feeling of running away from life because she feared Rodrigo. Now she was sitting in the same place, but everything was different. Perhaps it was God that had given her all these thoughts of returning to the place that helped shape who she was today. That brought a smile to her face because this was where she reinvented herself, and this exact location would always have a special place in Diana's heart.

"Can I get you anything to drink?" asked the waitress.

"I'll have an iced tea with lemon please." The waitress acknowledged her with a smile, then she came back with her drink. "Thank you," Diana replied, as she squeezed the lemon slice into her tea, then reached for some sugar. She used her spoon to mix the tea before taking her first drink. Diana enjoyed the scenery. Her attention was drawn to two families with children coming in for dinner. She smiled as she heard the children's conversations with their parents and the play fighting between the siblings. But then, like a ton of bricks, it hit Diana that she was childless, and tears fell from her face as her body tried to eject the pain in her heart. Growing up as a young girl, the thought of raising a family appealed to her, what girl didn't, since little girls were given dolls at an early age. Diana sighed, as she tried to regain her composure, but the pain soon turned to anger. It was an inner pain for Diana as she went through the process of her decisions. The waitress saw Diana's condition and walked over to her and placed extra napkins on the table. Diana managed a weak smile. She took a sip of tea, wiped her tears away, but the inner seething was still there. She'd been cheated out of motherhood, not by any one person, but because she was the leader of an immigrant smuggling organization. She stopped thinking and she nodded her head in recognition. It was that old saying, "for everything good in life, people had to live with their regrets." This is what she had to understand. There was a reason why she didn't marry and have children. As much as she wanted them, it was not in the cards for Diana Solis.

The waitress took her order, and once again, she was

alone in her thoughts. She laughed to herself, remembering that this trip was her swansong into retirement and here she was crying as if it was her last day on earth. By the time her dinner came, Diana had regained her composure. She ordered a Caesar salad because she wanted to eat light. She remembered the last time she had eaten here, and she recalled her emotional state at the time. Back then, her blood pressure was through the roof due to the inner battle that raged within her as she tried to build up her courage to face her ex-boyfriend, a human smuggler, drug dealer, and murderer. She saw Rodrigo kill a man in cold blood, so she knew what he was capable of. She had fought the urge to run away and never come back, but she knew Rodrigo and his many illicit connections. So she understood she'd never be free if he remined alive. Her friend, the Russian, had volunteered to eliminate him, but Diana needed to exorcise her own demons. And she did. Diana had taken a life, but it was in self-defense. That was the day Diana got her life back, and now her leadership was about to end. But it would be on her terms.

Diana finished her dinner, then had her iced tea topped off as she relaxed at the table. She found it strange that only a few hours before she'd been in her office replying to mail at her desk in El Paso, and now she watched the moon rising in Ventura. After dinner she took off her tennis shoes and carried them in her left hand as she made her way to the beach. The water was cold when the waves reached her feet and wet the bottom part of her pants. She didn't care, everything was going according to plan, and she was almost out of the immigrant smuggling business. As she walked the beach, she went back in time to when she was trying to muster the courage to take on Rodrigo. While she had been successful, she could still feel the cold fear of yesteryear, and she remembered her heart pounding in fear. It had been like nothing she'd experienced before. Her mind knew she had to find the courage within her to confront Rodrigo, but her heart and mind were frightened. One minute she was ready to face Rodrigo, the next she wanted to turn tail and run. Diana was happy with the end results, but she was surprised how fresh those emotions came back to her. She told herself to remember those feelings because what she did that day had been life altering. She'd been tested with the ultimate exam and passed. Diana had changed from that experience, and it propelled her to who she was today.

She felt proud of her accomplishments, both running a successful immigrant smuggling organization, and being able to step up to take someone on who was a mortal threat. Cold from her pant legs getting wet, she made her way back to her hotel. She showered and changed into pajamas. Diana's world was bright with an endless number of possibilities, and she would soon be free of running the organization. She'd come full circle since the last time she was here when she was filled with dread and terror. Now she sat on the sofa and enjoyed her current situation.

Diana stepped out onto the baloney. After a few minutes of breathing the ocean air, Diana came inside, sat on the sofa, and opened her laptop. On the screen was a Southern California map with information on the beaches from Santa Barbara to Laguna Beach. She was going to enjoy her mini-vacation, and, thankfully, it certainly was better than the last time she was here.

# # #

When the valet brought Diana's rental car to her, she tipped them five dollars, then placed her coffee on the console as she got into the car. It was an early Friday morning on the West Coast, and Diana was going to retrace the same steps she took years before. Since she was in Ventura, she took Highway One South, all the way to Dana Point; then like twenty-two years earlier, she'd make her way north, past

Ventura and into Santa Barbara.

It was a perfect California morning, and luckily, the usual marine layerhad not materialized, making it an even brighter day that had Diana reaching for her sunglasses. She drove to the beaches where she had stopped many years before, only this time to replace the feeling of dread with one of happiness. No, this was Diana's swansong, and she would say goodbye and never think of that frightening time again. Time heals all things, she was sure, and this was just one of them. Today she drove off in happiness and peace, but back then the same trip was like saying goodbye just in case Rodrigo had killed her. But she had found the courage to live, and Diana smiled at that fact. She looked forward to enjoying life because she had survived her mortal battle. Everyone faces their own battles, and if they come out alive, they are better people for it. That was Diana—she confronted her fears and survived.

After a while Diana headed back North on Highway One. Every thirty minutes or so she'd stop at a beach, retracing her steps from two decades earlier. And that's how the day went. Diana was witness to some fantastic views and the impending change in her life put her in a happy mood.

It was four-thirty in the afternoon when she arrived at Arroyo Burro Beach County Park in Santa Barbara. While she was a little tired from all the driving, she had finally made it to her last stop. She found parking then walked to the beach and looked out towards the horizon. She took a deep breath inhaling the salty air, smiled, and then said to the ocean, "See, I told you I'd be back." She had completed the itinerary she'd made many years before. To Diana, this felt like a victory lap because now there was no pressure on her, and those long-ago days when she didn't know if she was going to live or die were now long past her. The emotions she had during that trying time would always stay with her, both as a badge of determination to see the problem through and her bravery for being able to face her fears.

She stayed at the beach until six in the evening, then drove to her hotel. As she got to Ventura, she made it a point to stop and eat at the world-famous Andria's Seafood Restaurant and Market where there was always a line out the door. Diana liked to eat healthy but eating a little grease occasionally would not kill her, so she indulged in an order of fish and chips. Diana ate all her fried cod but left half of her fries on the plate. This meal was the topping on the entire trip. She had come back to the West Coast because of a promise she made to herself years before.

Diana called the airline and changed her flight. Instead of staying until Sunday evening, Diana would fly back to El Paso in the morning in time to have a late lunch with her friend Elizabeth. It had been a rewarding thirty-six-hour trip.

Chapter 35

Yulisa woke up at four-thirty for a six-twenty-five flight. She would have a two-hour layover in Las Vegas but would be in Seattle by noon. She would have plenty of time to settle into her hotel before a dinner meeting with Vanessa Villamontes. This was her first solo trip without Diana by her side. She felt confident and full of energy.

# # #

"Thank you for meeting with me tonight," said Vanessa as both women hugged. "I hope you had a good trip."

"I had a great flight and thank you for meeting with me."

"Diana and Margarito explained to me that you had time to meet with some of the groups waiting to come into the country," said Vanessa as they were being seated for dinner.

"Yes, I was there last week. I spoke to a person who had been waiting for a few weeks."

Vanessa frowned, then stated, "From time to time we have some hardheaded potential clients who are reluctant to sign their first contracts with us, but once they see the employees they get, they beg for me to send them more."

Their server took their drink order. Vanessa ordered a glass of Merlot while Yulisa requested a frozen margarita with salt on the rim.

"How often does that occur?" asked Yulisa after the server was gone.

Vanessa smiled, then said, "Only the first timers are scared to pull the trigger, but once they do, they know they are getting some trabajadores."

"Yes, the people I spoke with were full of confidence and ready to go," replied Yulisa just as their server returned with their drinks.

"Thank you," both said at the same time.

"So is Seattle where you are based out of?"

Vanessa smiled, then replied, "I don't work for the organization. I just help from time to time. I work for a company based out of New York City, and I get sent anywhere and everywhere." Yulisa had a shocked look on her face. Vanessa saw her expression then explained. "I get sent all over the country, so after work I meet with potential clients in need of dependable and hard workers for their businesses. I'm the one who writes up the contracts." Yulisa was still in shock. "Diana has always been after me to join the organization, but I'm as effective and convincing after hours too." Vanessa could still see the concern on Yulisa's face, so she continued, "I like the company I work for. I get to travel all over the place, and it allows me to line up contracts with employers all over the nation for Diana. Trust me, it works out best like this." She tapped her index finger on the table for emphasis.

"I'll take your word for it," replied Yulisa with a smile.

They ordered the seafood platter and shared it, then they ordered another drink. With dinner over, they got down to business.

Vanessa discussed the companies she'd been in contact with who wanted more workers. She also explained how close she was to getting new clients to sign on. Once the businesses were committed, they were rewarded with excellent employees. Yulisa could see why Vanessa liked her job as a headhunter for her company.

"Damn girl, you're perfect for this job," announced Yulisa.

Vanessa smiled and said, "Thank you. I love to travel, but I really love that I can use my skills to help the organization whether I'm in Seattle, Houston, Kansas City, Los Angeles, or parts in between." At the end of the meeting Vanessa reached into her satchel and pulled out some papers for Yulisa. "Here's my Six-Month Prospectus for the West Coast. It includes Seattle, Los Angeles, San Diego, the Southern San Joaquin Valley, and Phoenix." Yulisa tried to decipher the list, but it was hard to follow. "I figure, if we can reach twelve new businesses a month, the group rate could jump to almost twelve percent more than it is at present time." Yulisa nodded her head as she took in Vanessa's words, and suddenly she understood that there was still a lot of things she needed to learn.

The meeting broke up at five minutes past eight. Yulisa walked to the bar, ordered another margarita, and sat looking at the Seattle night. She could see the harbor with the boats bobbing up and down on the water. It had been a good meeting, and tomorrow she would meet with the Jimenez clan. As she enjoyed her drink and the scenery, she thanked God for her new opportunity. She was indeed grateful to God.

# # #

The next day, all the Jimenez's came to the hotel for lunch, minus Jenny who was in school. It took some work to get them to come because Rocio was insistent about cooking the meal herself, but Yulisa was able to convince her to enjoy a day off.

"Yulisa, te presento a Mercedes y Jacinto Jimenez," announced Reynaldo with a proud smile on his face. "Jacinto es mi nieto, y Mercedes su esposa."

Yulisa shook their hands, then welcomed then to the oval

table that had been prepared for them. They all ordered the surf and turf lunch, and when it arrived, everyone was impressed with the portions. There was silence as everyone began eating, but slowly the conversations started.

"Jacinto, how do you like your job and working for your tío?" asked Yulisa before taking a drink of her coffee.

Jacinto smiled, looked over at is wife and replied, "I love my job. Somos Jimenez's, we were born to be en la agua."

Yulisa smiled because they were practicing their English, which they had been trained to do before they arrived in their new country.

"El trabajo es goot, and I am learning new things every day."

"And how do you like working con su tío?"

"I like it a lot. He knows many things and tries to teach me more when we are at work."

"Que bueno. I'm glad que todo está bien. How is little Jenny doing in school?"

Mercedes put her hand on her husband's shoulder and answered the question. "Jenny is very smart. She loves school. She has made many new friends." Her face was filled with pride. "We want you to come over and meet her one day. She told me to thank you for bringing us into the country and giving us a better life."

Yulisa's eyes welled up with tears. What she really wanted to do was shout out in glee and high-five everyone in the restaurant, but after composing herself, she smiled and said, "That makes me happy. We love hearing stories like this because it makes everything we do worth it."

Jacinto and Mercedes looked at each other, then to his tío, then to his tía, and they all nodded their heads.

Their server came to the table holding a huge circular serving tray containing five plates of chocolate cake, and five new coffee cups. They continued their chat after their server left.

"So how long have you been with Diana?" asked Rocio, as her fork disappeared into the moist chocolate cake.

"Antes… I mean before, the organization, I worked at her office, so I have known Diana for about six years," explained Yulisa.

"Diana es muy chingona, said Reynaldo before his wife gave him a dirty look to make him correct himself. "Diana she is a very good lady."

Rocio sighed, then said, "Yes, she brought us over. Walked for almost twenty-four hours, but in the end, we made it. Pero fue muy difícil. It was the longest day of my life."

Yulisa took in all the information and thought how far the organization had come since the early days. "Jacinto, what do you do on the boat?"

"It depends. Sometimes I work with my tía in the kitchen, and sometimes I walk around the boat offering food and drinks to the people," he replied.

"¿Te gusta?"

"I like it a lot. I had some jobs antes where I came home dirty, but this job is about keeping everyone on the boat happy. Es muy fácil también. And to be able to work on the water, los Jimenez's were born to be on the water," replied Jacinto with a smile.

Yulisa then turned to Mercedes. She inquired if her family was getting enough support from the organization. Mercedes nodded her head that they had everything they needed. However, Mercedes brought up a good point that they were living with relatives, so Reynaldo and Rocio helped with things. To get the true answer to her question, she'd have to travel to other regions and ask families that were not living with relatives. Yulisa made a mental note and would discuss this with Diana later. "How do you like all the rain here?"

"You will get used to the rain, y mí gusta que no está tan caliente como en Colima," replied Jacinto."

"You'll get used to it. It took me and Reynaldo about a

year, pero ya, nada más es otro día," replied Rocio, who had lived in the Seattle area for twenty years.

Lunch was over at two in the afternoon, and Yulisa got to check off the two objectives on her list: the meeting with Vanessa, and a quick check-in with the Jimenez's family. Jacinto and Mercedes were hard-working people making the most of the opportunity they'd been given. Yulisa liked that Jacinto already had a working plan to work his way up on the boat and maybe have his own boat one day. He even shared a rumor that Reynaldo's boss was considering buying another yacht as he focused on his job trying to stand out with his work ethic. From what Yulisa had seen so far, the organization's vetting process was spot on.

# # #

Yulisa came out of the steamy bathroom wearing a white robe with a white towel wrapped around her hair. After meeting with the Jimenez's, she now had some free time. After she dressed, she did the touristy thing. She walked to Pike Fish Market, then glanced at the Space Needle. Later she went into the original Starbucks, and the aroma of coffee made Yulisa feel instantly alert. She sat in a corner looking out the window as rain continued to fall. She enjoyed the warmth of the coffee.

She smiled to herself as she looked around the building and pondered on how in the hell she'd been so lucky to fall into this job. And it just wasn't any job, but the top position in the organization. She could never have pictured herself in Seattle playing tourist, but here she was doing exactly that. In her heart, she knew that God was leading the way for her. She theorized that because of her tragic life, God was providing a new life for her. She was smart enough to know that she was just rationalizing since there was no actual proof. But as in all cases regarding God, she took it on faith. All she had to do was remember not to be reckless. She hoped that things would work out.

\# \# \#

Yulisa was back in El Paso by one on Wednesday. It had been an easy flight home, and she looked forward to meeting with Diana and passing Vanessa's Prospectus to her as well as filling her in on how the Jimenez Clan were doing. When she got back home, she looked over her notes. This was her job now, and she wanted everything to run as professionally as possible.

Chapter 36

Benny Benavides was happy it was Thursday afternoon. It had been a long, hot work week, but now it was winding down and almost party time. He saw his crew clean up their work areas for the day, which allowed him one last opportunity to fuck with the newbies. He turned off his truck, stepped out, and walked up to the youngest of his crew to berate him extra loud so that everyone could hear. "Carl Craft, what am I goin' to do with you kid? What did I tell you about the importance of cleaning your tools? Tools are your friend, so you must treat them with respect. Now look at this bullshit over here?" He pointed with his fingers. "This pipe wrench is fucking drenched with grease and is a safety hazard. Are you retarded, or just a little slow?" He looked around to make sure everyone heard him, and he had a pleased smile on his face.

"I'm sorry, I'll clean it up immediately," replied Carl as he retrieved a rag from his back pocket and then wiped the pipe wrench clean.

"Craft, let this be the last time I have to tell you. You do know that there are ten people waiting for you to fuck up so they could take your job? Be better tomorrow, Craft," said Benny with a scowl.

"All right, bring it up! Bring it up!" Benny waited until the men gathered. "We are finished with this site. So when we get back to the shop, you can pick up your checks and start getting drunk for all I care. Just don't be lagging on Monday morning or you'll be on my shit list. Let's go back to the shop."

Benny Benavides had been with the company since high school. He worked his way up from green roustabout, to motorman, to derrick hand to finally becoming a driller, or as he liked to call it, a tool pusher. He worked hard, and he'd always been abrasive. But the oil workers under his tutelage knew that he cared about them and their safety, though Benny had an unconventional way of showing it. Benny was old school. When a person was assigned to his crew, he worked with them and taught them, but he also expected hard work from all and for them to be a quick study. Those that had trouble paying attention to detail felt his wrath and quickly grew thicker skin working under Benny.

Benny had just turned forty-one years old. He was living his dream of working for a company where he could hone his leadership skills. He enjoyed being the leader of men. He loved that his worth in the company corresponded to the results the company earned under his watch. Plus, the company worked fast when a mechanical issue developed. Benny liked that his crew's progress could be tracked by increased oil production because Benny thought it showed the bosses that he had the respect of his team. He was tough on the greenhorns, but if a person was assigned to his crew, they knew they'd be treated fair. Sure, they got a lot of shit from Benny, be it that someone was a Raiders fan, liked music that Benny objected to, or if they were a bleeding-heart liberal, but if they landed on his crew, it was because they knew their jobs, and more importantly, were not a bunch of lazy shits that Benny detested with a passion.

# # #

"Okay, good work on this site. Ya'll kicked some ass and I appreciate it. I'm buying the first two rounds, so you fuckers don't be too late, or my generosity will quickly disappear," Benny announced. He looked over at the greenhorns who were standing next to each other, then said, "And to the fucking new guys," FNG's to the veterans of the crew, "you work in the oil fields, so don't be ordering any sissy drinks. We're beer drinkers!" The crew clapped and hollered, and even the newbies joined in.

The crew met at Greenhorns, a watering hole close to the oil fields. The bar was a prefabricated building, but the owner, Lawrence Lapinski, tried to put his own personal touches to the bar so everything was painted black to get more depth. He even brought in wood paneling from the seventies so his bar would stand out from the others that dotted the area. He wanted it to appeal to the working men in the area.

"It's about time, I was already looking at my watch and saying, 'what the fuck,'" announced Benny, before taking a drink from his frosty twenty-four-ounce mug of delicious Modelo. The whole crew was together, and their server took late comers' drink orders.

It was a festive day. This was the last day on site, the company was happy with their performance, and to top it all off, it was payday Friday. The mood was light, and everyone was enjoying themselves, as the start of the weekend had commenced for them.

"Hey boss, I had to talk Craft out of ordering a goddamn white wine," yelled Donald de Klerk, as he tried to show his comedic skills. Benny gave him the old finger across the neck and a dirty look.

Benny liked to use this bonding time with his crew to speak to the newly hired roustabouts, but he loved to use the term greenhorns. He understood that to them he was just a screaming asshole who got to stay warm in the winter and cool during the summer from the confines of his company issued Ford F-250. "Craft! Come over here and sit next to me," he said as he patted the seat cushion for emphasis. A tall young man of twenty-three with short brown hair appeared before him. "Ah, I see you've been doing some damage already. Look Craft, while I drink this truth serum with you, I want you to know that I've seen you work, and each week you will improve as you get to know more and more. Keep it up!" Craft listened to him and nodded his head, then Benny dispatched him back to the group with four quick pats on the back, which was code to Benny for 'get the fuck out of my sight.'

# # #

"Primo, are you home?" asked Brenda Benavides as she pounded on the heavy black screen door. After about a minute, she heard stirring inside and a muffled voice told her to hold on.

Slowly Benny opened the door while still trying to remove the lagañas from his eyes. "Prima! Come in!" Brenda was Benny's youngest cousin. She was nine years younger than Benny's forty-one. "Sorry it took so long to answer, I took my crew out and you know how things go, but you know what they say about the importance of bonding." He rolled his eyes in disgust.

"Mom wanted me to bring you some real food for when Brigitte stays with you. Ya'll can't survive on Micky D's alone."

Benny smiled at her and replied, "Thank you, but we don't always eat at McDonalds." He took the food containers and walked into the kitchen to put them on the counter. "Can I get you something?"

"No Cuz, I'm just following orders. Mom said, and I quote, 'Give Benny this food, last time I saw Brigitte, she had patas de araña. She must eat some real food.'"

Benny smiled at Brenda's comment. His tía was always so

dramatic, but she did have a way with words that even if the insult was directed at him, it made him laugh. "Can I get you some coffee?"

"Sure, I'll have a cup." Brenda walked into the kitchen and put two containers into the freezer. "My mom says to use blue container first."

"Sounds like my Tía Belinda is trying to get rid of some old food." He smiled and put his right hand up, then added, "That's a joke, or as kids say today JK, or so I've been told by my lovely daughter. So, ¿que haces?"

"After this, I'm going to do some phone banking to gather support for what is occurring at the border."

"The Kids?"

"How can you just say, 'the kids'? Do you know what this child separation is going to do to children's mental health?"

"Well, they should stay their asses' home in Mexico or wherever they come from," said Benny, as they walked into the living room and sat on the sofa.

"Primo, I know you like to sound like a chingón bad ass, law and order type who sees the world in black and white," replied Brenda, opening a box of chocolates that were on the coffee table. She took a bite before taking a sip of her coffee. "But the world is not black and white, there's a lot of gray. You don't know the circumstances of these people's lives. What would make people try and make such a dangerous trip if their lives were not already fucked up?"

"We can't save everyone."

Brenda looked at him and then gnashed her teeth together. She was wearing a white tank top and Levi shorts with her black hair was tied in a bun. She shook her head. "You are the only Benavides that puts money over people. When you make a comment like that, you sound cold blooded Cuz, and putting economics ahead of people? I know you were taught well, but I don't know what happened to your empathy gene."

"Chingado, stop talking politics."

"Cuz, it's not about politics, it's about thinking of others. You know there are more important things in the world than money."

"Look, my mom and dad went back to live in Mexico, and I stayed here and made my own way. Look at me now," he replied, his arms extended outward for emphasis.

"Yes, you're one big bad Tejano, but where is your humanity? All you seem to care about is the bottom line, and you have a price tag for everything," replied Brenda, as she shook her head. "All of our family was taught to have compassion. What happened to you, Primo?"

Benny slowly took in a breath, trying not to blow his stack and say something he'd regret later, so he searched for the right words. "Look, I get it, you were born with the biggest heart in the family, and I must have got the leftovers, and that's why I'm perceived as the chulero of the family. That's okay, I can be blamed for whatever, I really don't give a fuck, but that's who I am."

Deep down Brenda knew Benny had a heart, and he always contributed to the family when needed, but he was seen as the family viendido, or sellout. Benny embraced his Republican political stance of getting ahead by working hard. Brenda knew he supported his politics because he feared opening the border could somehow affect his way of life. Brenda knew he was scared and wanted to hold on to what he had for as long as he could. She felt sorry for her cousin because his identity was closely related to what he did for a job. "Look Primo, we'll never see eye to eye on this, but you're still my family and I love you. I don't care about all the crazy shit you believe." She tried to keep a straight face but failed. That made Benny smile, and he walked up and gave her a hug.

"Thank you, Prima, thanks for everything." Brenda was the diplomat of the family, a conduit for communication for the family. Benny always gave her some leeway about her beliefs because she had such passion, and they had always been close, so she never caught his wrath. One thing about his cousin, she always had a way of making him see her point of view.

Chapter 37

Monday was set up day for the new work site. The night crew had done most of the work, and Benny's crew made sure that everything was secure and safe. Everyone had their own responsibilities before the next shift arrived. Benny looked at Craft and was happy to see that he was the hard worker Benny thought he could be. The crew's last break was at four in the afternoon. Benny stalked around the site, making sure that everything was in order. As he checked the derrick, he heard his crew talking.

"Well Monday's about done," announced Delton Dawson, another of the greenhorns.

Donald de Klerk heard the comment, then said, "Jesus Christ, this is our first day here, why are you making a big deal about it?"

"I was just making small talk, trying to keep things positive," replied Dawson.

"Leave him alone de Klerk. What? Are you still hungover or are you just trying to make yourself feel better?" replied Paul Parson, the crew's floor hand.

"Parson, mind your business. I can say whatever the fuck I want," shouted de Klerk.

"Okay Hitler, I can see your having one of those days, but don't start with your Nazi shit today," said Todd Greene, the motorman.

De Klerk pounded his chest with the fist and said, "Now you want to start fucking with me for my beliefs?" He extended his middle finger into Greene's direction. "What, you want to defend those little wetbacks who want to leech off the government?"

"Oh, here we go again," said Greene, as he cupped his hands together then announced, "De Klerk's going full Hitler on us." He got laughs from some of the crew.

"All I'm saying is if you break the law, you had better be ready for the consequences," said de Klerk, calmly explaining himself.

Craft was quietly listening to the conversation. He looked at his tools and then subconsciously took the rag from his back pocket to clean them, then he grew bold and looked in de Klerk's direction and said, "They're kids, Adolph."

De Klerk ignored the comment, then said, "Where the hell are the parents? Why would they risk their children's lives by letting them go north unaccompanied?"

"You ever wonder why they would send their kids to the border alone. Perhaps their home life is shit, and they want a better life for their children," added Craft.

De Klerk was pissed, and everyone could tell from the deep breathing that made his chest heave outward and back in. "You shut the fuck up, newbie. Stay the fuck out of this."

"Calm down Adolph, everyone has their own opinions," warned Greene with his right hand extended out in the universal signal to stop. Break time was over, so the men went back to their stations and resumed working.

Benny had observed the argument from his truck, and seeing de Klerk was involved, he could only assume it was his usual racist shit. Benny and de Klerk were not too different politically, the only difference was that Benny knew how to get his point across while de Klerk vomited out his racial bullshit and made enemies at work.

# # #

The crew made one more round around the site to re-move any safety issues for the next shift when de Klerk began again. "I don't know why the media is making such a big deal out of the child separation at the border. The kids are provid-ed toys, probably more than they've ever had in their lives." He had a smile on his face.

"Damn dude, you're just so filled with hate," replied one of his co-workers.

Benny heard the comment from de Klerk. It made him recall the conversation he had with Brenda. She had told him how she heard snide remarks like the one coming from de Klerk with glee in their hearts at the emotional trauma be-ing inflicted on the children. It dawned on him that despite their shared political loyalties, he and de Klerk were noth-ing alike. While Benny believed in law and order, he also be-lieved people should be treated with compassion, especially the children who didn't have a say in the matter. "Goddamn Brenda," he said out loud. The talk he had with his cousin made him think of his family. Benny was the only conser-vative in a family of bleeding-heart liberals. He felt a cold chill on his back thinking that his family probably thought he was just another racist conservative pig. It made him sad to be seen like that. Whenever the family needed assistance, he was always there to help. In truth he voted with his wallet, and since his livelihood was tied to the oil industry, he made sure to support those candidates who didn't want to hurt the oil industry. But de Klerk supported conservatives because it punished immigrants. The more humiliation, the better, in his opinion.

Benny shook his head because he was still thinking about what Brenda had said. He had always been impressed with his younger cousin's passion for the things she fought for. Brenda Benavides was always trying to improve the world around her. She was unselfish, well read, and had excellent communication skills. Yes, she had opened Benny's mind to other reasons why immigrants would want to come to America, and it certainly wasn't to leech off the government, while watching daytime television and eating chocolates. It made him sad that his political party liked to scapegoat immigrants by calling them drug dealers, rapists, and lazy bastards. He sighed deeply, uncomfortable with the Republican stance that Latino immigrants were going to ruin America. It made him think about how much he was probably hated in his own family for the views that he held.

"Fuck those wetbacks kids, they should send their asses back the minute they catch them," shouted de Klerk as he stowed his gear into the work truck.

Benny heard what was going on and stormed towards de Klerk. "Look, shut your ass up with your racist shit, de Klerk." His patience was wearing thin for an employee nobody liked. De Klerk was a good worker and always punctual, but his constant comments about the tragedy occurring at the border alienated him from the other members of the crew. Benny was smart enough to know that de Klerk's views were probably shared with others on the crew, but only de Klerk was the one who said it out loud.

"Well, they should stay their ass home if they don't want to get locked up," shouted de Klerk to no one in particular. The other men turned around and ignored him.

"De Klerk! De Klerk! Guess what? Your bullshit earned you the night shift on Kern's crew for a month. You can spout your shit to them. I'm not going to have some asshole fuck with the mojo of my crew. We'll switch you out tomorrow."

"I'm sorry! I'm sorry! I take it all back," de Klerk pleaded. But Benny would not hear a word. He just put his right hand up because he would not change his mind.

Benny drove ahead of the crew truck to get the transfer paperwork to payroll. On the way back to the shop, he played de Klerk's comments in his head. It troubled him that in his arguments against immigrants, he used the same rhetoric as de Klerk, only a little more refined. His reasoning was strictly economical and tied to his job, while de Klerk was just a racist asshole, hoping to keep children in cages so it could inflict as much emotional pain on those seeking a better life.

Benny arrived at the shop and into the office to inform his superiors of his decision to switch de Klerk to the night shift. His bosses didn't care as long as production wasn't affected. Benny walked back to the shop just as the crew truck pulled in. He waited until all the men were together and then said, "Okay, men, we'll see you tomorrow. De Klerk, you'll start tomorrow on the night shift." Benny didn't bother to contain his smile as he hoped to piss off de Klerk.

On the way home from work, Benny called Brenda. "Prima, I'd like to talk with you. Can we have breakfast on Saturday morning?"

"Sure, ¿qué pasó?" she replied.

"You know, all your talk got me thinking."

"Ah, my Primo actually has a conscious?" she said playfully.

"Yeah, I guess you can say that."

# # #

They met at Johnray Kennedy's Cafe at nine. They looked at the menu as they sat in a booth. Their server brought them coffee.

"Well, what's up, primo?" asked his cousin as she poured cream into her coffee.

"When you came to my house, you said some things that really made me think. Then this week at work confirmed what you told me."

Brenda tried to recall what she said. "Confirm what?"

"All this shit going on with kids in the cages."

"What about that?" she asked.

"It makes me mad that my political beliefs are in line with all these fuckin' racists. Let me explain my view. If people can come in, then they could one day take my job. That is my real fear. Others though, they like these policies because they want to see immigrants punished punitively, the harsher the better. They say they keep the children locked up as a deterrent, but that's just an excuse to treat the children like shit because they don't look like them."

Brenda was shocked to hear such candid talk from her cousin. She smiled, patted his hands that were on the table, then said, "Awe, I knew my cuz had a heart after all." Benny looked at her and was not happy with her humor. Perhaps he'd made a mistake by opening up to her. Brenda seemed to read his mind and then turned serious. "No, cuéntame."

Benny looked in her eyes, cleared his throat and began. "All this shit we talked about."

Brenda interrupted him and said, "What shit are you talking about?"

"The kids in cages," he said more loudly than he meant to.

"What about that exactly?"

Benny sighed and looked uncomfortable. "I saw firsthand the glee of one of my workers as he talked about children in cages. You should have seen that asshole's smile. I could literally hear the joy coming from his voice as he laughed at the situation."

After they placed their orders, Brenda said, "And that's surprising to you?"

"I'm pissed that I have the same views on immigration as this racist pig co-worker."

"Is that the only reason you're mad? Maybe if you looked at this issue another way, it would give you a different prospective."

Benny shook his head. "No, I was wrong on this. Children should not be held accountable for their parent's actions… It isn't their fault, but they're facing the brunt of all this bullshit. It makes me sad." Just then, their food came.

A smile came to his cousin's face, happy to know Benny cared for others. Then an idea came to her. "So, all this is troubling you?" She cut the top off her biscuit and lathered the gravy on top of it before using her fork to take her first bite.

"It really does. I think you're a bad influence on me, making me think about this shit." He reached for the catsup and poured it on his country fried potatoes.

"Hmm, how much guilt do you feel?" asked his cousin as she began eating her Denver omelet. She looked him straight in the eye.

"The bottom line, I don't want to be associated with these racists in my political party. Your talk about family really got to me."

Brenda smiled then said, "What if I told you that I know an organization that helps immigrants. They are brought into the US and provided with jobs." She put her fork down to see his reaction.

"Have I heard of them?" He took a sip of coffee and then wiped his face.

"I doubt you've heard about them, but they've been around since 1995."

Now Benny was intrigued. "Tell me more."

Brenda explained to Benny about the La Lady Organization, and how they helped hard working immigrants to come to the US and prosper. "Look I know you're in shock, but if you wanted to help out, I know they take donations," she explained, as she scooped the last of her potatoes and dipped it in catsup. Brenda explained the vetting process and the training the people had to go through before coming to the United States. "Look, it's the real deal. They make sure these people are hard workers, give them jobs and support so that they can take care of themselves. All these people want is a better life and they are willing to bust their ass to achieve it."

Benny had a perplexed look on his face. "But how do you know all this?" He finished his breakfast and wiped his mouth before crumbling his napkin and putting it on his plate.

Brenda smiled. "Come on, you know I read the pulse of our people. I even send fifty dollars every month myself."

Benny was still in shock at how he and de Klerk had similar thinking, so he took his wallet out, pulled out two crisp hundred-dollar bills, and gave them to his cousin. "Can you please make sure they get this?" He wanted to distance himself from the dirty racist who he worked with. He was not one of them.

Chapter 38

"How'd you like dinner, Barb?" asked her husband Bradley Bell as he put the car in first gear.

"That's the best steak I've had in a long time," answered his wife.

Bradley smiled, because he loved to give his wife the good things in life. She deserved them, and he was happy to give her all she wanted. This dinner was special because Barbara's mother had begged to have their kids over for dinner, or else the Bell vehicle would have been at full capacity. "Did you see the news this morning?"

"I don't need to see the news to know what's going on."

"What do you mean by that?" asked the perplexed Bradley.

"All I see in the news are about children in cages. It's everywhere," said Barbara, as she reached into her purse for a tissue. "You ever wonder if God gets angry at us for allowing this to happen?"

"Barb, you know the US is using this harsh treatment as a deterrent. And as bad as it looks, maybe those people shouldn't make the trip up north," Bradley replied as they got on the freeway.

"Ha, deterrent? That would be believable if the architect of this policy didn't have Nazi leanings. I mean if he were still alive, I bet this administration would have Josef Mengele as the Camp Doctor," replied Barbara. She opened the glove box and tossed a few papers from her purse into it to show her displeasure.

"Look, I know the optics of it makes us look bad."

Barbara laughed sarcastically, then said, "Us? Are you part of the team?" Her mouth curled to one side, and Bradley knew she was pissed.

"Barb, let's talk about something else, my love." He reached for her hand and found her hand locked up in a fist. Slowly and gently he pried her hand open, and he felt Barb's resistance leave. Then a smile came to her face. "Always remember that I love you."

# # #

Wednesday was Bradley's favorite day of the work week because he always had a ten-thirty tee time to talk business with his buddies. The weather was a perfect seventy-two degrees with a slight breeze coming from the southeast. He enjoyed some fellowship with his friends, but he also liked to be competitive, challenging himself to play with his utmost concentration. All those hours of watching the PGA on television were conducive to him lowering his golf score from the low nineties to the mid-eighties.

Bradley was four over par after nine holes. They stopped and had lunch, having called the kitchen as they finished the seventh hole. He had his usual cheeseburger and fries while the others went with pastrami sandwiches. "Please pass the catsup," requested Thomas Tipton as he pointed to the red plastic bottle. He took the bottle and drenched his fries. "So what do you think about the news from the border?"

Charles cleared his throat and then spoke. "It's called deterrence. You must make it extra hard to be able to come in because if you don't, there will be a full-blown invasion." He took a bite from his sandwich.

"I don't know, it seems kinda cruel to separate children from their parents. That's the worst kind of trauma for kids," added Larry.

"But if there is no punishment, more of them will come," added Charles, his palms up trying to plead his case to his friends.

The debate continued on the back nine. On the par three fourteenth hole, everyone was on the green. As they went down the hill with their cart, Thomas said, "Hey Bradley, we haven't heard anything from you. What are your thoughts?"

Bradley looked up and saw that he was out, so he looked at the slope on the green and concentrated on his breathing. He practiced his slow pendulum swing and then stepped to address the ball. He went through his practice swing, looked at the hole that was four feet away, held in his breath and hit the ball straight into the hole. "My thoughts? My thoughts are that I just made a birdy putt." He pumped his fist in the air with glee. There was a short wait at the fifteenth hole, so Bradley piped in on the debate. "My thoughts are that they should not be separating families. If they get caught, just keep them all together until they are processed out of the country."

"But you have to make them feel some pain, that way we will be one less option for them," interjected Charles as he took out his driver and took a few practice swings.

"When they get caught, they must give their information making them ineligible to immigrate legally. That should be enough," added Thomas.

"I agree, lock them up together Anything else is being vindictive," said Bradley before putting a tee on the ground and then hitting a two-hundred-and-fifty-yard drive.

"Nice shot Brad. But if you just slap their hand, how is that a deterrence? How will that make them stop coming over? You must make it hurt to make them think about the consequences," replied Charles.

"And is it working?" asked Larry. He got ready for his tee shot.

"These things, they take time for the news to get back to the natives back home," Charles said with a wry smile.

"Really, now you're calling them natives?" inquired Bradley. "Look I get what you mean, but it just looks bad, and when people use these buzz words, it doesn't help anyone."

Bradley ended up shooting an eighty-five. He could have shot an eighty-four, but he shanked two easy pitches into bunkers. It had been a great day outdoors and the bonus was there were only two days left in the work week.

# # #

Wednesdays were also good for Barbara, as it was the day she had lunch with her friends. On this day they met for Mexican food at Casa Cantú. Candice Carlucci and Paula Peterson were friends from church while Wendy Winthope served with Barbara on the PTA.

They were seated and their server brought two bowls of chips and salsa, put the menus on the table, then placed four glasses of iced water with a slice of lemon on the rim of the glass in front of each of them. They immediately dug into the salsa and chips because Casa Cantú was known to have the best salsa in town. They all took turns updating each other on what happened over the past week as well as sharing the daily quarrels with their children as they tested the family boundaries in their quest to find their independence. Everyone was attentive and gave advice. Their server came back to take their lunch order. Eventually the talk turned to what was occurring at the Southern US border. "Every day it gets worse at the border," said Barbara.

Paula was in the middle of a bite, she chewed her food, then drank some water as a scowl formed on her face. "They need to stay in their own country. We don't need anymore, we're full."

Barbara was shocked by her friend's callousness. "Do you ever consider how bad their lives must be for them to take on such a risky journey?"

Paula sighed, then flicked her right hand out and said, "We're full. No vacancy."

The look on the faces of Barbara, Candice, and Wendy said it all. They looked at each other trying to come up with words to answer her. Finally, Wendy cleared her throat and stated, "But does the administration have to be so punitive? The ones hurt most are the children." Just then, their lunch order arrived, so it grew quiet as they had begun their meal. After a few minutes of silence, and without missing a beat, Wendy continued. "Plus, there are those in the administration who seem to enjoy the children's despair."

"Just stay home, and there wouldn't be any family separation," retorted Paula.

"You aren't seeing the big picture Paula, what is so bad that these people would gamble with their lives?" said Candice.

"That's not any of my concern," replied Paula, her arms folded in defiance.

Barbara shook her head, and with a sad voice sad, "Gee Paula, that's very Christian of you."

"Don't go there, Barb, you know I'm not like that. You know what I mean," said Paula with a furrowed forehead.

"Paula, I hear the economic argument about this. What is missing is showing dignity to others. If you want to lock them up, I'm with you, but lock the whole family, together," she explained.

Paula put her hand up and said, "Look, I'm sorry for all the grief, but they are breaking the law."

There were groans at the table for the age-old excuse for mistreating people for their indiscretions.

"I can understand Paula's position," added Candice. "We

see people coming in and our nation keeps getting worse. The more people they allow in, the worse we will be."

"Look, the world is a mess. Let's pray to God to help all people," said Wendy. After the prayer, the group stuck around discussing where next Wednesday's lunch would take place. Then each retreated to their own world.

# # #

The Bell kids' bedtime was nine in the evening. This was the time of night when the adults talked about how their day went. Bradley got to brag about shooting an eighty-five, and Barbara talked about what her friends had said over lunch. "Paula was so adamant that the administration was correct in separating families as a deterrent," reported Barbara as she put lotion on her legs.

"Charles was the same way, and kinda in a mean way, too," replied Bradley as he buttoned up his pajama top.

Barbara sighed deeply, then said, "I'll tell you one thing: some of our friends put the importance of having a sound economy over having compassion for all people, and they use immigrants as scapegoats."

"Yep, some of our friends are downright mean. It's all about the money. To them money trumps over anything else." Bradley looked at himself in the mirror one last time, then pulled the sheets back and got into bed. "I mean, I can see Charles point, but separating a child from their parents is barbaric." He shook his head and sighed deeply. "I say catch them but keep them together."

Barbara looked at her husband and nodded her head to show that she had heard him, but Bradley knew where she stood on this issue. "I think God is testing us to see what kind of people we are, and we are failing right now. Do you think it pleases God to see families broken up?" She hit the bed with both fists out of frustration. "Do you think God is happy with

Christians?" she asked as she put two fingers up in each hand to make an air quote. "They care more about money than about treating people with dignity."

"Honey, we're only in charge of ourselves. God knows everyone's heart."

"Well then, his heart is sad."

"Barb, we can pray for them to find their compassion. We have our faith."

# # #

Barbara was up at five in the morning. She liked her quiet time to start the day, but she also used the time to prepare lunches for her family. She went to the cabinet and took a coffee cup out just as the coffeemaker was finished brewing. Thank God for automatic coffee machines. When the last drip fell into the coffee pot, she pulled out condiments, lettuce, and deli meat from the refrigerator, then took out the bread from the pantry and placed it on the counter. She then poured herself the first cup of Joe for the day. She took her coffee black without sugar, like an old army sergeant, her husband liked to say. The first jolt of caffeine hit her system, and then her day officially started. She turned on the television and placed four pieces of bread on a plate and spread mustard evenly around each slice. As she opened the package of Black Forrest ham, a segment on the news shocked her. It was an undercover BBC video that had been taken inside a government facility where immigrant children were being kept. Every minute of the segment made Barbara angrier. She shook her head when she learned from the video that immigrants were being denied toothpaste, toothbrushes, and even soap. She slammed her hands on the counter. She knew exactly what was happening and tears fell from her face. She bit her lower lip upon hearing reports that girls were seen bleeding through their pants because they were denied feminine products. Yes, she thought, this is the first thing they do. It's easy to mistreat others when they are not viewed as equals. Barbara wondered if this was how the Nazis started, but either way, it was not good for humanity, nor Christianity, nor for her family. She felt an inner calling to speak out, to do her part to let people know that what was occurring at the southern border was a sin. Her husband walked into the kitchen and gave her a kiss.

"Good morning my love. Did you sleep well?"

Barbara smiled and said, "Good morning, yes I slept well, then I made the mistake of turning on the news."

"Well, what happened?"

Chapter 39

Barbara finished cooking a skillet of scrambled eggs, then reheated the bacon she had fried yesterday. Their kids came to the table for breakfast. Brooke Bell was a sixteen-year-old junior in high school, and her younger brother Bruce, was a thirteen-year-old eighth grader. When Barbara saw the kids enter the room, she turned the television off.

"Mom, we know about the BBC video, Vanessa texted me the link. Why are we being so cruel to people?" asked Brooke.

"Good morning, everyone, I hope we all had a restful sleep," said Bradley, as he finished buttoning his shirt.

Brooke ignored the question, and then said, "Dad, have you seen the BBC video?"

Her father sighed deeply, looked at his wife, and then said, "Yes, what is happening is a tragedy."

"How can America allow this? Why can't we treat all people with dignity?" Brooke was upset, and tears fell from her face. Her mother walked up to her and gave her a hug. She tried to soothe her daughter's concerns, but she was as disturbed by this as her daughter.

"I thought this was a Christian nation. Why are we treating others so bad?" asked Bruce, with concern on his face.

Barbara and Bradley looked at each other and they could see how affected their kids were by the video. All they could do was pray and ask God to comfort the families.

# # #

Brooke picked up Bruce from school. She was happy her parents bought her a car, but the downside was having to chauffeur her little brother around. "How was school today, Fart Breath?" Brooke smiled at her wittiness.

"Ha ha, in every class it was all about the video. It was all over school."

"Same here, it's just so sad and disrespectful that we can't show some decency to others. It really makes my heart hurt."

"Oh God, are you close to your period?" joked her brother. She stopped for a red light, gave him a dirty look, then punched his arm twice. "Okay, I'm sorry, I'm just trying to be funny."

"It isn't funny. Most of the students are against the child separation, but there are others who support what's happening," informed Brooke.

"Yeah, at our school too. I bet their parents are so proud of them," added Bruce sarcastically.

"Ah, hello little brother, where do you think they learned it?" said Brooke, as she turned left into their driveway.

Just before opening his door, Bruce asked, "What side do you think mom and dad are on?" He grabbed his backpack and got out of the car before slamming the door shut.

"I don't know, how about you ask them later," replied his sister.

# # #

Dinner was served at five-thirty. Barbara had prepared spaghetti with meat sauce, garlic bread, and a salad to start off the meal. There was small talk about how their day went and what was happening in school, but soon that question led to what troubled everyone at the table. "Dad, what do you think about what's going on at the border?" asked his son.

Bradley and Barbara looked at each other, then he cleared his throat and began, "What is happening is a calamity."

"Yeah dad, but how do you personally feel about it?" added Brooke.

"Well, it's complicated. You can't just let people break the law. There has to be law and order."

Brooke sighed loudly, then looked at her mother and back at her father before replying, "Come on dad, do you support it or not?"

"I don't support it. They should not separate the kids from their parents."

"But what about helping people in need?" asked Brooke.

"Well, it's a messy situation," answered her father.

Brooke sighed loudly to voice her displeasure but didn't say anything else. She ate her dinner in silence. Barbara asked questions about school, but both kids were disengaged, just eating robotically, and not looking up. Her brother was now more confused than before.

# # #

Later in the evening Bruce knocked on his sister's door to talk. He entered her room, then sat on a chair near the bed. He was sad thinking about children being taken away from their parents. It disturbed him that he would never know the extent of the fear they had. To him it was being done on purpose to punish people from trying to improve their lives. His sister could see he was upset and gave him a hug.

Bruce was troubled to hear his father's opinion on the border. He thought for sure that he would side with the families, but he still wanted them locked up together. The thirteen-year-old boy was confused. Growing up in church, they had been taught to have compassion and take care of those in need, but now it seemed that everyone was cool with separating children from their parents.

Brooke felt the same way. All those years of church and the teachings of Jesus had taught her that people should help those less fortunate, and now when people had the opportunity to help, all the compassion and dignity went out the window. To Brooke, and she was headstrong in her beliefs, the inaction of the Christian community showed they were nothing more than hypocrites who were Christian in name only. At the end of their talk, they prayed their parents would have the wisdom and strength to do the right thing. That's all they could hope for.

#

Barbara and Bradley were talking in the bedroom as they got ready for bed. "Did you see how upset Bruce was? I hate to see him like that," said Barbara as she took a drink from her bottled water.

"He's a tough kid," replied her husband.

"Brad, he's a sensitive kid with a heart of gold. You do know all those years of Sunday School has given him a compassionate attitude for those less fortunate. What did you expect to happen?"

"You don't think I know that?" replied Bradley. "We raised our children to have good values, and then they see how we treat those who need help. They must think we're the world's biggest hypocrites."

Barbara had a look of concern on her face. "How many of our Christian friends believe in what the government is doing, putting economics ahead of people? You know, I heard Pastor John talking with a parishioner, and he made a snide comment that these people should just stay home." She had a scowl on her face, and her husband knew she was fuming with rage. "Do you know how to fix Pastor John's attitude?"

"How?"

A sly smile came to Barbara's face as an idea crossed her mind. "All everyone seems to care about is money, even more than people, so what if we stopped tithing and instead give money to organizations who can help those people at the border."

"What?"

"Do you think God is happy right now? Do you think tithing to a church that goes against God's teachings should continue to prosper?" Barbara looked at Bradley dead in the eye.

He turned away and looked out the window, contemplating what his wife had said. "What do you mean stop tithing?"

"Bradley Bernard Bell, you know exactly what I mean," replied his wife, as she walked over to him and placed her hand on his shoulders. "Pastor John's comments really threw me. He's a man talking about living a Christian life, and he has an attitude like that? Have we been duped all these years?"

Bradley walked over from the window to sit down on the bed. His face was serious, and he was deep in thought. "Barbara, we can't stop tithing, what would people say?"

Barbara laughed out loud and smiled. "You're worried about what people will say? Who is going to remind Pastor John about compassion for the less fortunate? You do know if Mary and Joseph tried to come to America right now, the US would take baby Jesus away from them. Why do you care what people think? All we should worry about is serving God and teaching our children the true meaning of being a Christian."

Bradley nodded his head. His wife had made some excellent points. There was nothing he could say. She was right about everything, and it made him feel ashamed that she had to explain it to him. "Well, have you done any research?"

Barbara said she was in the process of looking those up. There were several organizations who helped immigrants and she would investigate it. She walked up to her husband and hugged him. Tears fell from her face and her husband comforted her as he heard and felt her sobbing and trying to catch her breath. "I can't get the look of Bruce's face out of my mind at his concern for the children. It makes me so sad." Then she smiled and said, "You know what? We raised our kids right. I'm glad that Bruce is sensitive, and I'm glad he cares for others."

Bradley smiled and nodded his head, "Yes, we did. You know I feel like a boob over the view I had on this tragedy." He shook his head in embarrassment.

"No honey, you're a strong man who wants the best for his family." She hugged him again and kissed him on the lips. It was getting late, and they both got ready for bed. "We'll have a talk with the kids in the morning."

# # #

Barbara was up early and had already prepared the day's lunches for the kids. Now she was working on breakfast of bacon, eggs, hash browns, and toast. She still felt sad remembering the fear in her son's eyes. Bruce was precious to her, just as Brooke was, but Brooke knew how to get her points across. She was feisty and had excellent communication skills while Bruce was just learning how to express himself.

Just then her husband entered the kitchen wearing black slacks and a white t-shirt. He walked up to his wife and gave her a good morning kiss.

"Good morning, honey." Barbara offered him a crispy slice of bacon.

He bit into the bacon and chewed for a moment, then said, "So, we're going to tell the kids we're going to do our part to help with this mess?" He poured himself a cup of coffee.

"We're going to tell them that we are following God's laws

about treating people with compassion, respect and dignity." The skillet sizzled as she put the hash browns on the stove. They looked at each other and smiled.

Both kids walked into the kitchen together, the smell of bacon was enough to entice them out of sleep. They hugged and kissed both parents, and then Bruce took out two glasses from the cabinet while Brooke retrieved the orange juice from the refrigerator—teamwork at its finest. "Have a seat, your mother and I need to talk with you." Bradley pointed to the chairs.

"What is it dad?" asked Bruce, confused as he had no idea why. Both siblings pulled out a chair and sat down.

"Your father and I have been talking. I know these current events are troubling to everyone, but we wanted to know you were right. This should not be happening. It goes against the teachings of Jesus. We want you to know we are against this cruel policy." Both kids looked at each other, shocked at what they heard. "It would be hypocritical to support such a barbaric policy, only meant to inflict pain. This is not what Christianity is about. So we want you to know that you were both correct in thinking about helping those less fortunate than us." Both kids smiled, and Bruce exhaled in relief, happy to know their parents choose the true Christian way of helping others.

Then Barbara shocked her kids even further by explaining how they were going to do their part to help people out of this situation. "I'd rather our tithing go to help people, and not to contribute to a church that has forgotten their mission." Brooke and Bruce looked at each other, not quite believing what they had just heard. Their mother continued, "It makes my blood boil to see politicians making this a partisan issue."

"Mom, you can hear the hate that some politicians have, all so they can please their political base and get re-elected," informed Brooke. Her mother smiled at her and nodded her head sadly. "But mom, you'll be happy to know that most of my friends think like we do." Her mother gave her a surprised look. "Yes, mother, our generation is more tolerant than yours, thank God. Everyone deserves to be happy if a person does no harm to others."

Barbara looked over at her husband and smiled, and he returned the smile because he knew their daughter was speaking the truth. "Yes, you're right, the future is bright if you follow God's rule of helping others. I apologize for my generation, as some people have forgotten God's mission and seem to worship money more than the teachings of God. Just know that our family will contribute to causes that help people because that's what Jesus would want us to do." The whole family smiled and came in for a group hug. The Bell family was raising compassionate and caring kids, and Jesus would be happy with them.

Chapter 40

Yulisa was busy running the day-to-day operations of the organization and relished the new experiences. Even though she was new to the job, she had an uncanny ability to anticipate issues. Yulisa Bermudez was born for this job.

Yulisa flew into Burbank, California, then rented a car and drove to Arvin, California to see if the organizational policies were meeting the people's needs. The Valaderes' were impressed that Yulisa would make such a long trip just to consult with them and to hear their experiences.

The Valaderases' felt the organization was there for them whenever they needed assistance. Vicente Valaderas was gainfully employed, and they had been placed in the newest apartment complex of this small agricultural town. To the family, everything had been provided for them. For Vicente, all he had to do was meet with the boss, sign a few forms, and he was part of the company. Earlier in the week, Vicente and his wife Oralia had talked about how fortunate they were to be taking advantage of the opportunities the organization offered them. All Vicente had to do was work hard every day, and the organization would take care of the rest. The Valaderases' felt safe and fully supported by the organization, and they made sure to report that to the new boss, Yulisa Bermudez.

After meeting with the Valaderases, Yulisa drove around the area. This was the Southern San Joaquin Valley, home to many foods that Americans eat on a regular basis, and Yulisa was in the middle of it. There was nothing but green fields of grapes, potatoes, lettuce, garlic, onions, and tomatoes, with Bear Mountain showing its presence to the East. Yulisa looked around the area and enjoyed her new surroundings. She would be everywhere, from the agricultural fields of Kern County to the cities of Los Angeles, San Diego, Phoenix, as well as Seattle, Houston, and Kansas City. Yulisa enjoyed exploring, and she looked forward to seeing many new places.

# # #

Diana relaxed on her living room sofa. It was Saturday morning, and she was working on what she'd do with all the extra time once she left the organization. She was dressed in blue sweatpants and her blue and orange UTEP sweatshirt. She put on a pair of socks as El Paso had finally turned cold in mid-November. She reached for her laptop that was on the coffee table, then balanced it on her knees. She resumed her search for places she always wanted to visit, and now there would be plenty of time. She surfed the Internet but couldn't help but wonder how Yulisa was doing with her new job. She knew she'd made the correct decision in choosing Yulisa to take over, but it was still hard for Diana to let go. Her cell phone rang, and she picked it up. It was her friend Elizabeth.

"Hey, ¿qué haces?" asked Diana.

"Just chilling here with a cup of coffee, finally enjoying a little fall weather. I just thought I'd call to see how you're doing now that Yulisa has taken over."

Diana smiled because she did not know what to do with all the extra time she now had. "I was sitting on the couch researching places I'd love to visit. But Bethy, I'm having a tough time letting go. I know the organization is in capable hands, but after so many years, it's hard to move on."

"Chica, you must let it go. You've served your time honorably and have helped so many people start the road to their prosperous lives."

Diana nodded her head in acknowledgement and said, "Yeah, you're right, but it's not as easy as you think."

"Well of course it's hard right now, but you'll adjust. It's your time now," explained her friend.

"Yeah, you're right."

"Want to do lunch at Jesusita's at noonish?" asked Elizabeth.

Diana looked at the clock on the living room wall. It read eight-forty-eight. "Sure Bethy, about twelve fifteen. It'll give me more time to continue my research."

"Well, you've earned it, now you just have to learn to relax," added her friend. "Okay, I'll see you just after twelve."

"Okay, bye." Diana was alone again. She needed to learn to take a step back, but it was a learning process.

# # #

Elizabeth was sitting at the table eating chips and salsa when Diana arrived. Elizabeth got up from the table and gave her friend a hug. "Hey girl!"

Diana smiled and said, "Thanks for the lunch invite." This worked out perfectly for her, otherwise she'd still be at home Googling places she'd like to visit.

"My pleasure. I'm so excited for you," replied her friend. Diana smiled at Elizabeth, but then her smile quickly disappeared. Elizabeth noticed immediately and asked, "What, what is it?"

Diana smiled sheepishly and looked down. "I didn't know it would be this hard to leave. I try to make plans to go on a trip, and a wave of sadness rushes over me."

Elizabeth looked at her friend and sighed. "Look, for the

last five years, I've heard you complain about how you wanted to find another leader for the organization. And now that it's happening, you're sad?"

Diana nodded her head hearing everything her friend had said, and it was exactly true. "Yes, it's hard to think of my life without it revolving around the organization."

Elizabeth laughed loudly, drawing attention from the other tables. "You're sad? What, just two months ago you thought Yulisa could be a Fed. And remember that Saturday morning, you called me hysterically because you thought you were going to get arrested. Come on Diana, you're free from all this now."

Diana felt bad because everything her friend had said was true. She'd be free of the stress, and her world would now be less hectic. But it was still hard to step away from something she started. "It's hard to say goodbye to a life that I've led for so long. You know what I'm saying? Old habits die hard. Shit, ain't that the truth? Don't get me wrong, I'm not changing my mind. I'm just trying to come to terms with this. It's hard to let go, it was so exciting and yet so stressful."

Elizabeth patted the top of Diana's hands and said, "Don't worry, you'll get used to it."

Diana smiled at her friend. She reached for her iced tea and took a long drink, then said, "Yes, I know you're right. It's just the finality about it, that's what gets me so emotional."

Elizabeth nodded her head and a smile crept onto her face. "Those early years were fun, but dangerous." She scraped the Mexican rice and beans on her plate with a corn chip, then scooped it up and ate it. "Little did we know it would all turn out like this." Her forehead furrowed as she thought of all the risks they'd taken.

Diana's sadness came from knowing it was now over. For the past twenty-seven years, her life had been directing operations for the organization, and in the early years, even bringing in immigrants herself. It was like starting a company, nurturing it, making sure it thrived, and now she was going to walk away. It was her choice, but it still caused an emotional loss in her heart. The only silver lining in all this was she left Yulisa to continue her work, and she knew her friend would continue the fight. Yes, the organization had been left in good hands, but Diana still felt like she was abandoning the organization, and her friendships would probably change due to her exit. "Yeah, those were some crazy times," she said with a smile.

They shared an order of flan with ice cream and topped off dessert with some excellent coffee. Elizabeth talked with Diana about her upcoming retirement at the end of the school year. She understood Diana's apprehensive feeling, too, because Elizabeth had been at same job for thirty years and stepping away, naturally created some anxiety. But nothing lasts forever, and change is inevitable. It was just something the two ladies would have to deal with.

After lunch Diana was in a nostalgic mood, so she drove around the outskirts of El Paso. She took Highway Twenty and headed north, just past UTEP off Interstate Ten. She took this road because her grandfather always took the Twenty, as he didn't like the race car like traffic on the freeway. She drove a leisurely fifty miles per hour, with agricultural fields on both sides of the road. When she wanted to feel closer to her grandfather, she always took the backroads. Yes, her grandfather hated traffic, but he enjoyed seeing the beauty of the crops—gifts from God he would always say. The organization would have never happened had he not left Diana an inheritance.

Diana smiled, knowing her grandfather would get a kick out of his money being used to help people. He always hated the government, both the United States and Mexico's, because he thought they were all corrupt. Diana knew he'd be proud of her, and she realized that the organization was as much a legacy of her grandfather as it was for her. She stopped at an old convenience store in Canutillo. She got out of her car, and climbed its wooden steps, the old boards creaking with every step she took. The inside of the store looked just as ancient as the outside. She walked to the coolers, picked up a diet Dr. Pepper along with a pack of gum, then went to the counter to pay. When she felt alone, she always stopped at this store, and somehow, she'd feel a closeness with her abuelo. Eventually the nostalgia wore off and Diana had to move back to the present.

The whole reason for Diana's sadness was her time in the organization was coming to an end. There were some friendships she'd built that she knew would wane as she stepped away from the top spot, and it made her sad, but that's how the world worked. Once a person left a position, their sphere of influence dropped, and friendships sometimes died. But Diana tried to look at the bright side. She was proud of herself knowing the people they brought into the United States were hard workers. The only thing these people wanted was an opportunity to show what they could do.

Diana was two minutes from home when she received a phone call from Yulisa. "Hola chica. ¿Qué haces?"

"Hi Diana, I just finished visiting with Oralia Valaderas in Arvin. Those questions I asked the Jimenez's in Seattle couldn't be answered, so I made a trip to ask another family."

"What do you mean they couldn't answer your question?" Diana asked, puzzled.

"I asked them if they were getting enough support from the organization, but Mercedes couldn't answer the question because they were already getting assistance from Reynaldo and Rocio," explained Yulisa. "So, I went back to your neck of the woods to find the answer."

"And what did you find out?" asked Diana.

"We're doing a good job, the Valaderases' are doing well, and they are happy with the support," reported Yulisa.

Diana smiled, happy with Yulisa's initiative in taking over

the reins of the organization. It was this kind of attention to detail that got Yulisa this job in the first place. Diana knew that the organization would be in good hands. "Yulisa, you're amazing. You're on top of your game, and the people you're helping are going to love you."

Yulisa was shocked to hear those words, and she managed to say, "Thank you."

Chapter 41

After speaking with Yulisa on the phone, Diana knew it was time to step away. Yulisa had taken over the organization without missing a beat. The organization was in good hands, so now she could move on with her life and enjoy the new opportunities that awaited her. Diana felt sad, but she was a realist. She knew the pain would last a while, but eventually it would be released from her body and mind.

Diana was mentally prepared for this moment. It was like a heavy weight had been lifted from her shoulders. She fought her way through her uneasiness, knowing that people would be in good hands. The last bit of doubt had been erased upon hearing about Yulisa's recent trip to the Bakersfield area. Most people would have made a phone call to get the answers they were seeking. Yet Yulisa knew that being new to the organization called for a hands-on approach with her being visible to the people brought in. To Diana this showed that Yulisa knew the importance of face-to-face communication, and Diana thought it was a brilliant move by Yulisa to show people that she cared about them.

Diana reached for her laptop, and started pricing month long vacations to Paris, France, as it was now time to hang it up. Diana smiled because now it was over, and she could have her life back. Her burdens had been lifted from her with clear visibility for miles. She looked outside at the blowing wind, as it attacked the leaves of her backyard tree. Diana had never felt more liberated. Everything she saw now looked different and clearer. She walked into the kitchen and poured herself a cup of coffee. Yes, everything looked different to Diana now, the result of clarity in her life.

Little did Diana know that her life would change upon hiring Yulisa Bermudez. Diana had never met anyone so in tune to people's needs than Yulisa. She had a knack for anticipating, then producing the items required to get the job done. Diana knew how dedicated her friend was to her job, and never did she let on about the tragedy and pain that she'd been living through. The more she thought of it, the more Diana was convinced that Yulisa had been heaven sent to her. Diana needed Yulisa, but Yulisa also needed Diana—it was a win-win situation.

# # #

Yulisa was feeling more confident. She was getting used to the job, and every day she learned more. The people Diana had placed in charge of various logistics for the operations were utmost professionals. They welcomed Yulisa with open arms, knowing she was as competent as her predecessor. She tried not to change anything and was open to suggestions. These people had done this for years, so Yulisa always listened to their approach on a particular problem, but this didn't stop Yulisa from trying to come up with other ways to run the operations as she was into improving and streamlining operations to decrease the risks for all involved.

Of all the jobs that Yulisa had had, this was the best for her in several ways. First and foremost, taking over for Diana and continuing the cause of helping immigrants was rewarding. But it also allowed her to stay busy so she didn't have time to dwell on her tragedies. Yulisa also liked that every day was different, be it visiting groups before making their trip up North, talking with mechanics on the transportation line, or viewing an operation from the air via drone. She loved her job and the mission it provided. Yulisa's phone rang and she picked it up, "Hello."

"Hello Yulisa, this is Vanessa Villamontes. I'm calling because I just finished talking with some potential sponsors, and they are now open to sign because they heard a few of their competitors signed up a few months ago and were happy with their employee's productivity."

Yulisa's smiled, and said, "So we can increase the number of people we bring in?"

"Yes, I'm sure of it. Employers are always hesitant at the start, but once they see what they get and observe the work ethic of the new employees, they tend to seek out more workers. This is what we saw today," informed Vanessa.

Yulisa nodded her head and replied, "Good. Here's hoping more companies hear about this and jump on board."

"Well, there's more good news," replied Vanessa. "Reynaldo Jimenez's boss is considering expanding his business by purchasing another yacht, which means they would need more crewmembers. It's not a done deal yet, but he's considering it."

"That's great news." Yulisa chuckled, before saying, "Thank God for that Jimenez work ethic." She reached for her writing tablet and wrote in the new information.

"So, are you getting used to your new gig, Yulisa?

"Truth be told, I'm having the time of my life. It's a huge learning curve, but I'm getting the hang of it now," replied Yulisa with a smile.

"I've talked with others within the organization, and everyone says you're doing an excellent job. Everyone is happy because they see no drop off," informed Vanessa.

Yulisa's eyes teared up upon hearing that news from Vanessa. It pleased her that she had the support of the members of the organization. "That's kind of you to say."

Vanessa thanked her for continuing to do an excellent job then hung up, leaving Yulisa alone in her own thoughts. Like anyone else, she enjoyed hearing praise for the job she was doing. She sat on the sofa and thought about how she walked into this position. She felt like it was created for her by God, there was no other explanation for this. God knew she was struggling, keeping perpetually busy as a way of not thinking about what had been taken from her. She was grateful to him for her good fortune.

Yulisa took in a relaxing breath and felt at peace with herself. Everything was going well, and every day on the job allowed her to gain more confidence. She looked around her living room and felt pleased. She'd stepped in for Diana and had shown she was up for the task. She was in a blissful state, a perfect blend of happiness, confidence, and determination. Everything was finally clicking in her life, and all the missing puzzle pieces seemed to have been found, except that her little Rosita and Sergio would never come back. As painful as it still was, there was nothing that could be changed. So the next best thing was to focus on the positive and change the things she could control. There was still a hole in her heart for the loss of her daughter and husband—it would always be there, but she had to focus on the present because that was all she could control. She was thankful for this opportunity, and she viewed herself like the immigrants that she helped bring into this country. All she needed was an opportunity to show what she could do.

Yulisa thought of the road that led her to Diana. She felt fortunate she landed the office manager position with Diana's realty company, which in turn catapulted her to where she was today. It was still hard for her to fathom that she was now the leader of an immigrant smuggling organization, but she had faith that God had opened this door for her and put her into this position. By nature, Yulisa was a humble person, always thankful for what God provided. She was confident in her abilities, owing it to her hard work and dedication. She was the type of person to let her actions speak for her. She never liked when people were arrogant and cocky because she knew at a moment's notice, a person's life could be turned upside down. She knew this from personal experience, so instead of tooting her own horn, she'd let others see the work that she put in.

Yulisa got up from the sofa, poured herself a cup of coffee, and then sat back down on the sofa. Her heart was content, or was as much as possible. She knew she was in a good place both mentally and physically, and that's why she was puttering around the house. This was a habit she picked up from when she was married—when she was in a perfect state of bliss with her heart full and her mind crystal clear. It was like she was born to do this job.

She reached for her yellow writing tablet. In between sips of coffee, she reviewed the notes, trying to find ways to improve efficiency. She wasn't going to immediately change anything, she'd just write ideas down to run by the staff in charge of that sector of operation. She'd let them point out the flaws in her planning. This was a good thing because it kept her mind active, and being the creative type, her mind was always looking for ways to improve. The next time she was in Mexico, she'd share her ideas with those with the intricate knowledge and responsibility of the operation and ask them what they thought of her ideas. She wasn't meddling, she just wanted everyone exposed to less risk, and the world revolves around innovation. The worst thing that could happen was someone would say her plan wouldn't work, then Yulisa would go back to step one and start over. It was a learning process, and change is constant in business. She enjoyed coming up with scenarios because even if they didn't work, she was gaining intricate knowledge from people with many years of experience under them.

Since Yulisa had taken over, she tried to read anything she could get her hands on about the early days of the organization. As Yulisa studied its history, she couldn't believe how risky the early days were, not to mention the physical exertion that workers had to experience to get across the border. The people who ran the early operations were now at the top of the organizational chart. They had been there since the organization's inception, so they knew their job. Yulisa read on. Eventually, their operations became more sophisticated with less risk. In 2004, the organization started giving each new person coming over their own driver's license/identification card along with a valid social security card in their own names. Yulisa wrote the new information into her notebook. She'd would make sure and ask Diana how she accomplished that feat. In 2011, the organization began utilizing Points of Entry at the Southern border. That made the work was much less dangerous and more convenient at the same time, and that's how it continued to the present.

Yulisa got up from the sofa and picked up her coffee, it had become cold, so she walked towards the kitchen to warm it up. As she waited for her coffee to be heated, she walked back to the coffee table and brought some papers with her into the kitchen to scan for information. Yulisa's job was to plan operations, so that's why she read anything she could get her hands on. She loved her new job.

Yulisa still had imposter syndrome, however, as she still could not believe she was the leader of the organization. Never in her wildest dreams could she have imagined doing this, but this is what she needed for her sanity. The loss of her daughter and husband was still painful to her, but somehow, she managed to cope through the loss, and Diana's job offer helped her to turn the corner emotionally. Yulisa was thankful because without this job, she'd still be living with her pain, which wasn't living at all. She walked back to her living room and sat down. The organization papers were spread out on the coffee table. Her phone rang and Diana's number popped up. "Hola chica, how are you?"

"Hi Yuli, ¿qué haces?"

"I'm glad you called. Listen, I have a few questions for you." Yulisa opened her writing tablet.

"Perfect. I want us to get together so you can see an actual operation and see how the people come into the country."

Yulisa's ears perked up upon hearing this. "Great, that's one of the questions I had." She drew a three-inch-by-three-inch box into her writing tablet where the information would go, once Diana explained it to her.

"Tomorrow, I'll pick you up at ten in the morning. Well spend the day shopping in Juárez, and then we'll cross the border at the Bridge of the Americas," Diana explained. "We'll be like three cars behind the group, and you'll get to see how they'll cross," explained Diana.

Yulisa tried to picture it. Would the group be nervous and arouse suspicion, or would they cross into the United States without any problems? "How do they cross?" Yulisa finally asked.

"You'll see tomorrow. We'll make our way back across the border just before six in the evening."

"I'm looking forward to it. It seems every day I learn something new," replied Yulisa. She looked forward to experiencing a group crossing, and all that it entailed. Her learning curve was steep, but Yulisa had the determination and intelligence to see things done once. After that, she was able to grasp the concepts because she was a quick study and paid attention to detail.

"I'm sure you'll be amazed at how we do it, but really, it's the people who do all the work preparing to meet The Man. It's their training that gives them the confidence and keeps their fear away. It's all about putting in the work. So when everything is on the line, they hold their heads up and take care of business," explained Diana.

"Yeah, that makes sense. I'm looking forward to seeing it."

"Okay, chica, see you in the morning," said Diana.

Yulisa hung up the phone, then closed her writing tablet and kicked up her feet up on the coffee table. She was done working for the day. Tomorrow another mystery of the puzzle would be revealed to her, and she was looking forward to it.

Chapter 42

Diana drove to Yulisa's house just before noon. The initial plan was to be in Juárez at ten, but Diana changed the time because there was no need to be there so early. Their mission today was to witness the crossing of the group, and that wouldn't happen until just before six in the evening.

They crossed into Ciudad Juárez at twelve-thirty and found public parking. They walked to the city plaza and took a seat on a bench that was covered in shade. The cool wind blew their hair around, as they watched people walk up and down the street. "It's such a beautiful day today," stated Diana, with a smile.

"The breeze makes it that much more enjoyable," replied Yulisa. She saw a family walk in front of them, the parents holding the hands of their children.

"So, you're ready to take over now, right?" asked Diana with a toothy smile.

Yulisa looked at her friend and smiled. "Yes, of course I'm ready." She stopped to find the right words, then continued, "I don't know how to thank you for this opportunity."

Diana smiled, put her arm around her friend, then said, "No, thank you. You're perfect for the job." Diana was lost in her thoughts, thinking about how all this would have turned out if she'd hired from within the organization. Yulisa was at the right place at the right time, and it had worked to Diana's advantage. She wanted to be the one to name her successor, and she had made an excellent choice. Diana snapped out of her deep thought and again said, "Thank you, Yulisa."

They explored the Plaza and all the goods for sale. It was like a bazaar with customers craftily trying to get deals as business owners shrewdly declined to sell their wares any cheaper.

Yulisa looked at the ground and grew nervous. Diana picked up on that and looked at her. "Qué te pasa, Yulisa?"

After regaining her composure, she cleared her throat and explained. "Diana, I don't know where I'd be mentally if I didn't know you. Rest assure that I'll bust my ass for this organization. That's the least I can do for what you've done for me."

Diana looked at Yulisa and then broke out in a huge grin. "I guess we're both winners here."

"Winner, winner, chicken dinner," replied Yulisa as they both broke out in laughter.

After some window shopping, they went back into shops to purchase what they were looking for—a purse for Diana and costume jewelry for Yulisa. They paid for their goods and had the shop owners hold their merchandise until they were ready to head back to El Paso.

It was now three thirty-five in the afternoon. They found a small restaurant called La Cocina and sat down for a late lunch. The restaurant had seen better days, the floor was old and worn and should have been replaced years ago. The tables were square with red and white checkered patterned tablecloths, and for some reason, there was a small lit candle in the middle of each table, but nothing could help its ambiance. "Have you ever eaten here before?" asked Yulisa, as she perused the menu.

"I haven't, but it comes highly recommended by a few members of the organization. I hear the asada tacos are excellent."

The waitress brought them glasses of purified water with lemon, then placed chips and salsa on the table. Diana absentmindedly put salt on the chips without finding out if it was needed. Yulisa took a chip, dipped it into the red salsa and took a bite. She then added more salt on the chips then the salsa. "The chips are sorry, huh?" stated Diana.

"Yes, but I hope the rest of the food is good," replied Yulisa with a hopeful smile.

Lunch was superb, Diana ordered the steak fajita plate and Yulisa chose the two-item combo plate that consisted of a carne asada soft taco and a shredded beef enchilada. Each plate came with a side of refried beans and Mexican rice. Yulisa gave the thumbs up sign, and said, "Props to whoever turned you on to this place. The asada is so tender."

Diana smiled, then put more salsa on her fajitas, and ate with a piece of corn tortilla. After chewing a bite, she washed it down with her iced water and said, "Beto always knew where to find the good eats."

"Beto?"

"He used to work for us until his retirement. He was our connection in Mexico for finding the people to bring in. He was always cool and never stressed out. Last I heard he was living it up in the Yucatán," informed Diana. "He was a good man. You'll meet more people like him, always focused on our mission."

Yulisa listened and made a mental note. She felt blessed to be working with such good people. Lunch was capped off with some coffee and a serving of flan. Though the restaurant needed repair, Yulisa felt comforted there.

Diana looked at her watch and calculated that they had two and a half hours before they made their way back across the border, so they ordered more coffee to kill time. Diana cleared her throat then began to open up to Yulisa. "I want to thank you once again for taking over for me." Yulisa put her hand up, signaling that it wasn't necessary, but Diana ignored her. "I'm so glad that you were open to taking over for me."

"Diana, you're the one who saved me. I was at the end of my rope when you offered me a lifeline. I mean, I would never off myself, but shit, a person can only stay so busy, and it was starting to not be enough. But then you saved me." Yulisa took Diana's hands into hers.

"Your work ethic is amazing, and you taking this job allows me to go out my own way, with my choice of who would take over." Diana smiled at Yulisa, then she finished what was left of her flan.

"Are you looking forward to your new life?" asked Yulisa as she took a sip of her coffee.

"Yes, and when I think of all the years that I put in here, I think of all the personal sacrifices I have made in my life. I'm pissed that I never got to be a mother. I missed out on a lot for all this," Diana extended her arms outward for emphasis. "It was worth it. But damn, I wonder what kind of life I would be leading had I never started the organization."

Yulisa acknowledged Dianas with a nod, sighed, then said, "Yes, you've given up a lot, but you've given many people better lives. I know it doesn't make up for your losses, but I always chose to see the positives in life."

Diana frowned, sighed, but nodded her head. She knew she couldn't go back in time and change her life. It was just better to acknowledge the pain and move forward. Her lost motherhood would always be a sore spot in her life, but nothing could be done about it. Yulisa was right in trying to see the positives in everything because there was not a damn thing Diana could do to change her life's circumstances. "You're right Yuli, I can't change anything. But I needed the opportunity to bitch and have someone listen."

"Oh, I have you girl, but perhaps you'll look at it in a different light," explained Yulisa.

Diana gave her a confused look and said, "How so?"

Yulisa shifted in her seat and sighed heavily. "Look, no one could ever replace the loss of motherhood, but if you looked at it another way, this organization that you've ran for over twenty-seven years is in fact your baby. You founded all this, this has always been your baby, and you have nurtured it."

A shocked look came to Diana's face, then she said, "Humm, I never thought of it that way." A smile curled up on her face. "Yeah, but I feel cheated out of the experience."

"You know me and my positive thinking, at least you never had to deal with shitty diapers," chuckled Yulisa. Both women laughed and felt a kinship. "I think we have a cosmic connection, because in my own crazy way, keeping the organization going is like caring for my little Rosita. I know she's gone, but continuing the organization is a way to keep her alive in my mind. I know you probably don't understand, or I'm not making sense, but I have weird ways of thinking sometimes." Diana motioned to the waitress that they were ready for the check.

Diana smiled, then said, "I understand what you mean, and it's not strange thinking. If it works for you, that's all that counts. I know the love you have for your family. Under your leadership, the organization is in excellent hands. Your work ethic and anticipation skills are superb."

For the next twenty minutes they laughed and joked, killing time until they met with the people preparing to come to the US. Both women were happy to clear the air and cleanse themselves of their individual pain.

# # #

Diana and Yulisa met with the group at the designated safe house in Juárez. There was excitement and nervousness in the air. Everyone felt it. Diana tried to calm everyone and reminded them that they'd been practicing for this moment.

There were twenty people coming over. There were four families of three, and two families with four. The ages of the children accompanying their parents ranged from ten to some as young as five. The children were tense, clinging to their parents' side. Yulisa saw two families having a prayer circle.

"¿Ya están listos para cruzar la frontera?" asked Yulisa.

Diana quickly translated to English, "Are you ready to cross the border?" The family looked at both women, smiled and nodded, hoping to convince themselves that they were ready.

The couple understood what Diana wanted, and the wife replied, "Yes, we are ready to cross and live in America."

Diana smiled and said, "Good, speak just like that and you will not have to worry." Diana patted the mother's back. She then turned her attention to her friend. "Yuli, in these times before the crossing, we always speak to the people in English. That way when it's for real, their stress level is lowered."

Yulisa nodded her head. "Yes, that makes sense, and I'll remember that from now on." She looked at the people as they lined up to exit the safe house and enter the vehicles that would take them to freedom.

Diana and Yulisa stayed to the side and observed the whole process. A surname was called, and the corresponding family would line up in front of a vehicle. There they got their final instructions and entered their vehicle, then waited until everyone had been briefed. With everything in order, Diana and Yulisa got into their vehicle and watched the six cars of different years and models get on the road. They were in the last vehicle so Yulisa could see the process the organization used to bring people across. They all drove around the city, then lined up at the Paso del Norte Bridge and waited their turn to cross. Diana could tell Yulisa was getting tense and said, "Now you know why we want them to be comfortable enough to speak English. They're in their cars trying to be as casual as possible. But you know, inside they may still have that sliver of doubt. We drilled them in English, so they could believe in the process. I mean, just look at you, all tense, looking like you don't want to be deported," chuckled Diana. "Just relax and see how it is done."

Chapter 43

"We're lucky we don't have a two hour wait in front of us. Right now it's only ninety minutes," informed Diana as she looked at Yulisa. "Relax girl."

Yulisa smiled and turned towards her. "I know, I know, but then I put myself in their shoes." She pointed to the vehicles in front of them.

"Trust me, they are all ready to make the trip. We drill pressure situations on them until we know they're ready."

"Have you ever been unsuccessful making it through the border?"

"We have a one hundred percent success rate so far, knock on wood," said Diana, as she playfully knocked on her forehead with her knuckles. "Look we have over an hour to wait from here, so relax," repeated Diana.

"I have a question. If people are coming in from Mexico, how did they get their passports, driver's license, and identification cards? Do you have your own printer?" asked Yulisa. She saw two teens walking on the sidewalk, heading towards El Paso.

Diana looked at Yulisa and then grabbed her hand. "Look, even I don't know where we get everything from, and I don't really want to know."

A wry smile crept onto Yulisa's face, and she asked, "You

have someone on the inside?"

"Yulisa, just drop it. There are some things better not known, so next question."

Yulisa stopped asking questions and thought about what Diana had just told her. Diana's insistence that she drop the subject scared her. She figured that someone in a state government office was helping, but then she deduced that groups were going to different States, which meant that the organization had help at the highest levels. A cold chill traveled down Yulisa's spine, and she managed to say, "Intelligence, you have someone assisting who's a Fed." Yulisa's eyes were wide with shock.

Diana interjected, "I'll answer any of your questions but that. That's for your protection. The less you know, the better." Yulisa's mouth was agape as she tried to process what she'd just heard. "Look, we have a good thing going, so don't mess with what's not broken. That is the only question I will not answer. But let's just say that when the US goes to the Real ID in a few years, know that it won't affect our, err, I mean, your operations," Diana said with a smile. "Just leave it alone, Yuli."

"I get the picture," replied Yulisa.

"Do you see those people walking towards El Paso on the walkway," asked Diana, pointing to the people on their right.

"Yes."

"Well, some of those people there are ours. It's a different group." People slowly trudged up the walkway, each step taking them one step closer to the United States. Diana looked at Yulisa to see her reaction.

"These people right here, they're ours?" asked Yulisa as she saw people carrying goods that they bought in Juárez.

"Yes, some of them are ours, I can't tell exactly who, but they are intermingled with the rest of the people walking into El Paso," informed Diana.

"Really? Ya'll got it going on." Yulisa was blown away. She

had no idea there was another group coming over. Yulisa thought the identifications issued were perfect if a pedestrian could come into the US with what the organization had issued them. Yulisa nodded her head at the organization's ingenuity.

"Ya'll?" stated Diana. "This is your baby now." She looked over at Yulisa and smiled. "By this weekend, you'll be aware of all our, err, I mean your operations."

Yulisa smiled and nodded her head.

# # #

Thirty-four-year-old Guillermo Gallegos was sitting next to his wife, Gabriela, as his eight-year-old son, Gabino, was sitting in the back seat waiting to cross the border. Soft calming music came from the radio to sooth their nerves. "Don't worry Gabino, it will be just like we practiced it. No tengas miedo, mijito."

"Yo sé, I mean, I know papá," replied the young boy. He looked at the cars in from of them, then at the pedestrians walking toward the border.

"Everything will be good," said Gabino's mother. She trusted the organization to get them across the border. She knew they invested a lot of time helping them to be comfortable enough to cross. She reached across the console of the car and took her husband's hand, both for strength to make it across the border and the love she had for him. She knew their family was fortunate enough to be chosen to cross, and they would not be in this car waiting to cross into the United States without the hard work and dedication of her husband. Because of Guillermo's work ethic, they were going to be rewarded with a new and prosperous life. She looked over at her husband and felt close to him. She squeezed her hand in his, then whispered, "¡Te amo, mi amor!"

Guillermo turned to his wife and said, "Yo también, mi

vida. We are going to have a great life." Their vehicle crept closer to the front.

They were now sixth in line to cross. They were the last of their group, which meant that the other five vehicles had already made it across, at least that's what Guillermo had figured since he did not see anyone being detained. The closer they got to the front, the more butterflies Guillermo felt flying around in his stomach. He tried to control his breathing so he wouldn't appear flustered before the Border Patrol. He opened the console and pulled the bottom portion of his temporary visa called the FMM. The visa had been whole at one time when members of the organization used it to bring the vehicle into Mexico. For this operation, a man, women, and young boy were used that looked like the Gallegos family just in case the border guards wanted to look at the videotape of them coming into Mexico. Now Guillermo and his family were making the return trip. They moved up about three car lengths and were now third in line. Guillermo took the three passports and visa form into his right hand, breathed deeply, and said a silent prayer. It took another twenty minutes, but they had finally made it to the front of the line. Guillermo rolled down his window for the Border Patrol officer.

"What is your citizenship?" asked the short, chubby Latino Border Patrol officer with a military style crewcut.

"We're Americans," they all said in unison. Guillermo handed the passports and visa to the guard.

"What was the nature of your trip?"

"We were visiting family," replied Guillermo.

The guard looked at the paperwork and all was in order. He handed the paperwork back to Guillermo. "Welcome back to the United States and have a good evening."

"Yes, same to you officer, and thank you," replied Guillermo. They drove across to El Paso, Texas, and into the United States of America.

"They crossed over!" yelled Yulisa. A smile on her face.

"See, we get these people ready to do this. They are constantly drilled so that they won't become tongue tied in front of the Border Patrol. The organization takes pride in preparing groups to deal with this kind of stress," said Diana. She beamed with pride.

Diana and Yulisa crossed over the border in the same line as Guillermo and his family. They were asked the same questions and provided the necessary paperwork to be able to cross, and soon they were back in El Paso.

"Now where are we going?" Yulisa asked.

"We're going to the safe house to meet the group. We have a tradition of having carne asada tacos on their first night in America," informed Diana.

"Well, I am hungry," chuckled Yulisa.

# # #

The dinner with the group was a celebration for all. The organization enjoyed another successful trip, and the people were happy that they would start their new lives in a few days, though the handlers in charge warned them that if they were within one hundred miles of the US border, they should expect to find other immigration inspection points. They warned everyone not to fall into complacency.

Yulisa looked around the back yard of the safe house that looked like a walled compound. It was a ranch house located on top of a hill, and the views of El Paso and Juárez were spectacular. It being a chilly forty-five degrees outside, they had a fire pit going. There was not a frown to be seen as everyone was celebrating a perfect day. Yulisa could see the faces of the people as they found warmth near the fire. Everyone smiled, some hugged, but all were relieved to be on the this side of the border. Families huddled together, quietly talking with each other and relishing how their lives were going to be better. Some families were excited about where they would live, and Yulisa could hear a mixture of joy and anxiety, but each had faith that they would be successful. Yulisa turned towards the glowing lights of the two cities and heard two men speak in Spanish. From what she could pick up, one man had a sadness of leaving his country and felt like a traitor, but the other man reminded him that their lives would have stayed the same had they remained in Mexico. The other man nodded his head and gave the man a bear hug. They looked out over the lights of El Paso and Juárez for a few more moments, then went to their respective families.

# # #

It was after midnight when they left the safe house. Diana drove towards Yulisa's home. "Well, what did you think about what you saw today?" asked Diana, as she made a left turn into Yulisa's neighborhood.

"Very impressive. The operation went off perfectly," replied Yulisa. She gave Diana the thumbs up sign.

Diana smiled because it would take Yulisa at least a year to figure everything out. She was smart, astute, and Diana knew she would read everything she could get her hands on about operational matters. "Well, now you know one of the ways we bring people in. We do it here, Eagle Pass, Laredo, Brownsville, Douglas, Arizona, Mexicali, the San Diego area.

"You guys are professionals, from step one to the final product. It's great to see people helping others as it's getting rarer to see such selfless attitudes these days," said Yulisa.

Diana smiled showing her toothy grin, then said, "When I started this a long time ago, I told everyone that we were going to put people first, treat them with respect and not as property to be shipped. Our success rate is possible because of all the drills and training we give the people. We prepare them to at least understand that they have a job to do consisting of learning, listening, and following directions."

"And does it work?"

Diana laughed lightly, and replied, "We use Catholic guilt, and it works really well." Diana turned into Yulisa's driveway. "Okay Chica, we'll talk more in the morning."

"Okay, have a good night," replied Yulisa before shutting the passenger door.

Chapter 44

Diana slept in until eight. Years earlier she could have lived off four hours of sleep, but the older she got, the more she needed sleep to replenish her energy. She stretched her arms over her head and tried to leave her grogginess behind. Diana was ecstatic that Yulisa was able to witness some of the ways the groups came into the country, though what she had observed was only a portion of the ways the organization brings its people in.

Diana dressed in some sweats and a hoodie as she had no intention of leaving her house today. She turned on the coffee pot and waited to have her first jolt of caffeine for the day. She looked out at her patio and saw the trees swaying in the wind from the typical El Paso weather. She saw a corner of shade appear on the patio table, then walked to the cabinet and pulled out a coffee mug. The coffee was only halfway brewed, but Diana couldn't wait any longer. So she poured herself a cup and put the pot back on the burner. She got a spoon and mixed the coffee to dissipate the bitterness of its strength, splashed coffee creamer into her cup, and walked to the patio door to open it. The wind hit her in the face, and her hair went everywhere. She pulled out the chair in the shade and took a seat. She took a drink of her coffee and looked around the yard. It was spotless with all the shrubs and flowers trimmed. The patio esthetics along with the events of last night put Diana in an excellent mood. Everything was going her way. Yulisa was a great choice to replace her, and she was learning on the job. Her work ethic was what made Diana know that she'd left the job in capable hands. And because of that, Diana was ecstatic with her thoughts on what she would do on her trip to Paris. It was only in the past month that Diana finally allowed herself to put herself first. She always knew that Yulisa was up for the job but proving that to the members of the organization was the final vote of approval. Diana was in a good place now, and a smile crept onto her face. She deserved her happiness for all she had done. She smiled and nodded her head, thinking how proud her abuelo would be of her and the smart way of using his money to start the organization. Yes, Diana Solis was happy to have her own life back. But Diana being Diana, she worried about Yulisa if she were ever caught by the authorities. Diana knew Yulisa would not reveal anything about the organization, but it gave Diana pause to put Yulisa in such a perilous situation after all that she had gone through a few short years ago.

The more Diana thought of the risks to Yulisa, the guiltier she felt for having placed her in this situation. She knew Yulisa jumped at the chance to take over the organization to control her own demons and there was nobody more competent than her, but Diana was bothered by the fact that Yulisa's life would be ruined if she were caught by the authorities. Diana searched deep within her soul, because putting Yulisa in such danger created a black cloud over Diana's heart. She felt it. She hated the feeling of putting a friend in danger.

She sat back down on her patio chair, the wind cooling her coffee and making a mess of her hair when an idea came to her that made her happy and warmed her soul at the same time. She'd have a conversation with Yulisa and tell her that if she were ever arrested, it would be okay to give her name to the authorities to lessen charges against her. That would mean that Diana would always be tied to the organization and she could still go to prison, but she thought that's the least she could do for her friend. She didn't like it much because she thought she'd be free and clear, ready to live life worry free, but Diana was selfless. She had fierce loyalty and would do what she could to protect Yulisa. Diana took the last sip of coffee, nodded, and then smiled. She was happy to have come up with this solution, though it was not to her liking. Diana knew how efficient and meticulous Yulisa was and would wager that she would not be discovered, but Diana would let her know about the offer if she were ever detained. Diana cleaned her house and tried to relax, thinking about what she would do with all her free time.

# # #

Yulisa had been up since seven. She got up and dressed in sweats, then went walking around her neighborhood. She had a treadmill in the living room, but there were times she wanted to breathe fresh air. As she powerwalked, she enjoyed the cool weather while she recalled what she had seen last night and how easily the group crossed the border. She wondered if all operations worked like this, or if different points of entry called for different tactics. After fifteen minutes, sweat started to run down Yulisa's face. She liked to get her cardio done in the morning because she felt it gave her more energy throughout the day. As she made the two-mile turn, she felt both physically and mentally strong. She was in a good place and would forever be in debt to Diana for extricating her from her personal hell.

Since agreeing to take over, Yulisa had been in a good mindset. Gone were the days of tears and sadness. Now her mission for the organization brought clarity to her. She saw things in a new way and enjoyed viewing things through this prism. Gone too, were the negative feelings. Now it was all about finding new and better ways to assist groups into the United States. The present situation was perfect for cohorts to enter, but Yulisa excelled at anticipating problems and was always open to innovation.

Yulisa finished her four-mile walk then took a quick shower. Her mission for the next several days was to read up on the organization's operations. First, to learn all the ways the groups came in, and second, to see if things could be tweaked to become more efficient. But Yulisa was no fool, she would modify operations only when needed because she had learned that old adage, 'don't fix what ain't broke.'

Yulisa stopped what she was doing and looked around her living room. She smiled and thanked God for putting her on her current trajectory. She was happy to keep her mind on the job because it allowed her to focus on things she could control. She was so tired of reliving the pain of losing her family and knowing there was not a damn thing she could do to change the circumstances. Thus, she was grateful to God and to Diana for changing her life.

Yulisa looked at the files of the people who had already crossed the border, where they had entered the United States, their employment, and their pictures. She studied the faces, looking at a husband and wife with a six-year-old boy, then a four-year-old girl. Everyone smiled in the pictures, and she wondered how their lives in America were going. She looked down at the photo again and concentrated on the father's eyes. She saw fierce determination in them and hoped the family had found their American Dream.

She dug through the files and found Reynaldo and Rocio Jimenez's photo along with their daughter. She knew personally that this family was a success story. Reynaldo a boat captain and Rocio a chef. More importantly, Reynaldo was a pipeline to those with fishing experience in Mexico. He was always looking for new crew members, and the organization utilized him to employ some of those new arriving groups.

Yulisa smiled and nodded her head, seeing the shrewd move by the organization to place people in occupations they already had experience in. Yulisa thought of Reynaldo and Rocio Jimenez's nephew, Jacinto, and his family. From what she read in his file, he worked well with others and was dependable. Jacinto Jimenez would still be in Manzanillo, Colima if he didn't possess the strong work ethic that got him noticed and nominated. Yulisa figured the organization's success rate was high because of its vetting process. When considering if workers were deserving, the organization was known to knock on neighbor's doors to ask about a person's character: if they were boozers or if they noticed anything strange about their behavior. To be chosen, a person had to possess a strong work ethic, be focused, and preferably have a family. The Organization brought in singles only on special occasions because higher ups knew that some single men liked to drink and sometimes lost their focus. No, the organization only wanted people who knew what they already wanted out of life.

The phone rang, which brought Yulisa back from her thoughts. It was Diana and she wanted to meet for lunch at Adrian's Tacos at one in the afternoon.

# # #

Yulisa met Diana for lunch. After they placed their order, they found a table and sat down. Yulisa was still talking about how easy it was for the group to cross the border. Diana was quiet and reserved, unusual in a person who asked to meet for lunch. After a few minutes time Yulisa noticed and asked, "¿Qué te pasa?"

Diana looked at her, and then she sighed, slammed her palms on the table and opened up. "You know I'm so grateful that you are taking over for me. The organization is in great hands, but I've been thinking about something." Just then the server came with their lunch.

Yulisa sat up straight in her seat. "What? What is it?" Her eyes were as big as saucers.

"I'm so appreciative of you Yuli, you'll never know how much it means to me that you have stepped up for me."

"Yes?" replied Yulisa with anticipation.

"Well, I know that it won't happen, but if you are ever detained by law enforcement, you have my blessing to implicate me. Just give them my name and it'll go easier for you," replied Diana.

Yulisa's mouth was agape, not quite believing what she had just heard. "What's all this talk about getting caught?"

Diana smiled then continued. "I have so much respect for you, that I don't want you to be caught holding the bag, if things ever go south. I've looked deep within myself, and if for some reason you are arrested, you can give them my name. Tell them I'm your boss."

Yulisa's forehead farrowed then replied, "What?"

"I was the one who got you involved in this right? You had no idea about what I really did, and I feel responsible for putting you at risk."

Yulisa shook her head. "Diana, I would never put the finger on you?" Yulisa laughed. "I'm game for whatever happens. What we are doing is important, and I would never rat on you. Come on, I'm Tejana, and my family taught me about loyalty. I appreciate you saying all this, but it's not fair to you. You founded this organization—you have done enough. Plus, you released me from the hell I was living in. Consider yourself free. You have served your time. Enjoy your retirement, and I don't want to talk about this anymore." Yulisa put her right hand up for emphasis.

Chapter 45

Over the last six weeks of the year, Diana concentrated on her realty business. She was in serious talks to sell her business and retire from all her responsibilities. Every day she got closer to her goal of full retirement. She gave Yulisa space to allow her to become comfortable with the daily aspects of the job and let her put her own touch on the job as the leader of the organization. Diana felt proud she chose Yulisa as her choice for her replacement. She heard that some organization members were pissed at Diana's decision, but they understood her point that hiring from within would lead to turnover at the top every five years or so. Their objective was to help get people to America, and not just sit on their asses, collecting a paycheck until retirement. No, Diana was ecstatic about choosing Yulisa as her replacement.

# # #

As the year ended, Yulisa used her time to read up on all aspects of the organization. She read about the new group that would be reporting to the Language Institute in early 2019. She researched the Points of Entry that would be used and read the history of the ingenious ways the organization used to bring its people into the United States. Yulisa raised her eyebrows and shook her head—the early days of transporting people were dangerous and carried enormous risks. Compared to how groups crossed the border today, it was like night and day. Yulisa was wise and knew that if a business was to endure, it had to change with the times. This is what the organization did when they had to modify their entry routes to meet the group's needs. Yulisa had been in business long enough to see that good companies understand that change is progress—those unwilling to change where often the first ones to die out.

Yulisa sat on her sofa with a pile of organization files in front of her. She flipped them open and read. There were pictures of people before they were brought over, a little history on them, then information on where they were sent, and what company would employ them. She wondered how all the people who had been brought in were doing. She made a list of people she'd like to visit to see how life in the United States was treating them. She looked out at her living room and smiled, remembering the hell she'd been living with. While this job could not bring back her family, it had given her a new attitude, and she thanked God for taking her out of the darkness that she'd been living in. Yulisa recalled the chat she had with Diana about if she were ever caught. Under no circumstances would she inform on the person who'd given her new life. She remembered the old one, busting her ass at work during the day then coming home to cry away her sadness. That's how her life was until that fateful day that Diana offered her a new life. Since then, her days were focused, as there were missions to complete. She'd forever be grateful to Diana, and if, God forbid, she ever got pinched by law enforcement, she'd remember those sad, shitty days before Diana's job offer chased the darkness out of her heart. Because of that, Diana's secret would remind hidden from view.

Yulisa continued to read the files. From time to time, she looked up from her reading and smiled as she enjoyed the life she was now leading, all thanks to Diana. Diana's job offer had changed her life, and happy tears fell from her face because her life now had new meaning and allowed her to live with purpose.

# # #

Diana was at home surfing the web on vacation deals to Paris. She was happy that she'd finally have time for herself, and this lifelong trip would start the next chapter in her interesting life. She hoped Elizabeth would be able to join her, and she smiled as an idea popped into her head. If she had to, she'd fly Antonio, Elizabeth's husband, to California to visit the Dallas Cowboys Training Camp in late July. Diana laughed, because she knew he'd jump at the chance.

She went back to searching for the perfect vacation. Though she had loved Paris ever since she was a little girl, she also wanted to see other European cities. If she could find a package that included, London, Paris, Munich, and Berlin, she'd jump on it. Until then she continued with her quest. All this planning made Diana recall her experiences in the organization. She smiled recalling some of the people she had met, but the organization would carry on without her. She was happy to relinquish the leadership role because she had done her time and knew Yulisa was perfect for the job. The organization would be in capable hands for many years to come. Diana was so wrapped up going through memory lane that she took a binder off the shelf. The binder had information from all the missions she participated in. Diana flipped a page and saw a picture of the Garcia family. The information indicated they crossed the border in Arizona in 1999. Diana remembered that mission because they came in on December 30. The mission was changed from the regular time and date so that everyone could have New Year's Eve off. That's why she remembered this family, and she wondered how they were doing now, some nineteen years later.

Diana flipped the pages and stopped on the Reynaldo, Rocio, and Mari Jimenez file. Now this mission Diana remembered by heart. It was a grueling twenty-four-hour experience through the mountains and desert of Mexico and Arizona with eighteen of those hours walking through driving rain. Of all the missions Diana led, the one with the Jimenez's was the one she would remember the most because of how hard it was. Plus, the Jimenez's had a special place in her heart because they'd been helpful in placing people with fishing experience with them. Diana knew these were good people who understood the importance of helping others. That's why God had blessed them with a great life because they always thought of others.

Then Diana went back to what she would do with her life after she got back from her Paris trip. Mostly she would rest, she thought, as she was both physically and mentally tired. She was looking forward to stepping back and just take care of herself, but that's something she was not used to doing. Diana would stay at her realty company until she could sell it—hopefully before her trip in mid-June. She knew there would be adjustments in her life, but she was looking forward to what God had in store for her. She looked at the clock on the wall that read twelve thirty. She picked up her cell and called Yulisa. The phone rang twice before Yulisa picked up. "¿Qué haces?"

"Hi Diana, I'm just sitting around doing research, you know, doin' my homework."

"Yeah, I've been reminiscing about some of the missions we did when the organization was in its infancy. Man, that was some hard work, some of the hardest shit I've ever had to do," stated Diana. "The organization has come a long way from how it started," she chuckled.

"Well, thank God for technology, right?" added Yulisa.

Diana stayed silent for a bit, then said, "Well, that's a double-edged sword. Yes, it's good that we use the technology we have. But so does law enforcement, and they don't have the budget constraints that we do. Still, operations are better and less risky than they were in the past. Anyway, I called because I'm giving you my two weeks' notice." Both ladies laughed. "But really, this organization is in excellent hands, and I know you'll continue to assist our hard-working people and help them with their American Dream. Trust me Yuli, you are ready, and you're going to be chingona at it, too."

Yulisa smiled at the comment as she knew this day would come. She always had an intuition about things happening before they occurred. Like thinking, 'I wonder when I'll hear back from them,' then mysteriously, the letter she'd been waiting for would come by mail. Yulisa figured that Diana was letting her take control of the organization a little at a time with no pressure. Now the time had come for her to officially take over and Yulisa beamed with pride. "Thank you, Diana, you'll never truly understand how you saved me. Your offer to follow in your footsteps has shined the light back into my life."

"Yuli, you'll be great. I've never seen anyone with more work ethic than you, and I've seen many people within the organization who worked hard. You have this. And take this as you want, but I would never leave the organization if I thought it would flounder. I know it's in excellent hands, and the groups will see how much you care for them."

Yulisa took a deep breath as she tried to retain her composure from the words she'd just heard. "I'll serve with pride and won't let you down, Diana." She choked back tears of happiness.

"Yuli, I know you will be great. The bonus of hiring you is that you'll hopefully stay another twenty years. Had I hired from within, the leadership position would have a turnover rate at the top every five years or so. I wanted to have continuity, and that's why I went with you."

Yulisa understood Diana, and she thanked God again for allowing then to meet. She knew how fortunate she was to be in this position, and she knew that God was taking care of her. "Well, thanks again." Her composure was back and her voice strong.

"Okay Yuli, I just wanted you to know what I planned. You'll officially take over on the first of February, have a good day."

"Okay Diana, thank you for the heads up." After getting off the phone Yulisa went to the organizational chart and found Elizabeth's phone number. She'd call her and ask if she'd help set up a going away party for their friend. Yulisa felt a pang of apprehension from the talk she'd had with Diana. From now on she'd be responsible for everything that occurred within the organization. It would be under her watch, and it was her ass that would be on the line. She understood the immense responsibility, but she was confident that the status quo would remain in the organization because she was sure of her abilities and was good at motivating others. She understood everything evolved over time, and it was always good to be out in front of that change and anticipate issues before they became a problem.

Chapter 46

Getting Elizabeth to help with Diana's going away party worked out perfectly. Elizabeth said she'd handle all the invites and offered up her backyard for the festivities. She told Yulisa that this would be the second party that was thrown in Diana's honor. With Elizabeth taking the point on the party, Yulisa began looking at the upcoming schedule to send the next group to the Language Institute. Yulisa had seen the importance of learning English when they witnessed the border crossings a few months earlier. As Yulisa continued to read, she liked that the cohorts were encouraged to learn English and had to pass tests, to make sure they could handle the stress of speaking with a Border Patrol officer. Yes, Yulisa was impressed with how the organization prepared the groups for their trip across the border.

She continued to read organizational materials, be it past operations, the names and pictures of the groups brought into the US or reading up on those in the organization. On more than one occasion, Yulisa shook her head after learning of some of the organizations ingenious planning. There was a reason why the organization had not been discovered, and Yulisa attributed it to excellent planning, plus a little bit of luck. She hoped the luck would continue under her watch.

Yulisa got up to get some coffee, then was hit by her emotions. Her life seemed to be illuminated now—every step forward bathed in clarity. It was a far cry from when she was lost in her grief, not understanding how to deal with the losses in her life. Now her life was filled with light, the darkness replaced with purpose, with hope, and with the need to help others. Meeting Diana had changed her trajectory in life. She dropped to her knees in the living room, brought her hands together in prayer, and gave thanks to God for putting her in this situation and removing the darkness from her life. She would never be able to repay Diana for giving her another chance at life.

# # #

Diana's party was the last weekend in January. Elizabeth hosted the party outside, but there were enough heat lamps that nobody felt the cold. The yard was decorated festively with wine, liquor, and beer flowing throughout the night. The menu for the evening consisted of New York steaks, baked potatoes, Caesar salad, and dinner rolls. The party was an intimate affair with hugs everywhere. That made sense to Yulisa since some of these people had been working in the organization from the beginning.

Diana's parents flew to El Paso for the party. Both were happy that their daughter would finally retire from her risky endeavors, but proud of the work she'd done. They understood the personal sacrifices their daughter had made to help others to improve their lives.

Diana got the shock of her life when she saw Reynaldo and Rocio Jimenez come through the side gate. They had flown in from Seattle for Diana's celebration and were considered personal friends with her—the memory of her leading them to freedom would be forever etched in their memories. They hugged and talked for a while, with smiles on their faces the entire night. From a distance Yulisa could see the personal bond they had, and she hoped to have that same kind of connection with the future groups she would be helping.

As the night wore on, the party and music grew louder as everyone enjoyed themselves and celebrated Diana's leadership. Yulisa was now part of this family, and she was up for the challenge. She respected Diana too much to screw this operation up, plus the attitude she had for work would never allow her to.

At the end of the night, Diana thanked everyone. It was an emotional goodbye with lots of tears, hugs, and Mexican gritos. Diana had been smiling the entire night, happy with the intimate company of those who had risk their freedom to help others. But now she was relieved that she no longer had the pressure nor responsibility. She hoped she could teach herself to let things go because the organization was in capable hands. She didn't have to worry anymore. The party started to break up at around two as some organization members mingled together waiting their turn to say their personal goodbyes to Diana. She had done her time and now deserved to live in happiness.

People were still talking to Diana as it approached three in the morning. It was like nobody wanted to leave. It was a tribute to Diana that organization members didn't want the evening to end, but little by little, the crowd began to disperse and soon it was only Diana, Yulisa, and Elizabeth.

Yulisa didn't want to overstay her welcome, so she walked up to Diana to let her know she was leaving. Elizabeth sensed the mood and walked away to clean up.

"Well chica, are you ready to take over?" asked Diana with a smile. Her eyes were red from crying.

Yulisa smiled, then replied, "I am Diana. I'll make you proud."

They embraced, sharing a sister hug. Diana looked at Yulisa and was reminded of herself at Yulisa's age. There were many similarities between the two, but perhaps the most important was that both ladies had learned at a young age to pay attention to detail and that trait had served them both well. "Yuli, remember, if things go to shit and you're arrested, give them my name."

"I'll remember that, but it won't be needed." Both ladies hugged again.

"Yuli, you take care of our baby. I've nurtured it, now it's your turn."

"Our baby? You're the mother of this organization, you raised it, cared for it, and modified operations so there would be less risk. I'm just the caretaker, but I'll care of it and love it just like my little Rosita." They hugged again. Tears flowed down both faces. "Okay chica, I'm heading out. Please stay in touch."

Diana nodded her head and said, "Yes, we'll stay in touch. You take care Yuli." Yulisa smiled and waved, and then walked to her car, leaving Diana alone with her own thoughts. The moment she'd been waiting for was finally here. She was now free of any organizational responsibilities. While she felt some apprehension at the newness of all this, she nodded her head and a smile came to her face. Diana Solis wondered what tomorrow would bring.

Acknowledgements

La Lady Fund, nor any of my other writing, would have seen the light of day without the help of my late, great friend, Fred Rue Jacobs. He guided, encouraged, and challenged me. I will always be grateful for his tutelage.

I also want to thank my friend, Chan Bayless, who helped me with editing. I truly appreciate your quick turnaround time.

Many thanks to my friend, Jorge Alberto Maldonado Morales, for his valuable assistance in making sure that the Spanish language used was correct.

I would also like to thank my editor and publisher, Russ López and Shawmut Peninsula Press for taking a chance on *La Lady Fund*—especially during these difficult times. It is great to see people with some intestinal fortitude.

Lastly, I want to thank my grandson, Adrian Puentes, for the constant reminder that you must put in the work if you want to succeed, be it writing or playing the guitar.

www.ingramcontent.com/pod-product-compliance
Lightning Source LLC
Chambersburg PA
CBHW070745160726
48004CB00001B/59